# CITY of FIRE

# CITY
## *of*
# FIRE

Thomas
Fitzsimmons

A TOM DOHERTY ASSOCIATES BOOK
NEW YORK

This is a work of fiction. All of the characters, organizations, and events portrayed in this novel are either products of the author's imagination or are used fictitiously.

CITY OF FIRE

Copyright © 2009 by Thomas Fitzsimmons

A Forge Book
Published by Tom Doherty Associates, LLC
175 Fifth Avenue
New York, NY 10010

www.tor-forge.com

Forge® is a registered trademark of Tom Doherty Associates, LLC.

ISBN-13: 978-0-7653-5933-9
ISBN-10: 0-7653-5933-2

First Edition: March 2009

Printed in the United States of America

0  9  8  7  6  5  4  3  2  1

*For Maureen, Robert Emmett, Patricia and Carol.*

*Thanks to our parents, Madeline and Tom, we all know how to spin a yarn.*

# CITY *of* FIRE

# CHAPTER I

Solana Ortiz was frightened that night, but not for the obvious reasons. Not because she feared the wolf packs of starving dogs that prowled the alleys and streets of the South Bronx, even in the stifling August heat. Dogs that watched her as she made her way from the subway and turned toward her residence, their attention roused by the pungent scent of the Chinese take-out food she carried home.

The time had long passed when Solana feared the glassy-eyed crack addicts who were loitering off to her left in a cave-dark tenement doorway. And there was the slicked-back, homeboy Romeo at his usual street corner post, grabbing his crotch, undressing her with his eyes, whispering, "I'll pay you ten dollars to suck it, baby. You know you want to."

Solana Ortiz had a specific fear.

She feared a man.

A man who began haunting the ghetto neighborhood six months ago—cruising the streets at all hours in a black Lincoln Town Car—soon after the multinational Gold Organization purchased the ten square city blocks on which Solana's apartment building stood. That's when the fires began and her neighbors began to flee.

Solana's intuition told her the man in the Lincoln was somehow responsible for those fires. It would take someone like him—he radiated an implacable evil as tangible as a gunshot—to burn people out of their homes.

Her senses on full alert, Solana walked with the rambling crowds down Hunts Point Avenue toward the sparsely populated south end of Hunts Point. Spent crack vials, like so many wasted lives, crunched beneath her feet. Blaring salsa music and the crowing of cock-fighting roosters mixed with the tremors of boom-box gangsta rap and pounded her ears. Laundry in shades of orange and yellow, red and green, yellow and purple, hung from fire escapes. Illegal street vendors hawked aromatic Hispanic fast food: *pastelillos, bacalaos, cuchifritos*. Rickety display tables featuring "designer" T-shirts, knockoff handbags and five-dollar wristwatches lined the curbs. Aggressive peddlers worked the crowds offering all sorts of black market goods: stolen iPods, credit cards, trail-mixes of drugs.

A fleeting melancholy touched Solana as she veered right onto Coster Street and passed the place where, five years ago, four white New York City cops gunned down her upstairs neighbor: a gentle, unarmed sixteen-year-old black youth who she and her mother baby-sat as a child. Riddled his adolescent frame with eighteen armor-piercing rounds. By mistake.

Although the horrific incident had long since faded from the collective memories of her neighbors—as quickly as the boy's blood weathered from the sidewalk—she commemorated his death every year by placing a small bouquet of flowers on the spot where he was killed.

Solana blessed herself, said a short prayer and kept moving. She passed abandoned, disemboweled buildings, deep dark canyons cluttered with the charred shells of burned-out cars—the ghetto equivalent of monkey bars for children—and worried that her building would be the next to burn.

Solana turned right onto East Bay Avenue, heard a loud

noise. She looked across the street, through vistas of charred building debris, down a shadowy, trash-strewn alley. A bulky plywood door had crashed open and the man Solana feared stepped from the basement of a boarded-up tenement. Solana slowed, watched from the safety of the crowd as the man brushed dirt off his suit jacket, stuck an unlit cigar in his mouth, picked up a heavy-looking chain and used it to secure the basement door. As he clumped from the alley to the street a group of toughs scattered before him. A dawdling beggar gaped up at the man, dropped his hand-out hand, spun on his one good heel and peg-legged away.

What made the man stand out was not his tall muscle-bulging frame or his peculiar facial features, which looked at odds with one another, like mismatched puzzle pieces out of scale. No, it was the fact that even in this insufferable heat he wore a dark, freshly pressed business suit.

The man knocked a persistent marijuana hawker out of the way as he walked to the curb. He leaned against his shiny black Lincoln Town Car, lit the cigar, flicked the spent match to the tenement stoop and glanced in Solana's direction.

She averted her eyes, turned to a vendor's display table and pretended to inspect some merchandise.

"How much?" she said to a black-as-coal African merchant as she fingered a cheapo scarf with a Hermes label, one eye on the suited man—she could almost feel his dark, probing eyes moving over her like wet slugs.

"Fifty dollars," the merchant said without enthusiasm. He swatted a mosquito that had landed on his neck. "But for you a special deal: thirty-five dollars."

"I'll give you three dollars."

"You insult me," the merchant said. "Ten dollars."

Solana let go of the scarf, walked to the end of the block, stepped off the sidewalk and crossed the street through bumper-to-bumper traffic. She shimmied between two parked cars, onto the opposite sidewalk and heard the jingle of a dog collar. Slowly she turned and found herself facing a pack of dogs led by a huge Rottweiler—icicles pierced her heart.

"Nice Lobo." Solana knew the one-eyed beast's reputation—an abandoned attack dog whose drug-dealing owner had had its voice box cut out so when it attacked it did so without warning. Solana knew if she exhibited fear, Lobo and the pack would attack. *Stay calm*. But the blood left her head, her knees weakened and her body quaked. Finally she remembered, too late, the bag of Chinese food. The dogs must be after the food.

A German shepherd charged toward her, fangs bared.

Bystanders froze in fear, some scattered.

Solana saw movement out of the corner of her eye; the suited man was moving with the speed and agility of an athlete. He knocked several bystanders aside and kicked the attacking dog, sent it skittering back into the street. The pack went wild: barking, growling, advancing until the man made a sudden quick charge toward them.

The dogs turned and dashed away, tails between their legs, all but the one-eyed Rottweiler. Lobo held his ground, stood defiant, sniffing the air, capturing and memorizing the man's scent.

His scent. Solana was all at once enveloped in it. A vaguely familiar odor—a man's cologne. Napoleon. Strong. Expensive.

"Get the hell out of here," the man said to Lobo with a ragged, cigar-stained voice. He picked up a chunk of broken sidewalk cement and flung it. The jagged concrete opened a gash on Lobo's head. The Rottweiler made a gasping sound, staggered, and on unsteady legs, managed to scurry away, leaving a trail of blood behind it.

"Hello, beautiful lady," the man said to Solana. "I'm Pete. From Queens."

Solana nodded almost imperceptibly and tried to move on.

Pete from Queens blocked her. "In case you don't know it, I just saved you from being mauled, maybe worse." The seams on Pete's suit jacket threatened to split as he folded his massive arms across his chest. "A simple thank-you would be in order."

"Thank you." She smiled tightly.

"You're welcome." Pete looked her over. "What's your name?"

Solana didn't want to tell him but was afraid not to. "Solana Ortiz." She slipped her hand into her Gucci-knockoff shoulder bag, felt for the long hat pin she always carried for protection—a surprisingly formidable weapon. But Pete stepped gallantly aside and allowed her to pass.

"Have a safe and lovely evening, Solana," he said.

Even though she felt her legs could not carry her, Solana managed an air of self-assurance as she walked slowly to the end of the block, turned a corner onto Manida Street, out of Pete's sight. She collapsed onto a stoop and fought the urge to be sick.

Solana sucked in several deep breaths and forced herself to sit upright, aware that any further show of weakness might draw predators. As the nausea passed she thought about the fact that this Pete actually *had* saved her from the dogs. She wondered why he'd bothered. Then realized she might soon find out. Pete had been ogling her for weeks. Now he knew her name. It was only a matter of time before he discovered where she lived.

"Fire!" someone yelled.

People started running toward East Bay Avenue.

Solana pushed off of the stoop and walked to the corner arriving just in time to see Pete from Queens's Lincoln make a quick right turn and disappear down Tiffany Street. She looked down East Bay Avenue. The boarded-up tenement she'd seen Pete leave was engulfed in flames.

# CHAPTER 2

Night. A man enters a shabby tenement, eyes darting. He moves down a dimly lit hallway. Stops. Listens. The place is quiet. He lights a match in an effort to locate a name on a row of ravaged mailboxes. The flame reveals the face of police officer Eric Stone. Hardboiled. Handsome. A killer's eyes. A badge hangs from a chain suspended around his neck. The flame flickers. Blue smoke swirls. The flame dies.

Stone pauses to allow his eyes to adjust to the darkness. He checks his Glock 9mm automatic—thirteen armor-piercing rounds in the clip, one in the chamber. He slips it back into his shoulder holster, glances at his watch, takes a deep breath.

Stone moves quietly down the hall, turns a corner and stumbles over a sleeping drunk who bolts upright. Yells an obscenity. Upstairs a guard dog barks. A man screams for the dog to shut up. A baby starts to cry.

Stone silences the drunk with a raised hand—a threat. He stuffs some cash in the drunk's hand. "Beat it."

The drunk fingers the loot. Rolls to his feet. Staggers away. Stone moves farther down the hall, eyes fighting the darkness, and finds the apartment he's looking for. He approaches it, puts his ear to the door, hears a TV—a news-cast in Arabic. Cautiously, he tries the door. It's locked.

Stone removes a credit card from his pocket, slips the card into the door crack above the knob, trips the lock. *Click.*

Blam! A .357 Magnum discharges from the other side of the door. Metal splinters and wood chips slice through the air.

Stone is hit. Blown off his feet. He crashes against a wall and falls onto the tenement floor.

All at once the lights go out. Absolute darkness. A boom-ing intercom-voice yells, "Cut! That was beautiful, gang. Beautiful. Let's see a playback."

The lights come up and the still silence on the set of *Law & Order* erupts into choreographed movement and con-versation.

"Hey, Detective Stone," the veteran actor who played the drunk said. "C'mon, get up."

I OPENED ONE eye, squinted into the overhead floodlight. "I'm playing the moment."

"You give good dead, Beckett," the actor said. "For an Irishman."

"You're too kind," I said.

The old actor offered a makeup-grimy hand and helped me to my feet. I'd practiced the scene with the stunt coordinator—throwing myself back against the makeshift wall and hitting the ground—a dozen times. But I still managed to land hard on my left arm. I massaged the elbow area; nothing broken, but it hurt.

"It would never happen like this in real life," I said. "Real cops don't take on lunatics alone."

"So you've been telling everyone."

"No one listened."

"That's because reality is no excuse for bad story-telling," the actor said. "Never forget that."

"Thank you, people," a faceless voice called out over the control booth intercom. "That's a wrap for today. Call time tomorrow 5:30 A.M. Oh, except you, Michael Beckett. Officer Stone is persona non grata."

"Good riddance," a bearded, thick-necked teamster sneered. The hulking ex-con—he'd killed a man in a barroom brawl—had taken an instant dislike to me my first day on the set. Not that his attitude bothered me. The vast majority of people on the show couldn't have been more accommodating. But there are people in the world, especially those with criminal records, who simply hate cops.

I took a mock bow and gave the teamster the finger.

After two months, and eight episodes, I'd started to feel at home on the set of *Law & Order*. The show was a ratings phenomenon and for good reason. Although the show's cops and district attorneys were preposterously bright, honest and dedicated, for my money, it was the best police series on network television.

I moved off the set, noticed the sound stage's digital wall clock. *Late again.* Hurriedly I stepped over power cables, scooted around a group of production assistants, cleaved through assorted tradesmen, knocked into a steel boom tripod and stubbed my toe: *searing pain.* I saw stars. The tripod toppled. Glass shattered.

SOLANA ORTIZ AND Tina Roe, sitting high above the sound stage in the glass-enclosed *Law & Order* production office, stifled giggles as Michael Beckett hopped in pogo-stick circles, clutching his foot. For a moment he actually looked vulnerable, a side of him they'd never seen.

From the moment Beckett walked into the Silver Screen studios three months ago to audition, along with hundreds of actors, for the featured role of police officer Eric Stone, it was obvious to everyone that he was somehow different.

And it was not due to his Celtic good looks, natural acting talent, or the fact that he was, in real life, a highly decorated New York City cop. It was his attitude.

While the other leading men consistently oversold themselves—especially during the nerve-wracking callback process—Beckett acted like he didn't give a damn if he won the part or not.

"I'd do him," Tina said, fussing with long fingernails that made it almost impossible for her to type. "Anytime." Tina was in her twenties, married with children and dressed in clothing better worn by a slimmer woman.

Solana made a barf sound. "You'd do Gumby." From what she'd observed, Tina was awed by just about every man.

"Beckett's a gentleman," Tina said. "Always dresses nice. Gotta be better then the last guy you dated; the one you told me about, the one who hit you."

"OK, so I'm attracted to bad boys," Solana said.

"And hard-luck cases, and lost souls—"

"Beckett's conceited, arrogant—"

"He's always smiling."

Solana scrunched up her face. "That's 'cause he thinks he's God's gift." The fact he was a white cop didn't help matters. In Solana's world, white cop was synonymous with murdering racist.

*A raised voice.*

"Uh, oh," Tina said.

Solana and Tina watched as a scary, ex-convict teamster pointed to the fallen boom tripod and said something harsh to Beckett. Beckett barked something back.

The teamster made a quick, hostile move and Beckett got into the guy's face. The two men squared off, locked eyes. And then, for some reason, the teamster's aggressive posture lessened. He took several guarded steps to the rear, turned and walked timidly away.

"Don't look now, girlfriend," Tina said. "But if I were you, that's the man I'd want to protect me from—what's his name, the scary guy you think is starting the fires?"

"Think?" Solana said. "I see him walk out of a building. Five minutes later it's on fire."

"Girl," Tina sighed, "we been working on this cop show long enough to know, you don't actually *see* him start the fire, you got nothing but circumstantial evidence—which is why you need some professional help." Tina folded her arms across her considerable bosom. "I mean," she said, "you live in the South Bronx. From what I hear Beckett's a cop in the South Bronx."

Maybe Tina was right. Although like most ghetto residents Solana was mistrustful of all police, if Beckett could back down that musclebound bully, maybe she could convince him to investigate Pete from Queens.

"Quick." Tina handed Solana her clipboard, pulled back her chair and forced her to her feet. "He's coming this way."

"But what should I say?"

"With *your* body, girl, you don't have to say anything." Tina fluffed Solana's thick, dark hair, unbuttoned her blouse one more button.

"This is stupid," Solana said, re-buttoning what Tina had just unbuttoned. "I barely know the man."

"Lips," Tina said.

Solana applied lipstick as Tina ushered her out of the production office and closed the door behind her. Solana hesitated, looked and saw that Beckett was only steps away. She took a deep breath and clanged down the dozen or so metal steps that led to the sound stage floor.

"Michael?"

I heard someone call my name and turned around.

She was stunning: the tiny waist, the rich, firm swell of goodies above and below. I did a 360 to see which lucky "Michael" was in the vicinity.

"Me?" I pointed to myself.

"Your name is Michael." Solana smiled as she approached. "Isn't it?"

I felt an adolescent stomach-churning excitement corkscrew into my heart. "You're Solana?"—as if I didn't know.

"Solana Ortiz," she said.

"Solana." I tasted her name as I said it, took near-carnal pleasure tongue-fondling the word. *So-lana.* "That's a beautiful name."

"Thank-you."

I hit her with my most earnest smile and imagined her lying naked: latte skin in contrast to a white Caribbean beach.

"I'm impressed," Solana said.

"With what?"

"You. Guys like him"—She gestured to the ex-con teamster —"don't usually back down from anyone."

"That a fact?"

Solana nodded. "He sensed something."

"That I am a gentle soul. Kind to animals."

"Of course." She smiled into my eyes. "That has to be it."

*What was going on here?* Although I'd been wildly attracted to Solana since first laying eyes on her, she'd hurt my feelings time and again by being cold to me and, even worse, indifferent. Now she was talking to me, flirting even. I glanced over her shoulder, checked the wall clock—I sure didn't want to go play cops and robbers.

"You going to work?" Solana said.

"I'm late as is."

"Then I'll make this quick. Our executive producer really liked your work. Don't be surprised if you're booked for future episodes."

"Really? So, Detective Stone might not be dead?"

"I'll let you know if I hear anything. What's the best phone number to reach you?"

I wrote my numbers on Solana's clipboard.

"Also, I'd like your professional advice on a certain matter."

"Oh?" All at once I sensed that this was not about resurrecting Detective Stone, or Solana having a sudden, personal interest in me. She wanted something. I re-checked the sound stage clock. "Can we talk tomorrow?"

"You get to work. I'll call you."

She smiled and touched my sore arm in an intimate way and I felt something pass between us; or had it?

"Call me anytime," I said.

The surge of frenzied, star-struck autograph hounds and the brutal summer heat almost sent me scurrying back into the Silver Screen Studios. I slipped on my new designer sunglasses, walked past fans who demonstrated a disheartening lack of interest in my autograph, and scanned the Chelsea Pier roadway for taxis. There were none.

I saw an opening in traffic and jogged across the six-lane West Side Highway and spotted a taxi pulling to the far curb. As a businessman stepped from the back seat, I stepped in.

"Ten eighty-six Simpson Street," I said. "The Bronx."

The driver, a turban-wearing middle-aged Arab, looked at me in his rearview mirror. "I am off duty."

"Your off-duty light isn't on."

The driver flipped the off-duty light on.

"Now, look, pally—"

"I will *not* take you to the South Bronx," the driver said with a pronounced accent.

I didn't have to ask why. The South Bronx was the most violent of high crime areas. Dozens of taxi drivers were robbed, assaulted, even murdered there every year.

"I'm a cop." I whipped out my shield. "Sorry, but you're gonna have to take me."

The driver shook his head. "I am off duty."

"All right," I sighed. "I guess I gotta do a taxi inspection." I looked around the cab. "This back seat isn't as clean as it should be; that's a $50 fine. I noticed your tires are a bit bald; that's another $50. Your air conditioner obviously isn't working; that'll bring your fines up to, what, $150?"

"You do this because you think I am Muslim."

"I'll bet your meter runs fast; they'll suspend your hack license for that."

"I am not Muslim. I am Sikh."

"I don't care if you're Muslim, Jew, gentile or worship sun gods. All I care about is getting to the fucking Bronx."

The driver said something foreign that sounded unkind. He flicked the meter on, switched on the air conditioner, and muttered something in English about a flea-infested camel pissing on my ancestor's graves.

"Go straight," I said. "Turn right on 57th Street. Left on York. Take the FDR Drive at 63rd to the Willis Avenue Bridge to the Bruckner Expressway."

The taxi eased from the curb and moved north in moderately heavy traffic. I sat back, adjusted my off-duty gun for comfort, thought about the way Solana Ortiz had touched my sore arm—delicately—decided that something *had* passed between us.

I wondered what advice she needed. Since she was part of the *Law & Order* writing team, she probably wanted to consult me on proper police procedure—I hoped I had the answers. But even if I wasn't booked as an actor again, being one of the show's police consultants would be fun, and maybe profitable. I'd probably have the opportunity to work closely with Solana—and then I'd make my move, invite her to drinks, dinner.

I checked my wrist watch, muttered a curse. My partner, Vinnie D'Amato, would be angry that I was late, again. I pulled a cell phone from my jeans pocket and dialed the 41st Precinct switchboard.

*"Forty-one. Officer Schultz speaking."*

"Schultz. It's me."

*"Beckett. Lemme guess. You're late, again."*

"I am truly awed by your psychic abilities."

*"Yeah, yeah. I'll tell D'Amato. He ain't gonna like it."* Schultz hung up. I put away my cell phone; *I didn't like it either.*

Although I'd yet to tell a soul, I confess that I was having serious doubts about remaining a New York City cop.

Considering the fact that I joined the NYPD reluctantly (I didn't know what else to do after being discharged from the Navy), in some ways, I still liked being a cop. The prestige that comes with carrying a gun and badge in the number one police force in the country, 42,000 officers strong, was part of my being. My father retired after thirty-five years as a New York City police lieutenant. My father's brother retired after thirty-seven years as a sergeant. Several uncles on my mother's side were New York City cops. Two of my cousins had only recently been sworn in: one to the NYPD, the other to a Rockland County PD. Even my kid sister Shannon planned on someday joining the NYPD.

Most of my close friends had been law enforcement types before my stint on *Law & Order*. Now I was starting to fraternize with an eclectic mix of actors and tradespeople and enjoyed, for the most part, being privy to their cocooned, violence-free lives and naive worldviews.

Conversely, although I reveled in the broad diversity of my newfound friends, I most likely would never get too close to any of them. They were outsiders. I had been raised trusting only cops, and for good reason. Only cops knew what I knew about humankind's dark side: the depravity, the savagery, the unimaginable cruelty and evil.

As a veteran observer of countless blood-soaked crime scenes I felt that I'd experienced violence in all its grotesque forms and knew there was a sameness about it—be it a crime of passion, greed, or a terrorist attack—there was a mind-numbing senselessness. And I knew that caustic awareness, combined with a cop's inherent heart-hardening cynicism fueled by a baffling revolving-door system of criminal justice, had had an adverse effect on me. I had long ago stopped believing in fair play, stopped caring about the very people I was supposed to protect and serve. I was becoming intolerant, even numb to the plight of crime victims and the sufferings of the disadvantaged.

My experience on *Law & Order* changed things.

The thrill of working on a prime time TV series, hob-nobbing with TV stars, working with beautiful actresses had lightened my heart, caused me to spring out of bed every morning looking forward to each new day. I began to realize there was a world outside the police force, some-thing I had never before seriously considered.

All at once the exhilaration of my last day on *Law & Order* and my perplexing encounter with the criminally beautiful Solana Ortiz evaporated. I felt empty, adrift. I was on my way back to the South Bronx to don a uniform and bullet-proof vest and patrol the highest crime area in America. A place where the sound of gunfire was as fa-miliar as the stench of rotting garbage. Where cops had a free hand and, because the powers that be wished to con-tain violent crime in the ghetto, supervision from "down-town" was virtually nonexistent.

In some parts of the United States, cops retire after twenty years without ever pulling their weapon. In the South Bronx, I drew my gun almost every day.

The taxi driver slowed in heavy traffic. I glanced to my left and saw a limousine turn into the West Side heliport; the millionaire's heliport. I caught a glimpse of the limo's license plate.

"RJG," I said to myself. The vanity plate initials stood for R. J. Gold.

I recalled with a touch of nostalgia the days when, much to my chagrin, I was known to some as R. J. Gold's "beard." Gold, myself and his mistress, Janet Roth, a former Ms. Hawaiian Tropic, would ride around town in Gold's limo, fly in his private 727 to his Las Vegas casinos, see heavy-weight fights, the best entertainment.

Those were good times.

I turned my attention back to the traffic, sat back, mas-saged my sore elbow, and thought about the fact that al-though I'd occasionally seen his limo racing around Manhattan, I hadn't socialized with Gold in years.

We crossed 57th Street, accessed the FDR Drive at 63rd Street. As we approached the Willis Avenue Bridge I glanced out the taxi's rear window and watched as Manhat-tan gradually slipped away. The South Bronx loomed ahead; its appalling, anthill density put tension on my face. I could feel my shoulder and neck muscles begin to bunch; my posture changed. My eyes became more vigilant.

# CHAPTER 3

Police officer Vinnie D'Amato nosed his ten-year-old Toyota into a vertical parking space half a block away from the 41st Precinct stationhouse. He killed the engine, stepped out into the muggy afternoon air and, even though the area swarmed with convicted car thieves, did not bother to lock up: the last person caught stealing a cop's car was escorted to the 41 basement and nearly beaten to death.

D'Amato crossed the cratered street, swatted at a formation of dive-bombing horseflies, and breathed in the usual neighborhood stench. Heat radiated off the soft, tire-rutted blacktop. It would solidify as night and slightly cooler temperatures claimed the Bronx ghetto.

D'Amato wove though a crowd of sullen, shirtless young men and foul-mouthed, provocatively attired adolescent girls who were dancing to boom box salsa music. Helmeted kids on skateboards streaked down the sidewalk. A well-fed middle-aged couple exchanged harsh words in Spanish. Several cats fought a stray dog over a scrap of food. A fighting rooster crowed somewhere in a nearby tenement.

D'Amato walked past clots of ever-present colicky stoop

dwellers guzzling beer and noticed that the stationhouse was the only building on the block that did not have a stack of rotting garbage piled in front of it.

The neo-Florentine 41st Precinct stationhouse had been built around the turn of the last century. The bulky, flat-roofed fortress was covered with ugly concrete slabs. There were bars on the windows and, because angry mobs still sometimes stormed the stationhouse, there were thick steel shields behind the bars.

Shrill voices warned D'Amato to sidestep a group of irate civilians as he entered the beehive-active 41st Precinct. The cavernous, dirty and dimly lit space was painted institutional green; time and again dust and peeling paint particles rained down from the ceiling.

"Hey, D'Amato." Schultz, the five-time-divorced, perpetually pissed-off cop assigned to the 41 switchboard, shouted above the din. "Beckett called. Late, again."

"Fuck!" D'Amato threw his hands up. "He say how late?"

"When're you gonna get it though your thick, guinea, wop, grease ball, dago, I-talian head, I ain't your fucking answering service."

"Blow me," D'Amato said and headed to the metal staircase that led to the fourth floor locker room. He was getting sick and tired of covering for the increasingly self-absorbed, forever-late-for-work Beckett. Coming up with excuses: phony dental and medical emergencies, subway delays. Beckett was never late for work before he landed the part on *Law & Order*.

D'Amato headed to his locker, changed into uniform and was strapping on his gun when a skinny, smart-aleck rookie cop several lockers away said:

"I see you still carry an old six-shooter." He was pointing at D'Amato's Smith & Wesson, four-inch barrel .38 revolver.

D'Amato smiled tolerantly at the rookie. "Automatics

can jam." D'Amato buckled his gun belt. Then shoved his backup gun, another four-inch .38, into a waistband holster.

"Not if you keep 'em clean."

"Oh, yeah?" D'Amato tweaked his Pancho Villa mustache. "Couple of years ago, me and Beckett respond to a bullshit landlord tenant dispute. We get out of our RMP, totally relaxed, a couple of Joe-gloms, and two pit bulls attack us."

Half a dozen cops in various states of dress had stopped to listen to D'Amato's yarn.

"We don't know it at the time, but the dogs are trained to go for the throat. So the dogs charge, leap for our throats. Beckett pulls his automatic, it jams. I pull my .38 and kill both dogs. One shot apiece." D'Amato paused for effect. "Midair."

"Midair?" the rookie said. "Wow! Those had to be the luckiest shots ever."

"Luck, my ass." D'Amato stuck his memo book in his rear pants pocket. "I'm good." He picked up his nightstick, walked out of the locker room, and headed down to roll call.

"That was bullshit," a light-skinned black cop, slipping on his uniform shirt, said to the rookie.

"What's bullshit?" the rookie said.

"D'Amato's whole story."

"How do you know?"

"You gotta be kidding," the black cop said. "Look, pally, no one, and I mean no one, could shoot two pit bulls dead, midair."

"So, he was putting me on?" the rookie said.

"No," the black cop said. "He was lying."

"Look, kid," a pasta-plump Italian cop said. "No one's saying D'Amato's a bad guy or a bad cop. Just don't believe anything he says. And I mean ever. *Capisc'*?"

SHIT. D'AMATO REARED back and stopped just short of entering the sitting room. Captain Ward, the straight-arrow,

275-pound veteran precinct commander with the personality of a speed bump was standing at the podium alongside the roll call sergeant, and Michael Beckett was nowhere to be seen. Not that Ward's presence was that unusual. The captain attended roll call a couple of times a month in order to read "special orders" from headquarters, or just to show his face. Problem was that if the captain became aware that Beckett was not present he might mark him AWOL and team D'Amato up with a rookie—who could be an informer from the Internal Affairs Bureau (IAB)—or worse, a female officer. And there was no way D'Amato was about to risk his personal safety by working with a freakin' woman.

D'Amato waited until the last possible moment, then slipped inside the jam-packed sitting room and ducked behind a couple of old-time potbellied cops.

"Listen up," the roll call sergeant said and the men quickly came to order—no fart noises, catcalls or smartass remarks: the captain's presence had its advantages.

"Anderson," the sergeant said.

"Here," Anderson said.

"Andrews."

"Here."

"Barnes."

"Here."

"Beckett."

"Here," D'Amato said.

"Where?" Captain Ward scanned the ranks. "Show yourself, Beckett."

"Here." D'Amato stepped out from behind the big cops and into view. "I mean Beckett's here: not here here. He's upstairs changing."

The captain scowled. "He'd better be—"

THE SHRILL WHOOP of sirens greeted the 4-to-12 tour as they left roll call and exited the station house. D'Amato watched as several RMPs skidded to a stop. Cops alighted, dragged out several battered prisoners, and marched them into the 41 Precinct.

D'Amato checked the time. Where the fuck was Beckett?

A yellow cab, a rare site in the ghetto, rolled down Simpson Street and pulled to the curb. The rear door swung open and Beckett stepped out. Walsh saw him. So did Coyle and Talbot. So did Ryan, McShane, and the rookie policewoman, Destiny Jones. All looking like a band of ragtag mercenaries in piecemeal uniforms—there was no enforcement of the uniform regulations in the ghetto—rather than squared-away cops. They applauded as they climbed into their police cars. Derisively, sure. But applause just the same for Beckett who in his expensive designer sunglasses and tight jeans looked every bit the television actor.

All at once D'Amato could feel Captain Ward standing directly behind him.

"If bullshit was electricity you'd be a powerhouse, D'Amato," Ward said.

"SORRY I'M LATE, Captain," I said as I moved toward the station house steps and tried my best not to stare at the captain's newest pompadour toupee. This one looked like a red river otter was sitting on his head. I bit back a laugh and rendered a sloppy hand salute. "There was a purse-snatching incident down on Tiffany Street," I lied. "I was forced to take police action."

"Police action." Ward laughed a little. "Good one. I'm docking you four hours pay for being late."

"What?"

The captain stepped close to me, lowered his voice. "If you showed me some respect," he said reasonably. "I mean, you haven't made a collar in months. Hell, you haven't written a single ticket."

"I'm in a slump," I said. "It happens."

Ward scrunched his face. "Know why every cop awarded the Medal of Honor is put on the fast track to the detective division, except you?"

"I can't handle my booze—no, I got it. I'm overly educated?"

"Bingo!" Ward's finger was in my face. "It's your wiseass attitude." The captain turned and stalked back into the stationhouse.

"Up yours," I said under by breath. Most superior officers treated me with deference, cut me some slack because of my medal. Not Captain Ward. It seemed he never missed an opportunity to bust my balls. It was as if he could look into my soul and knew the awful truth: I was a fraud who did *not* deserve to be awarded that goddamned Medal of Honor.

"He's tyrannical," D'Amato said. "But with a heart of titanium."

I looked at my partner and could not stop the reluctant smile that bloomed on my face. D'Amato was smiling from ear to ear, his fists on his hips. The sleeves of his short-sleeved shirt rolled up around his almost muscular arms. His shirt opened strategically to the third button revealing his almost hairy chest. His array of breast-bar police medals: seven Meritorious Police Duty (MPD), forty Excellent Police Duty (EPD) and Pistol Expert were displayed on his chest. His .38 was worn gunslinger style, low for quick draw.

"Hey, Beckett." McShane strode over to me and, without saying another word, threw a punch—*what the hell?* I blocked it and shoved McShane away.

His partner, Ryan, charged D'Amato, knocking him into a parked car. D'Amato grabbed Ryan and twisted him into a headlock. A dozen other cops quickly intervened and pulled us apart, restraining us.

"What's your problem?" I said to McShane.

"You two scumbags didn't back us up last night."

"You had enough backup," I said. "What, you need us to hold your hand?"

McShane exploded, struggled in vain to break free of the cops holding him and get at me.

There had been a burglary run late in the tour. McShane and his partner had called for backup, and several radio cars responded. Anxious to sign out, get home to my fax machine, and check out my *Law & Order* script, I convinced D'Amato that McShane and his partner were sufficiently covered—because they were.

"I'm cool," McShane said, calming down. "I'm cool." The cops who were holding him reluctantly let him go. He took a step toward me and got in my face.

"You two're gonna need backup someday. Don't be surprised if no one shows up." McShane and Ryan walked off toward their radio car.

The other cops went about their business. And the narrow-eyed looks on their faces said that they were not happy about what had just been said. D'Amato and I were being accused of being slackers. Slackers had urine poured into their lockers, their cars were vandalized, they were awakened at home in the middle of the night by harassing phone calls.

I watched McShane slide into his RMP's driver seat. He flipped me the finger. I flipped him back.

D'Amato said, "You should've decked that prick."

"I'm an actor," I gestured dramatically, placed a hand to my brow. "Not a fighter."

"*Were* an actor." D'Amato had one eye on Destiny Jones as she sashayed to her Westchester Avenue foot post. "You were killed off. Right? Tell me this was your last day on *Law & Order*."

"Maybe not. The producer liked my performance. They're not sure about killing off Detective Stone."

"Great." D'Amato scowled. "That's just fucking great."

"What's your problem?"

"You're a ghetto cop wearing $400 sunglasses, your watch costs more then my fuckin' car—it's embarrassing."

"You're just jealous," I said.

D'Amato sneered. "Jealous of you? Please—"

I didn't like the way D'Amato said that. Since getting the gig on *Law & Order*, I had run into a few jealous or resentful cops, but I never expected that from my partner. "You got something on your mind?"

D'Amato frowned. "You gonna get dressed, or what?"

"Be right down," I said.

"I'll alert Page Six," D'Amato shot back.

I walked into the stationhouse and headed for the locker room.

D'AMATO STEPPED INTO the street in search of his and Beckett's radio car—fucking Beckett. Although he'd never admit it to anyone, Beckett was not totally off base— D'Amato *was* jealous. But not because Beckett was an actor on a prime time TV series, or had won the prestigious NYPD Medal of Honor. It was his partner's carefree bachelor life style.

Beckett lived on the fashionable Upper East Side of Manhattan in a tastefully decorated, rent-controlled (20 percent of market value) apartment. He did not own a car. Had no real financial responsibilities other then his penchant for clothes and dining in the better restaurants. He could party every day, take home a different female every night. He answered to no one.

Whereas D'Amato answered to a nagging wife, lived fifty miles from the city in a rundown A-frame—there were car payments, insurance, a crushing mortgage, never-ending emergency home repairs and ever-rising real estate taxes and property assessments. Add to that the overwhelming financial responsibilities that went with rearing two young daughters; D'Amato's threadbare wardrobe was vintage Wal-Mart.

But even with their differing life styles, he used to be able to talk to Beckett. Pictures of him and Beckett hung all over his Massapequa Shores home; on the walls, on the fireplace mantle. There were pictures of them at police barbecues, beer bashes, bachelor parties. They used to be inseparable, during work and after. Beckett was godfather to his eldest daughter. But since he landed the part on *Law & Order* things had changed. Beckett no longer had time to hang out with D'Amato or the other cops. He was often preoccupied, uninterested in police work, aloof even. It was obvious to D'Amato that his partner now thought he was too good to be a cop. Not that Beckett had said so, not in so many words.

"Hey, D'Amato." Two cops in civilian clothes, heading home, were cackling like adolescents. "Your TV star partner gonna put on lipstick tonight?"

"Up yours," D'Amato said. He allowed no one to criticize Beckett but himself.

No one.

# CHAPTER 4

Zeke Taylor was feeling lower than a snake's belly in a wagon rut. He was losing face in front of his two younger brothers, Bo and Bubba, something he just could not tolerate.

Zeke, twenty-three, scuzzy, long brown hair, the eldest of the three Taylor boys and the one with the most tattoos, was getting really pissed off at the ig-nor-amus in the new, green Jaguar driving west across New York City's Queensboro Bridge. No matter how hard Zeke slammed his derelict 1972 brown Ford into the rear of the four-door luxury sedan, the dumb ass wouldn't pull over.

Bo, twenty-one, in the passenger seat habitually scratching his crotch, wearing a soiled "I Eat Pussy 'Cause It Looks Like a Taco" T-shirt, and Bubba, nineteen, in the back, shirtless, were snickering. Zeke kept losing more and more face by the second. And that meant it was time for him to get mean. He squinted, focused on the Jaguar's driver, burped up squalls of three A.M. Jack Daniel's and anchovy pizza, and mustered up his dark powers of positive thinking.

One month ago, Zeke, having served time in prison for a string of brutal armed robberies, was released from a

Mississippi chain gang. The warden, who thought of himself as a progressive reformer rather than the practicing sadist he was, ordered that *every* inmate read the national best-seller, *Think Positive*, before they were discharged.

Zeke, his conviction reversed on a legal technicality, and with only days until his release, buckled down and read the entire book in one night.

It changed his life forever.

Zeke's cellmate, Hambone, snored. Before reading *Think Positive*, Zeke would drop from his bunk in the middle of the night and punch Hambone in the face until he stopped snoring. Once Zeke hit Hambone so hard and so often he not only stopped snoring, he almost stopped breathing. But hell, that wasn't Zeke's fault. Snoring drove him nuts.

But after Zeke read *Think Positive*'s chapter about "how to develop lasting friendships," he decided the next time Hambone snored, instead of beating the snot out of him, he would approach him like a gentleman and see if they could resolve the problem without violence.

That night Hambone began snoring. This time Zeke eased down from his bunk, gently shook his cellmate awake, and informed him of the snoring dilemma. Zeke told his justifiably alarmed bunkmate how snoring made him lose sleep which made him angry, which made him violent. He then suggested several remedies which might alleviate the problem. Like sleeping on his stomach, or on his side, or switching to a larger or smaller pillow.

Hambone, certain Zeke had lost his cotton-picking mind, suggested that Zeke "go fuck hisself."

At first Zeke's feelings were hurt. But he recalled the chapter in *Think Positive* about "how to turn any challenge into a new success." Zeke chided his cellmate for using foul language and responding to his attempt at diplomacy with such hostility. He suggested, in the strongest possible terms, that Hambone read *Think Positive*.

And then Zeke beat the snot out of him.

Zeke was discharged from prison a few days later with the clothes on his back, the *Think Positive* book, and his chain-gang pay. He purchased the brown Ford from a local used car dealer, then raced home to a dilapidated tobacco farm in Tupelo, Mississippi, birthplace of Elvis Presley. There, with the aid of his chain-smoking, bourbon-guzzling, snaggletoothed, common-law wife—she actually had a decent body if you overlooked the zits and mosquito bite scabs—he honed his positive thinking skills and developed:

- A positive mental attitude: He became positively positive he was gifted with an e-normous brain.
- Sound physical health: He could drink a quart of moonshine and still walk a straight line.
- Harmony in human relationships: He now hit his wife with an open hand instead of a closed fist.
- Freedom from all forms of fear: Zeke wasn't scared of nothing except maybe his wife, the crazy bitch. He slept with one eye open.
- The capacity for faith: Zeke knew beyond a doubt that he could sell sunglasses in a coal mine.
- A willingness to share his blessings: If Zeke had a quart of moonshine, and you knew he had it, and he knew that you knew he had it, he'd share it.
- An open mind on all subjects: Long as you agreed with Zeke's idol, the Grand High Exalted Mystic Wizard of the Klu Klux Klan.
- Self-discipline in all circumstances: Zeke stopped mixing drugs and booze. Well, sort of.
- The capacity to understand others: Zeke now understood all white Southern Baptist males.

A few weeks later the new and improved Zeke knocked his wife unconscious with an empty Jack Daniel's bottle. He hocked her TV and stereo, and stole what few dollars she had managed to squirrel away while on welfare. Then Zeke picked up his two younger brothers, who worked at a nearby Dairy Queen, and made straight for the land of Oz, New York City.

Zeke had learned while on the chain gang that the pickings were ripe as a month-old melon in the Big Apple. He also learned that New York law enforcement was stretched so thin that the undermanned police force took hours to respond to reports of a crime. It was almost impossible to get arrested for anything, unless you was a rag-headed terrorist, a nigger, or just plain dumb as dirt.

Using the prison library computer, Zeke spent part of most every day researching his future home. He pulled up maps and New York City newspapers and studied the five boroughs with an interest only a criminal mastermind planning a crime spree worthy of Jesse James could muster.

From fellow inmates, he culled a catalogue of criminal intelligence: where to buy guns, fake IDs, to whom and where to fence stolen goods.

Zeke figured if he was gonna test his newfound powers of positive thinking, New York City would be the positively perfect place.

Zeke reread the section in *Think Positive* on "how to win the job you want" and came up with this bump and rob scam—which had been going smooth as a gravy sandwich until today. Zeke would simply permit the Ford to roll into the rear end of a car in front of them—a Mercedes, Jaguar, Porsche or even a Lexus would do—and drivers would brake to a stop, jump out of their vehicle and start screaming. Then Zeke, all smiles and apologies, would take the driver to the side of the road to exchange insurance information, stick a gun in his face, rob him of cash and jewelry, steal his car. Then the Taylor brothers would take off like jackrabbits in coyote country.

By the time the short-handed New York police got wind of the robbery and car theft, the Taylors were up in the

Bronx's Black Cat Social Club—a place highly recommended by Zeke's fellow prison inmates—fencing the stolen goods.

Now Zeke's brothers were laughing out loud at him.

Zeke began yanking on his left ear, the one with the swastika tattooed on the lobe, the one he always yanked when he got mad. And Zeke was getting madder by the minute. For the life of him, he couldn't figure out why the Jaguar's driver didn't respond appropriately to being rear-ended.

Zeke hit the gas and the brown Ford slammed yet again, into the Jag's bumper: a hungry duck after a junebug. But instead of pulling over, the Jag's driver flashed Zeke the finger. Bubba and Bo were laughing hysterically.

"Y'all think this is funny?" Zeke said.

"Better 'en Redneck TV," Bubba said.

"Better 'en winning first prize in a tobacco spitting contest," Bo said.

Zeke punched Bo in the mouth.

Bubba guffawed.

Zeke pulled his .38, pointed it at the back seat.

"Keep laughing, asshole, see what happens."

Bubba stopped laughing.

Zeke stuck the gun back in his waistband, then decided to take positively positive action. He stomped on the gas. And the resulting impact smashed the Jaguar's rear lights and dented the trunk. The Jag swerved. The driver slammed on the brakes and made a skidding stop in the middle of the Queensboro Bridge.

NEW YORK CITY First Grade Detective, Robert Doyle—no one would dare call him Bob, Rob, or Bobby—was supposed to be catching up on paperwork in the 41st Precinct squad room. Instead he was trapped in standstill west-bound traffic on the Queensboro Bridge.

Doyle's usual biweekly appointment at a men's tanning/hair salon—he always scheduled the appointment on city time—had run behind schedule. If traffic didn't start moving soon, he'd be late signing out, which could make him late for that evening's black tie affair.

Doyle ran his fingers though his only-just dyed hair and chided himself for deciding to use the 59th Street Bridge, an ancient, crumbling, forever-under-repair overpass that connected the borough of Queens to the east side of Manhattan.

Doyle told himself to stay calm. He put the car in park and checked that the rented tuxedo, draped over the passenger seat in a plastic suit bag, contained all the customary accessories: tie, cummerbund, gold cufflinks—everything was there. He zipped up the suit bag and then inserted a CD in the CD player. He hit "play," sat back and tried to relax by humming along to Bach's Trio Sonata No. 1. Thirty seconds later he flipped out, punched the dash board. "Damned traffic!"

Doyle shoved open the car door. He stepped out, looked ahead, and saw the source of the tie-up. A two-car accident between a junk 1972 brown Ford and a new green Jaguar was choking off traffic flow. Probably a minor accident, but the imbecilic drivers had decided to stop in the middle of the bridge to inspect the damage.

Doyle checked his wristwatch, let go an exasperated moan and decided he'd had enough. He slammed his car door shut, remote-locked it, and paraded up the road to the accident scene.

Always tanning-bed brown, Doyle was attired in a dark Savile Row business suit, white shirt and tie, and looked like an English aristocrat, not a cop. He was past fifty, alarmingly out of shape—an obsessively private, fussy, self-absorbed elitist who claimed to socialize exclusively with high society and/or the beautiful people. Not—heaven forbid—other cops.

Doyle saw a large, well-dressed black man shove a scroungy white guy. The black guy screamed that the scroungy guy was a "jackass." The scroungy guy called the black guy a "field nigger." Other irate drivers had gotten out of their cars, were surrounding the two quarrelling men, and picking sides. Tempers were at the boiling point.

"Hold it." Doyle produced his gold detective shield and loudly ordered everyone back to their cars. But the black guy and Scroungy charged each other like rodeo bulls. Doyle wedged himself between the two, grappled and pushed them apart. That's when the first punch was thrown. Scroungy threw a roundhouse punch that struck Doyle in the face and toppled him. But Doyle, a former Syracuse University middleweight boxing champ, was back on his feet in an instant. Scroungy, quick as a weasel, ducked a Doyle right cross and glancing left hook. Then someone jumped on the black guy and other drivers joined in. Fists started flying and the donnybrook was on.

A dozen motorcycle cops, heading to United Nations escort duties, roared up the Queensboro Bridge along the white center lines through the standstill traffic and stumbled onto the melee. They stopped, dismounted their Harleys, waded into the crowd and used batons to break up the brawl. A burly motorcycle sergeant lumbered over to Doyle.

"You okay, Doyle?" the sergeant said.

"I'll survive."

"Hell happened here?" the sergeant said.

"You!" Doyle brushed the sergeant aside, lunged and cracked Scroungy across the mouth, staggering him.

"Identify yourself," Doyle said.

Scroungy steadied himself by leaning on a delivery van. "My name's Zeke Taylor, sir." The expression on his face said his jaw and feelings were hurt. "I didn't mean to hit you, sir. I was aiming at the nigger."

Doyle noted the swastika tattoo on Zeke's left ear lobe and the one that read "God Sucks" on his left bicep. He grabbed Zeke by the neck, slammed him face first against the side of the van, spread-eagle, and frisked him.

"Gun." Doyle pulled a .38-caliber revolver from Zeke's waistband and stuffed it into his own right trouser pocket. He peeled Zeke's hands off the van one at a time and hand-cuffed them behind his back.

"You're under arrest, Zeke." Doyle manhandled Zeke back to his car, unlocked and opened the rear door, grabbed a handful of Zeke's greasy hair and hammered his head against the car doorframe.

"You have the right to remain silent, Zeke." Doyle crammed his dazed prisoner into the back seat and shut the door.

"Would you mind dispersing the traffic?" Doyle called to the motorcycle sergeant with his usual lockjawed pomposity. "And be quick about it. I'm attending a black-tie function in a few hours. I'd rather not be late." Doyle took a moment to straighten his silk tie, then eased himself into his car, started the engine and waited impatiently.

"Heck's Doyle's problem?" a cop asked the sergeant.

The sergeant pursed his lips. "You mean besides being an asshole?"

The cop chuckled. "Besides that."

"Rumor is, a sick wife."

"How sick?"

The sergeant shrugged.

"Still," the cop said. "That's no excuse."

Bo AND BUBBA Taylor exchanged fretful looks, backpedaled, and melted into the mess of mired cars and irate motorists.

"What're we gonna do?" Bo said, waving his arms at the cop's car, trying in vain to catch the dazed Zeke's waning attention.

"Stop waving," Bubba said. "You'll get us all locked up."

"But what about Zeke?" Bo said.

"I'll think a something," Bubba said. "Let's git."

Acting invisible, the Taylor brothers retreated to the safety of their brown Ford, locked themselves in, and waited for the traffic to start moving.

# CHAPTER 5

Their eyes gave them away.

Pete from Queens considered the patrons of the Black Cat Social Club, located at Casanova Street in the Bronx.

Take the dreadlocked Jamaican posse smoking dope and playing cards at the next table. Or the furnace-eyed tub of lard Tookie Jones and his gang of Stoners, swilling shots of tequila at the bar. Or the pimp du jour with eyes like a vacant lot, cleaning his fingernails with the gleaming blade of a stiletto, in the company of several totally bored, over-the-hill whores. Their eyes spoke volumes, the hostile, glazed orbs of psychopaths.

But what impressed Pete most about the Black Cat Social Club—besides its foreboding exterior, pumped-up air conditioning and musty stench of stale beer—was the decorating theme. There was none.

Inside, the place was dingy, painted iridescent red, lit with a dozen miniature plastic Tiffany lamps and furnished with a menagerie of dilapidated tables, plastic chairs, three-legged bar stools and dusty imitation plants. Rotting carpet and blinking Christmas tree lights complemented the decaying nude centerfolds Scotch-taped to the roach-splattered plywood walls. The bone-rattling jukebox spewed a mix of oldies, modern day rap, reggae and classic country western. Pete couldn't help but feel comfortable here. It was just like home.

The Black Cat Social Club, like hundreds of other fire traps in the Bronx, was actually an unlicensed bar. By terming the place a "private social club," the owner could skirt the strict State Liquor Authority fire, health and safety laws.

Pete had moseyed into the Black Cat Social Club that morning in an attempt to locate the owner, renowned for her nefarious contacts: an ex-con transsexual named Mario Vitelli, also known as "Mona Love."

Pete and Mona had been raised in the same middle-class neighborhood in the Ridgewood section of Queens, and had both attended Grover Cleveland high school, though not together—Pete was years older. They were not friends.

Far from it.

Mona's father, Mr. Vitelli, was a low-level Mafia associate, degenerate gambler, gavone, and all around pain in the ass who, in a matter of months, parlayed a small debt into a $50,000 loss to Pete's employer, a Queens bookmaker. When the bookmaker demanded the minimum monthly vig, Mona's father, under the impression that his mob associations made him untouchable, laughed at him, told him to go fuck himself and added, "You can't get blood from a stone." The bookmaker had smiled at Mona's father and responded with an ominous "We'll see about that."

With the permission of a Queens consigliere, the bookmaker sent Pete, a recently discharged Army MP, to collect.

Sixteen-year-old Mario/Mona was home the evening Pete crashed through her family's front door and demanded the bookmaker's money. Mr. Vitelli told Pete to fuck off. So Pete locked Mona and her mother in a bedroom, beat Mr. Vitelli to a bloody mush, then dragged him out into the wintry night. Mona's mother called the police. But Pete was never arrested. And they never saw or heard from their husband/father again.

So, that morning, when Pete arrived at the Black Cat Social Club, clamped a tree-root hand tight around Mona's delicate neck and informed her that he had a torch job he needed to outsource, Mona was all ears.

Pete wanted men with the following qualifications: reliable but not too bright. And Mona quickly assembled a collection of slow-blinking reprobates and ex-cons in need of Pete's cash. But after several discouraging interviews—Tookie Jones struck Pete as too ruthless for his own good, and he couldn't warm up to the doped-up Jamaicans—Pete was anxious about the possibility of disappointing his boss.

Luckily for Mona, the front door of the Black Cat scraped open and two rednecks, Bo and Bubba Taylor, rolled in.

Pete watched as the Taylor brothers, in a sweat-covered panic, moved hurriedly through the crowd to the bar. They waved to Tookie Jones and his Stoners, then wedged themselves between a pair of octogenarian alcoholics.

"Cops got Zeke," Bo shouted to Mona over Johnny Cash's "Folsom Prison Blues." His words, tight with excitement, came rapid-fire. "You gotta help us get 'im out."

"The hell I do." Mona hated the very sight of the Taylor brothers. Knew that, because of their outspoken racist views, it was only a matter of time before someone killed them.

Mona placed six shots of rotgut tequila, a shaker of salt, and wedges of lime in front of Tookie Jones's crew.

Tookie flexed a fat bicep as he threw back his drink. "What happened, dawg?" he said to Bo.

Bo stuck his right hand down the front of his jeans and scratched his crotch. "We had a car ac-cident on the

Queensboro Bridge and Zeke wound up fightin' some big nigger."

A half-dozen black faces with murderous eyes pinned the Taylor brothers.

"Cops showed up." Bubba scooped up a fistfull of stale bar kibbles from a bowl and stuffed them into his mouth. "Found his gun."

"Possession," Mona said cheerfully.

"That's a mandatory minimum one-year prison sentence in New York State," Tookie said.

"That sucks," Chico, one of Tookie's Stoners, said.

"Gol-darn right it sucks," Bo said.

"I'd get a good lawyer, I were you," one of the octogenarians volunteered.

"Mind your business," Bo said, in the old man's face. A ploy so no one would notice him artfully swipe ten dollars of the man's money off the bar. " 'Fore I stick my size twelve up your wrinkled old His-panic ass." Bo jammed his right hand, the one with the ten, in his pants pocket, clawed his crotch. "We ain't got no money for no Jew lawyer, Miss Love."

"That's too bad." Mona forced a frown. "Unless you got friends in the police department." She strangled a laugh. "Don't suppose you know any friendly cops?"

"Hell no," Bo said.

"You, Miss Love?" Bubba said.

"No, but—" Mona looked toward Pete, then back at the Taylors—now here were a couple of dimwitted potential arsonists, exactly what Pete wanted. Mona grinned at the Taylors. "I know someone who might."

"You do?" Bo said.

"Follow me," Mona said and escorted them to Pete's table by the wall under a sagging plastic palm tree.

"Pete," Mona said. "This is Bo and Bubba Taylor."

Pete grunted. Mona made herself scarce.

The Taylors, awed by Pete's appearance, stood frozen.

"Sit," Pete said.

The Taylors eased onto plastic chairs.

Bo offered Pete a grimy hand. "Pleased to make your acquaintance, sir."

Pete let the hand hang there. "State your business."

"Well, sir." Bo cleared his throat. "Our brother, Zeke, got his-self arrested for possession of a firearm."

"Yeah. Miss Love," Bubba said, "told us you might have a friend in the New York police department."

"So?"

"So," Bo said. "We was wondering, maybe your friend could make Zeke's gun charge go away?"

As Pete sat back his plastic chair creaked. Its legs buckled but held. "What's in it for me?"

The brothers exchanged vacant looks.

The theme song from *Deliverance* played on the jukebox.

"What do you want?" Bo said.

"We got no money," Bubba said.

Pete scrutinized the Taylors. "I need an empty building set on fire. Got a problem with that?"

"Hell no," Bo said.

"None," Bubba said.

Pete handed the Taylors a piece of paper with the address of a building at Coster Street and Viele Avenue typed on it. Bo and Bubba studied it like they were reading a menu written in French.

"You can read," Pete said, "can't you?"

"Yes, sir," Bo said, not the least bit offended.

"The building is abandoned. Burn it to the ground. Tonight. That means after dark." Pete searched their greasy faces and wondered when they had last bathed. "Questions?" He snatched the piece of paper back.

"Burn it. How?"

Pete slapped fifty dollars on the table. "Buy some gasoline. Pour it on the stairwell. Light it. Run like hell."

"Any particular kind of gasoline?" Bo said.

*Oh, brother.* "No," Pete said. "Your choice."

Bo squinted in thought. Then nodded like he finally understood. "How 'bout Zeke?" Bo said. "Can you get him outta jail?"

"Consider it done."

Bo and Bubba jumped to their feet, let out a rebel yell, slapped each other high-fives.

"Thank you, sir," Bo said.

"Thank you very much," Bubba said.

"Meet me here afterwards," Pete said. "We'll go pick up your brother."

"Yes, sir." Bo snatched the fifty.

Pete watched the Taylors join Tookie Jones and his gang at the bar and couldn't suppress the smug, baleful smile that spread across his face. Although he'd always made a habit of doing his own dirty work—no co-conspirators meant no one to turn state's evidence and testify against you in court—the Taylors were a timely necessity, albeit a short-term one.

After the fire, he would intercept them outside. Take them for a ride. Kill them. That way they could not deny the forthcoming allegations that they were responsible for the entire string of South Bronx arsons.

Pete walked out of the Black Cat into the late afternoon sun and turned south in the direction of Coster Street. He wanted to arrive early in order to secure a good spot from which to watch the fire.

# CHAPTER 6

A group of helmeted, skate-boarding eight-year-olds nearly knocked me over as I left the precinct and stepped onto Simpson Street. I jumped back and high-fived one of the jubilant, pint-sized desperados as he raced by. I heard laughter, looked across the street and saw Juan Langlois, a level-3 predicate sex offender and drug dealer whooping it up with a group of pre-teens, handing out cold soft drinks—frustration and anger hit my bloodstream like a shot of Irish whiskey.

Juan was first imprisoned for rape and sodomy at age sixteen. After he'd spent three years behind bars, I arrested him for sodomizing an eight-year-old boy. He told the newspapers I framed him and swore revenge adding the charge of threatening a police officer to his list of crimes. Yet here he was back out on the street after a mere five years in prison.

My first instinct was to roust that degenerate, slap the piss out of him, kick his ass out of the neighborhood, maybe even break a few bones in the process. But I knew that, since the recidivism rate for level-3s was near 100 percent, the only way to stop Juan was to take him into an alley, put a bullet in his brain.

I joined D'Amato and we walked to our RMP which the cops from the previous tour had left parked on the far end of the block. We heard drums. Looked and saw a crowd surrounding several frenzied young men pounding different-sized percussion instruments, really into it. The resulting primal composition was haunting, strangely erotic: sounds of the barrio.

"Question." D'Amato had to raise his voice to be heard above the drums. "I begged you to fix me up with that broad on *Law & Order*, the sultry one who plays the ADA."

"I remember."

"Why didn't you?"

I looked at him. "You're married."

"A man needs a mistress just to break the monogamy."

"Your idea of romance is taking a date to a porn film."

"Yeah. Women love porn films."

"I rest my case," I said.

We arrived at our blue-and-white.

"Telling it straight, Beckett. I wish they'd kill you off that show for good." D'Amato went round to the driver's side. "Maybe then you'd get your mind back on police work."

*Police work.* The words pinballed in my brain. I glanced around at the hulking tenements, at the impoverished ghetto denizens and felt like I was suffocating, trapped in a netherworld I had somehow transcended.

It was at that precise moment I decided to resign from the New York City Police Department. I no longer wished to minister to the sick and dying, or solve people's marital problems, or discipline punks, break up fights, chase bad guys, or be involved in a gunfight ever again. I felt worn, my legs leaden with fatigue.

"Hey, dickhead. You listening to me?"

I sort of nodded. "I'm listening."

"What'd I say?"

I focused on my friend. "That I'm the person you admire most in the world."

D'Amato smiled. "Exactly."

We opened the RMP's rear doors—the rattle-bang rig smelled strongly of body odor and faintly of vomit. We began the usual chore of searching the auto for discarded contraband, weapons, or recording devices planted by the Internal Affairs Bureau, IAB. We pulled out the rear seat, checked under and behind, then checked the front before getting in.

I settled into my seat. The familiar broken springs dug into my buttocks and thighs. I positioned my 9mm Glock, then clicked the safety off my backup gun, which was tucked in my waistband—a 9mm Browning—half-cocked it, and decided this would be my final tour. Finito. *No mas.* At midnight, I planned to walk into Captain Ward's office, hand in my gun and shield, tender my resignation, sign out on the roll call sheet for the very last time.

"Hey, earth to Beckett."

I glanced at D'Amato. I was not ready to tell him about my decision to quit. He'd try to talk me out of it. "How's the family?" I said, trying to steer the conversation.

"What?"

"Your wife and kids?"

"They're great. Why?"

"Just asking." I shrugged. "I need a reason?"

"How about me?" D'Amato said belligerently. "Ask how I am for a change."

I glanced sideways to see if he was kidding. "All right. How are *you*, Vinnie?"

"Fan-fucking-tastic," D'Amato said.

I tossed my summons book up on the dashboard. We each placed our nightsticks on the floor, alongside our seats for quick access.

D'Amato opened his summons book, flipped a few pages. "I'm almost outta summons."

His summons book joined mine on the dashboard.

"Tonight's gonna be like old times," D'Amato said.

"After the tour, we'll head to a titty bar and get absolutely pulverized. What do you say?"

The last thing I wanted to do after work was hang out in some sleazy topless joint. Don't get me wrong. There was a time when I was into titty bars. Not any longer. "Let's see how we feel later."

D'Amato started the engine.

Out of habit I switched on the inadequate air conditioner: warm air blew in our faces. The radio belched static and the voice of the NYPD dispatcher, Central, filled the RMP.

*"Central to all units, holding fifty jobs in the 41 Precinct. What units available?"*

"Holding fifty jobs" meant that fifty calls to 911, everything from violent disputes, felony assaults, burglaries and armed robberies had yet to be responded to.

"Screw 'em," D'Amato said. "Lets get coffee first."

*"41 Ida. Central to 41 Ida."*

"Tag," I said. "We're it."

"Aw fuck," D'Amato said.

I picked up the radio. "41 Ida."

*"41 Ida. Respond to Coster Street and Viele Avenue. Smoke condition. Advise if fire department is needed."*

"That ain't our sector," D'Amato complained. "And it's clear out in Hunts Point. Hell're they calling us for?"

He was right. "We're on Simpson Street, Central," I said into the radio. "Anyone closer?"

*"Negative, Ida."*

I shrugged at D'Amato. "10-4."

"Smoke condition," D'Amato snarled. "We're cops, not firemen. Why don't they give it to the goddamned fire department in the first place?"

I stymied a snide comment that would have set D'Amato off. D'Amato had had a problem with firemen ever since one of them charmed a voluptuous jughead away from him at a St. Patrick's party last year.

I switched on the RMP's flashing lights.

D'Amato shifted into drive. Stepped on the accelerator.

"THIS IS IT," I said. "Viele Avenue. Make a right." I switched off the flashing lights. D'Amato made the turn, squeezed past a double-parked Con Edison (gas company) truck, then slowed. A large crowd was blocking the street.

"Ah," D'Amato bellowed. "My people." He opened his arms—Moses parting the Red Sea. "I will lead the animals across the Bronx River to the Promised Land. Co-op City."

I looked up the street which, with its burned-out buildings, resembled Berlin after the Second World War. The crowd had gathered in front of a tenement and was looking up at something, pointing.

I scanned the boarded-up five-story brick tenement. Saw faint wisps of black smoke seeping from all around the perimeter of the roof.

"We've got a working structural fire," I said. "Call the fire department."

"It's an abandoned rat hole." D'Amato put the car in park. "Let it burn."

Ignoring D'Amato, I said, "I'll start moving the crowd back." I hurried from the car, cut through the throng to the tenement entrance.

A frail old-timer, wheezing from smoke inhalation, lay prone across the front stoop. He squinted up at me with red, vein-flogged eyes.

"Squatters. Upstairs." The old-timer gasped. "I tried. Smoke's too thick."

*The building was occupied.*

A cold sweat chilled me, my emotions an intense mixture of duty-sense and anxiety. Eight years ago, while off duty, I had inadvertently walked into a burning building and stumbled upon two children home alone. I carried them to safety, was felled by smoke and nearly killed—which was the reason I was awarded the Medal of Honor.

I knew what smoke and fire could do. I'd rather face a room full of armed psychos than enter that tenement. I scanned the street, listened in vain for Fire Department sirens.

"Fifth floor," the old-timer said.

I groaned. Years of kicking down South Bronx doors in hot pursuit of fleeing felons had left me with torn cartilage in both knees—stairs were the enemy.

"You gotta hurry." The old-timer tugged my trouser leg. "A girl in a red dress and an infant."

*A girl. An infant.*

I ran into the tenement.

Relying heavily on a handrail for support, I climbed the broken stairs to the second floor. Smoke grew thicker and the pervasive stench of gasoline nearly choked me. I heard noise above, a whooshing sound. Smoke was being drawn rapidly up the stairwell. I remembered a phenomenon a fireman pal had warned me about: an exploding fireball sometimes called a "flash-over." If this was a flash-over, the building could blow up. I would be incinerated.

The whooshing sound became louder, more intense, and I was convinced a flash-over was coming. I hobbled back down the stairs. Charged out to the street. Dove head first for the safety of the pitted concrete pavement.

Boom! The building exploded in flames. Windows blew out. Fragments of brick and jagged glass shot through the air, slicing into the crowd like a million tiny razors. People started screaming, trampling each other in their panic for cover. Flames licked the sky. Thick black smoke rolled.

I looked up to the fifth floor just in time to witness a horrifying site: a female in a red dress, all but engulfed in flames. She held a bundle out the window for a brief moment then dropped it—the infant.

To me, the infant dropped in slow motion, tumbling through the air, gaining speed—I had to try to catch her. I pushed to my feet, took a step, but my right knee buckled and I hit the ground hard and scraped it on the broken concrete.

Suddenly, from out of nowhere, appeared D'Amato. He was sprinting. Cutting zigzag through the crowd like a wide receiver. Knocking people aside. His eyes homed in on the falling infant. It was going to be a miracle. D'Amato always came through and he would now. I could always count on D'Amato. He would save the infant.

D'Amato left his feet, flying through the air like a goddamned eagle. It was an Olympian effort, D'Amato diving to save the infant.

D'Amato hit the ground, empty-handed.

A woman screamed, covered her eyes.

A collective hush silenced the crowed.

I did not want to believe what I saw. I pushed himself up—aches bit into my elbow, hands and knees. I shoved my way through the crowd, stepped over D'Amato, my eyes never leaving the child.

D'Amato struggled to his feet, really hurting. "I had her." His voice trembled. "I thought I had her."

We looked on in horror.

The infant was impaled on a spiked wrought iron fence. Blood was trickling out of her back, neck and buttocks.

"Christ," D'Amato whispered.

Fire engines began to arrive on the scene.

I stepped close to the infant and saw faint movement in her chest. She was still breathing. Could her heart and lungs be undamaged? There was a chance.

Then we heard it, a heavy grinding sound. Debris fell around us. We looked up. The entire north wall of the building was buckling. What was left of the tenement was about to crash down on us, on the infant.

"Beckett, D'Amato," a fireman yelled from an arriving fire truck. "Get out of there!"

People ran for their lives.

"Get to the car, Vinnie."

D'Amato did not question me. He bolted. I slipped my hands under the infant, lifted her straight off the iron spikes into my arms and ran as fast as I could.

We jumped in the RMP, adrenaline a magnet between us. D'Amato screeched away from the curb just as the building collapsed with a deafening roar. We did not look back.

"She's a DOA," D'Amato said, careening down the street, narrowly missing two uniformed gas company employees.

"Shut up and drive." My chest, pants and hands were soaked with blood. The kid was emptying its life all over me. I pressed my fingers on the wounds in an attempt to stanch the free flowing blood. I lowered my mouth over the little nose and mouth in my arms and began resuscitation, the siren screaming, the police car speeding through traffic.

D'Amato radioed ahead, telling Central to have a trauma team standing by at the hospital.

We arrived at the hospital in just four minutes. We burst through the emergency room doors and I gave up the child to the waiting physicians. We watched, helplessly, as the trauma team laid her on an examination table and searched for signs of life.

There were none.

A doctor turned to us. Pulled plastic gloves from his hands and shook his head. "I'm sorry," he said, as if we were the infant's parents. "She's gone."

I threw the switch from numb to very numb.

"You're bleeding," the doctor said.

At first I thought he was referring to the infant's blood that had soaked my shirt and pants. But then I saw that both my elbows and the heels of my palms were scraped raw: the price of skidding on concrete. I could also see blood where the knees were torn out of my uniform pants.

"You need to clean those wounds," the doctor said and handed me some gauze and a tube of antiseptic.

I thanked him and walked out of the emergency room into the blinding late afternoon sun. We drove in silence back to the 41st Precinct stationhouse.

# CHAPTER 7

Solana considered the oily face of a wild-eyed panhandler shuffling through the unventilated subway car and concluded that the idiot had a death wish. Begging for spare change from intrepid ghetto residents, many of whom worked sixteen-hour days for minimum wage, was tricky enough. But being pushy, getting in people's faces and demanding a handout was asking for the worst kind of trouble.

"Hunts Point Avenue," a voice droned over the subway's static-laced PA system. Solana abandoned her seat, wedged though the jam-packed car toward the exit, hoping that she'd make it off the train before the panhandler—a lanky man who spoke in a clipped, agitating manner—imposed on the wrong person and the inevitable happened: an angry exchange of words, a brandished weapon, bloodshed.

The doors parted and Solana rode a wave of passengers from the subway car. She smiled wearily as she passed several young men who formed a semi-circle on the crowded platform, singing a cappella amid the roar of speeding trains—they sounded pretty good. She pushed her way through the turnstile, climbed the stairs to Hunts

Point Avenue and spotted Pete from Queens's black Lincoln Town Car stopped at a red light.

Pete glanced toward the subway station.

Solana ducked behind a newsstand, routing a pride of battered cats and scattering a collection of empty cat food cans with her foot.

The traffic light changed.

Solana peeked.

Pete waved at her.

Caught, Solana gave a small wave back.

She left the cover of the newsstand and hurried north on Southern Boulevard, looking over her shoulder every few steps. She tripped over a baby stroller, crashed head-on into a meter maid who cursed her for not looking where she was going, and saw the Lincoln round the corner and steer in her direction.

Pete was following her.

Panic.

Solana dashed into a restaurant doorway and cowered: her body began to shiver, her legs grew weak. She stole a look and saw Pete's car cruising closer—how to escape? She was about to take refuge in the restaurant, maybe flee by a back door, head to her apartment using a roundabout route, when she saw a cop car pass and turn left onto Westchester Avenue. Solana realized she was only a few blocks from her neighborhood police station.

Pete's Lincoln prowled by. Solana read the Lincoln's license plate number and memorized it. Then she broke from the doorway and began to run.

The only time she'd been anywhere near the 41st Precinct was to protest the police shooting of her upstairs neighbor: the unarmed youth shot eighteen times by mistake. The news stations had covered the week-long protest where the always predictable sound-bite-hungry community activists, led by the Reverend Al Dullard, had made their appearances clamoring for justice. But when the news cameras left, so did Dullard and the community activists. The boy's family was left to grieve alone.

The 41st Precinct, a dingy, depressing place, was filled with busy cops and anxious civilians when Solana rushed in. She paused to catch her breath, looked around at the men dressed in blue—a few were leering at her—and wondered if the cops who had murdered her neighbor were among them.

Solana made her way across the muster room, past two obese black women who were holding each other, crying hysterically, past a white cop and an Hispanic couple involved in a loud, heated argument, something about a missing welfare check. The man shoved the woman. The cop told him to stop. He didn't. The cop bounced him off a wall. Across the room another cop was berating a man who'd apparently left his children home alone.

"What?" A cop standing behind the high-top desk alongside an overwrought desk sergeant was scowling at Solana. The name SCHULTZ was written on a name plate below his badge.

"Does Michael Beckett work here?" Solana said.

"Who're you?" Schultz said.

"A friend."

Schultz looked her over, head to toe. "Well, whaddya want?"

"Is he here?"

"Negative. He's out on patrol."

A phone rang. Schultz stepped over to a switchboard, answered the call, barked at the caller, then hung up. "Can you fucking believe it?" Schultz said, thoroughly exasperated. "A man my age, getting obscene phone calls." He looked at Solana. "Is it an emergency, lady?"

"A man's been following me," she said.

"He outside?" Schultz glanced to the street, placed his hand on his gun butt, and started to come out from behind the desk. "I'll take care of it."

"No. He's up on Southern Boulevard, I think."

"You wanna file a complaint?" Schultz said. "That office over there." He pointed across the room. "See Officer Neary."

"I don't know if I want to file a complaint," Solana said.

"Okay," Schultz said. "Whaddya wanna do?"

"I've got his license plate number."

"Congratulations."

Solana was taken aback. "Pardon me?"

"You got the guy's plate number. So what?"

Solana thought about how police officers are portrayed on TV and in movies: polite, helpful, courteous to the public—this cop, Schultz, was downright rude.

"Can you find out who owns the car if I give you the license plate number?"

"We can," Schultz said. "First you gotta file a complaint."

"You can't just tell me?"

"Look, lady, we can't access motor vehicle information unless there's a complaint filed."

"There's no way I can find out who owns the car?"

"I didn't say that—you got access to a computer?"

Solana said she did.

"There're all sorts of resources on the Internet," Schultz said, "from what I hear."

"What kind of resources?"

"For Christ sake, lady, I dunno. Type in 'license plate check' in a search engine. See what comes up."

"Thanks," Solana said. "For nothing."

"Anytime—you wanna leave your name for Beckett?"

Solana thought a moment. "No."

Solana found herself amid a chain gang of foul-mouthed, handcuffed prisoners being loaded into a curbside paddy wagon as she walked out of the 41 stationhouse. Ignoring their obscene comments, she stepped to the curb, scanned the street for Pete's black Lincoln. Not there.

A police car pulled up. The passenger side door opened and Michael Beckett stepped out. Solana gasped, her hand shot to her mouth. Beckett's face, arms, and shirt were stained with blood. His pants were torn at both knees. Solana's first instinct was to approach Beckett and see if he was injured, but she could tell by the way he moved that he was not badly hurt. Beside, she wasn't about to let the neighborhood gossips see her fraternizing in public with a *pendejo* cop.

Solana thought about following Beckett into the station-house, but the pained look on his face made it clear that now was not a good time. She turned, hightailed it north and disappeared into the multitudes dawdling along Simpson Street.

# CHAPTER 8

"Infant make it?" an FDNY fire marshal and old friend named Michael Collyer queried as D'Amato and I entered the 41 Precinct clerical office.

D'Amato shook his head.

"God help us," Collyer said and blessed himself with a burn-scarred hand, making the sign of the cross.

I heard someone sneeze, looked at the half-dozen black and Hispanic prisoners sitting on the floor in the precinct holding cell awaiting processing before being taken to court. A scroungy, tattooed white guy was standing at the front of the cage, smiling like an idiot, wiping his runny nose with the back of his hand.

"Howdy, officer," the white guy said.

"Who's the skell?" I asked the clerical man, a swizzle-stick-thin cop named Neary.

"Doyle's prisoner," Neary said.

"What?" D'Amato feigned shock and amazement. "You saying a 'defective', I mean *detective*, actually left a pub long enough to do police work?"

"Hard to believe," Neary said. "Isn't it?"

"Post it on the Internet," D'Amato said.

I turned to Collyer. "You here on the Coster Street fire, Marshal?"

"Affirm-a-tory." Collyer's eyes were on my bloody uniform. "Filing the report now." He snatched the arson report from Neary and handed it to me. "Found a couple of eyewitnesses."

"Witnesses?" I said skeptically. "Locals?"

"Get real," Collyer said. "Two gas company employees. They were supposed to seal off the main gas line in the burned building. Never got the chance." Collyer's report stated:

> At time and place of occurrence, witnesses (listed on attached UF #49) said that two unknown white males, 19–25 years old, 5' 10" tall, thin, stringy blond hair, dressed in jeans, one in a T-shirt, the second shirtless, were seen loitering in the vicinity of Coster Street and Viele Avenue. Witnesses further state that the males were observed entering the building carrying a red 5-gallon can of gasoline. The fire appears to have been encouraged by the presence of a highly flammable liquid propellant. Lab analysis of debris to follow.

"Where're the gas company guys now?" I said.

"Upstairs looking at mug shots," Collyer said.

"They recover the other body yet?"

Collyer shook his head. "A woman in a red dress. She was the infant's mother, according to witnesses. A child herself really. They said she looked around fifteen years old." Collyer took his hat off and scratched his freckled bald head. "There's still a couple hundred tons of rubble to dig through."

I handed the report to D'Amato, who scanned it, then handed it back to Collyer.

"So it was arson?" D'Amato said.

"Definitely." Collyer handed the report back to Neary.

"How amusing," a voice said, and all eyes turned to the clerical office entrance.

Detective Robert Doyle ambled into the room. "You speak as if that were a divine revelation of some sort, Marshal." Doyle was decked out in a tuxedo, pleated cerulean shirt, matching cummerbund and bow tie.

D'Amato elbowed me and whispered, "Check the hair."

I did. Doyle's formerly thinning white mane was now a sickly reddish brown. Since Doyle was one of those detectives who apes his TV and movie counterparts—you know, the superhero detectives who save the world while we uniformed dolts do their bidding—adopt their language and manner of dress, I wondered which actor he was emulating. Not that I gave a rat's ass. I didn't like Doyle or his phony, patrician manner. Add to that the fact he treated most other cops with amused condescension.

And Doyle didn't like me.

"I suspect even a layman, like my friend Steven Spielberg, would arrive at the very same conclusion." Doyle was fanning himself with what appeared to be a gold-embroidered invitation.

"Friend?" the scroungy guy in the cage said.

"Correct, Zeke," Doyle said. He took a quick look at my torn uniform trousers and bloody shirt but made no comment.

"No lie?" Zeke said. "You and *the* movie producer, Steven Spielberg, are friends?"

All eyes were on Doyle.

And he played the moment. Shot his cuffs: gold cufflinks came into view. "That is correct. Steven and I are quite close." He waved the invitation. "I'm attending a banquet in his honor later this very evening."

"May I see the invitation, sir?" Zeke gushed.

"You may not." Doyle put the invitation away.

D'Amato said, "I read about that bash in the *Post*. Any

moron who's stupid enough to fork over $1,000 a plate
can attend."

"You are such a mirthful fellow, D'Amato," the detective said. "Next thing, you'll urinate on my shoes." Doyle
moved to Neary's desk, swiped a hand across a corner
checking for dust, then sat. "Question, Marshal Collyer.
Have you uncovered any solid leads?"

"Only descriptions," Collyer said. "And I'm positive
the propellant was gasoline."

"Yes," Doyle said. "That's about what I expected."

"Give Collyer a break, Doyle," Neary said. "And while
you're at it, get your pompous fucking ass off my desk."

Zeke hee-hawed.

Doyle turned to Neary. "I realize that this may be a difficult concept for you to grasp, Officer Neary. So, listen
closely." Doyle spoke as if to a retard. "Profanity commu-
nicates one's lack of good breeding."

"Kiss my Irish ass," Neary said, and then his head tilted
quizzically. "What'd you do to your hair?"

Doyle stiffened.

"It's the color of dog shit."

"He's right." D'Amato laughed. "You give the word
'shithead' a whole new meaning."

Doyle looked like he'd swallowed a hair brush. "The hell
with all of you." He stepped to the holding cage, opened it,
dragged Zeke to a chair by Neary's desk, slammed him onto
it, and began the paperwork that would process his prisoner.

"Who owns the Coster Street building?" I asked Collyer.

"The Gold Organization." Collyer went on to say the
building was part of ten square city blocks of mostly abandoned tenements recently acquired for renovation by the
mammoth real estate concern. "They also own the abandoned building over on East Bay Avenue that was gutted
recently."

I took a moment to consider the information. "You saying you see a pattern?"

"Still investigating," Collyer said. "Understand, there are only thirty fire marshals for the entire city of New York. The fire department answered over 480,000 calls for help last year. We'll top that this year. These abandoned building fire investigations are pretty low on our agenda."

"The East Bay Avenue fire," I said. "That arson?"

"Again, still investigating," Collyer said. "The responding fire lieutenant told me it looked like a couple of squatters started a cooking fire that got out of hand. But he discovered the remains of what could be a simple arson instrument: matches rolled around a cigarette."

"Was Coster Street vacant for long?" I said.

"Only just abandoned," Collyer said.

"Which explains why the gas company guys were there," D'Amato said.

"Neighbors said that the girl and her infant probably moved in yesterday," Collyer said. "The arsonist probably didn't know anyone was in the building."

"Or didn't care." I recalled the stench of gasoline. Envisioned the girl in the red dress, a human torch. And the infant who, minutes ago, died in my arms. "What type of person purposely sets fire to a building?"

"Well, there're different types of arsonists," Collyer said. "There's the classic pyromaniac. A guy with an 'impulse control disorder.' He can't resist the urge to deliberately start fires. Then there are 'fire starters.' They do it for attention. Usually young males with emotional problems. And then there are criminals who use fire for the purpose of insurance fraud, or to cover another crime, such as homicide—we could find another body, or bodies in that debris."

I hadn't thought about that.

"And lastly," Collyer said, "there's the most common variety of arsonists: 'strippers.' They're mostly local youth gangs. The Savage Nomads, Crips, Bloods, Stoners. They set fire to abandoned buildings, like Coster Street, to prevent reoccupation. Then they return and remove the valuable copper wire, brass pipes, and fixtures. Sell them for cash to buy guns or drugs."

"In my opinion, the fire was set by a youth gang," Doyle said with authority.

"Why's that?" I said.

"According to statistics, youth gangs commit the vast majority of abandoned building arsons. The use of a highly flammable propellant—gasoline is cheap and plentiful—fits the strippers' normal modus operandi. A professional arsonist, or a person committing arson for profit, or to cover a crime would take great care to make it look accidental. Correct, Marshal?"

"For the most part, correct, Detective."

Collyer turned to me. "I heard you two guys know the head man at the Gold Organization, R. J. Gold."

Neary looked up from his paperwork. "I thought the Gold Organization was a brand name. You know, like Coke or General Motors. There really a Mr. Gold?"

"A mystery man," Collyer said. "Like Howard Hughes was in the end. Avoids the spotlight." He looked at me, then D'Amato. "What's the story? You guys know him, or what?"

"I've been in his company half a dozen times," D'Amato said. "Beckett knows him better then I do."

Everyone in the room looked at me. I shifted. The wounds on my elbows, hands and knees itched. It was all I could to stop from scratching.

"How well you know him?" Collyer said.

I gave Collyer a blank look, wondering how much he already knew.

"Look, Beckett, a couple of city cops socialize with a billionaire," Collyer said. "Word gets around."

I sat on a short wooden bench.

Collyer sat next to me. "How well do you know Gold?"

I leaned forward, sore elbows resting on sore knees. "I thought I was his friend once."

Collyer let that sink in. "How'd you meet him?"

"He was infatuated with an ex-girlfriend of mine, Janet Roth. She happened to mention to him that her ex was a cop. Gold phoned me, invited me to his office—he wanted to meet me for some reason. Check me out, I guess."

"What kind of guy's he?"

I shrugged. "Like any other guy. More competitive than some."

"Bull," D'Amato spat. "Tell him."

I shot D'Amato a sharp look.

"Yeah," Collyer pressed. "Tell me."

I sat back and crossed a leg. I glanced out of the clerical office gathering my thoughts. I saw a man with a small knife sticking out of his back stumble into the station house, stagger through the various pockets of crime victims and witnesses, and collapse into the arms of Officer Destiny Jones.

I said, "Suppose you tell me what you know about Gold, and I'll tell you if it's true, maybe fill in the blanks."

Collyer thought a moment. "Only thing I know about him is that he's politically connected, an elusive sort, faceless, colorless. He owns an airline, ships, hotels, commercial real estate, gambling casinos. There was a newspaper story a few years back claiming that some of his financing came from the Yakuza."

"What's that?" Neary said.

"The Japanese Mafia," Collyer said.

"Far more sophisticated than the American version," Doyle said.

"I read somewhere that Gold's a scratch golfer," Collyer said. "Plays a lot and for big money. Say, you ever play golf with him?"

"Yeah," I said. "I played with him a couple of times."

"For money?"

"No." I shook my head. "But I watched him play for money several times."

"Wow," Collyer enthused. "That must've been great. He as good as they say? I read somewhere he could play professionally."

"He thinks so," I said noncommittally.

"Golf's my game, you know?" Collyer beamed and executed an imaginary swing.

"Know what the word 'golf' stands for?" D'Amato said. "Gentlemen Only . . . Ladies Forbidden. The Scots invented the game."

We all looked at D'Amato for a long moment.

"Well," Collyer said. "That's about all I know. Your turn, Beckett."

"All right." I looked directly at Collyer. "I don't know anything about his investors, Japanese or otherwise—the way I see it, all billionaire businessmen are gangsters anyway."

Heads nodded in agreement.

"But when R. J. Gold plays golf for money—"

"Yeah?" Collyer was hanging on every word.

"He cheats."

# CHAPTER 9

"Cheats?" Collyer said.

"That's what I said."

"When?" Collyer demanded. "How?"

"Five or six years ago," I said. "A small stakes game at Wing Foot. Again during a couple of big money games. I've seen him move the ball to get a better lie."

"That doesn't make sense," Doyle said. "Why would a rich man cheat at golf?"

"Good question," I said. "Ego. Plain and simple. Gold hates to lose at anything."

"Tell me more," Collyer said.

I got to my feet and began to pace the narrow office. "Well, Gold has two daughters. He's a good father. He can be a regular guy at times. Generous. But he can also be adolescently insecure, vain, obnoxious, pretentious, petty, egocentric, shallow, phony, insensitive, stubborn." I paused for effect. "He can be cruel."

Doyle said, "If he's so insufferable, why were you, er, friends with him?"

I paused to consider the question. I had genuinely liked Gold when first we met: his surprising self-effacing sense of humor. Although, after I'd conducted a comprehensive background check on him for my ex Janet—he really was rich, and very married—I had to admit a part of me envied his "lucky sperm club" credentials. I'd been raised in the Irish Catholic working class Woodlawn section of the Bronx. Gold had been raised in an elite world.

Born in the affluent Riverdale section of the Bronx, Gold had attended blue-blood schools like Dalton, New York Military Academy, Wharton. Spent his summers in family-owned villas in France and Italy. Yet, to Gold's credit, he did not share the same "entitlement" complex as other rich kids in his age bracket. Those who graduated Ivy League colleges secure in the knowledge that they would enjoy a "winking" entrée into any profession they chose. Gold, in contrast, had begun his own construction business after college and worked tirelessly at amassing a personal fortune. Eventually he took over the Gold Organization from his aging father. But the hard won success had apparently changed R. J. Gold, and not for the better. Word was, as his wealth and power increased he was developing an over-bearing arrogance.

"Excitement," I said in answer to Doyle's question. "Before I began palling out with Gold, I'd never been in a private limo, or flown in a helicopter, or a custom jet."

"Me neither," D'Amato said.

"So you two took advantage of a friend who was rich and powerful," Doyle said.

"It wasn't like that, dickhead," D'Amato said. "We didn't 'take advantage.'"

"Really?" Doyle droned. "And your contribution was—?"

"Financially," I said, "nothing, nada, zilch. Gold wouldn't even allow us to leave tip money, not that we could afford to."

"Gold took Beckett to the Super Bowl," D'Amato said with barely disguised envy.

"So?" I said. "He took us *both* backstage at Broadway premières and rock concerts."

"Sounds like you guys miss the lifestyle," Collyer said.

"Big time," I said.

"Who wouldn't?" D'Amato said.

"Not to offend," Doyle said. "But what was in it for Gold? I mean, a man of his stature, why associate with you two?"

I had been asked the question before. I did get offended. But I answered just the same. "At first I thought we'd hit it off, that he took a liking to us. Then I realized he was using me."

"How?" Collyer said.

"He was married, courting my ex. Hiding the whole affair in plain sight—that's why he took me everywhere with him. I didn't realize it at first, he was using me as a decoy. I was Gold's 'beard.' "

"When you found out," Collyer said, "what did you do?"

"Nothing. I played along. I was addicted to the lifestyle."

"Well, that certainly explains it," Doyle said smugly.

"I take it you two don't socialize with Gold anymore?" Collyer said.

"It's not like we run in the same circles," D'Amato said.

"But he doesn't call you?" Collyer said.

"We don't call him," I said.

"Any specific reason?"

"Yeah. Gold screwed Janet over," I said. "He and I argued about it. I told him to go fuck himself." I tried to be matter-of-fact but knew I wouldn't be able to control the resentment in my voice. "The prick took advantage of her," I said. "Then dumped her. Hard. That's Gold's normal modus operandi. Exploit a business associate, acquaintance, friend or lover until they've outlived their usefulness, then cut all ties."

"Sounds like you hold a grudge," Collyer said.

"Life's too short." I shook my head. "What's past is past. I've got no problem with Gold."

"Okay," Collyer said. And when he spoke again his voice

was just above a whisper. "Know anything about Gold's business?"

"Next to nothing," I said.

"You, D'Amato?"

"No."

"The papers reported that the Gold Organization bought the tenements in the South Bronx for the purpose of renovation," Collyer said. "That they're gonna fix them up so low income people can live with dignity. You believe that?"

I shrugged. "Why not?"

"In your opinion, is R. J. Gold ruthless?" Collyer said.

I thought about the reporter who wrote that bombshell Yakuza story. I was in Gold's office when he told his CFO and lawyer, Tomo Nagasue, to destroy the guy with frivolous lawsuits. "I don't care how you do it," Gold said, "Just keep him in court for twenty years." Gold had Nagasue sue the newspaper, the publisher and reporter both corporately and personally. Eventually, the publisher and reporter were forced to file for business and personal bankruptcy.

"He'll destroy anyone who crosses him," I said.

"Think he'd force people out of their homes?"

"What do you mean?" I said.

"There's been rumors," Collyer said, "about forced evictions in Gold buildings; threats, intimidation. Since most of the tenants are illegals, no one's made an official complaint."

"That's absurd," Doyle said.

"If he wants to build high-rise structures instead of renovate," Collyer said, "he'd make a hell of a lot more money."

"Motive," D'Amato said.

Doyle threw his hands up. "That is perhaps the most preposterous theory—look, a wealthy individual like an R. J. Gold would not resort to forcible evictions. He would simply buy people out of their leases. Believe me, I know. I've socialized with dozens of wealthy individuals—"

"Socialized?" D'Amato made a face.

"Correct. Socialized, and I know how they do business."

"Bent over?" D'Amato said.

Doyle scowled. "Buffoon."

"The Gold Organization would have no reason to buy the tenants out," Collyer said to Doyle. "According to the newspapers, the Gold Organization is buying that land with government loan guarantees. The terms and timetable are specific. They must begin construction, renovate the existing structures by a certain date, and maintain them as low income housing units. The existing tenants aren't supposed to relocate, not long term anyway."

"What if the existing buildings were destroyed?" I said. "You know, no longer habitable. Could he demolish them, put up all new, modern apartment buildings?"

Collyer smiled, sort of. "If the existing structures were condemned, and the Gold Organization maintained the original minimum building foundations, I believe they could erect high-rise structures without fear of forfeiting the government loan guarantees."

D'Amato looked at Doyle. "Motive, doofus."

"I still think the theory is ridiculous," Doyle blustered. "Strippers are far more plausible."

"And that's what bothers me," Collyer said. "Everything points to strippers. It's all too obvious, a little too neat."

"I hate to agree with doofus," D'Amato thumbed toward Doyle, "but Gold's worth, what seven billion? No way he'd be involved in some arson scheme."

"Maybe you're right." Collyer looked at me. "What do you think?"

I took a moment. "I've gotta agree. There's no way Gold would be involved in arson."

# CHAPTER 10

Dusk. The clean uniform shirt I had changed into was already soaked with sweat. I rummaged distractedly through the RMP glove compartment, found some left-over White Castle napkins and used them to wipe the sweat from my neck and brow. "Can't believe this heat."

"You okay?" D'Amato steered the RMP down Aldus Street.

"Yeah," I said. "Sure."

The police radio droned in the background.

I had used the tube of antiseptic that the doctor at the hospital had given me to clean my scrape wounds, soap and water to scrub the infant's caked blood from my face and bare arms. But there was no way to scrub away the memory of the little one's velvety skin against my face, the taste of its sweet breath. I couldn't shake the mix of panic and powerlessness I felt as I forced air into its tiny lungs.

"Earth to Beckett."

"Uh?"

"Did you know, the record for male orgasms is sixteen in one hour? I had twelve once myself."

I saw a group of pre-teen girls practicing synchronized

rope jumping in a refuse-strewn schoolyard. I marveled at their raw athletic talent and found myself wondering if any of them possessed the fortitude necessary to claw their way out of the ghetto. Or would they wind up homeless, destitute, like the child-mother and infant who died in my arms?

I adjusted the sweaty bulletproof vest under my shirt. "What was with Collyer?"

"What do you mean?"

"Say the odds are 90 percent that strippers started that fire."

"Say 99 percent," D'Amato said.

"Alright, 99 percent. So why's he focusing on Gold?" As we drove on, I checked out a raggedy panhandler whose battered face I'd never seen before. There was no telltale weapons bulge. He wasn't hassling people and seemed harmless enough.

"Covering all bases?" D'Amato said. "He said there were rumors of forced evictions."

I looked at D'Amato. "Maybe."

"Think he knows something we don't?"

"Maybe."

I knew well the "unofficial" Police Officer's Guide to Investigative Procedures 101: *The most obvious criminal suspect is more often than not the perpetrator*. In this case, youth gangs. But the fire marshal Collyer's line of questions gave me pause.

"Say for the sake of argument that the forcible eviction rumors're true," I said, "and that some of the tenants at Coster Street were forced out. Gold Organization employees could've been involved in that fire."

"Yeah. That's 'if' the rumors're true." D'Amato fiddled with his mustache. "And then there's *still* a 99 percent chance that strippers set that fire *after* the tenants were kicked out—problem being, there's no way to find out for sure."

"We could talk to the former tenants."

"They're illegals," D'Amato scoffed. "They're scattered all over the city by now."

He was right.

"Why? What're you thinking?" D'Amato said.

"That we should investigate."

"What's this 'we' shit?" D'Amato said. "Who's gonna patrol our sector while we're off playing 'defectives'? McShane and Ryan sure as shit won't cover us; they'll pour piss in our lockers. Besides, that's Collyer and Doyle's job."

"Doyle has his mind made up."

"And for good reason."

"Yeah, you're probably right."

We both eyeballed a group of male teens dressed in discount hip-hop fashion, doing their adolescent best to look tough, dangerous; wannabe gangbangers.

"Still," I said, "there's no harm us poking around."

"Yeah, there is. We've got no business running an independent investigation."

"No," I said. "We don't."

"Hell, you're already on Captain Ward's shit list. If we get caught, Ward'll skin us—*me*—alive."

"Yeah," I said. "He will—unless we solve the case. And you know what that could mean; more medals."

"Medals, uh?" D'Amato chuckled as he drifted around a double-parked post office truck. "This is amusing, you know?"

I glanced at him. "What is?"

"*You* trying to con *me*; *me* of all people." D'Amato waved Hi to a couple of heavy-set female postal employees. "Before you waste anymore of your bad breath, partner, I gotta know: this vendetta about R. J. Gold, or the dead infant?"

"Whaddya mean, vendetta?"

"I mean I don't believe what you told Collyer, that you've got no problem with Gold."

"I don't."

"Yeah. Sure—this about Gold or the infant?"

"The infant."

"Okay," D'Amato said. "Long as we understand each other." D'Amato made a turn. We scanned the faces on the street alert for sudden movements; people scattering, quick stepping away from cars or into buildings.

"All right," D'Amato said. "I'm in. What do you wanna do? Slap around some youth gangs?"

"I prefer the term, 'interview.'"

"The Bloods' headquarters is the closest."

But when we arrived at the Bloods' clubhouse, a mailman informed us that the gang had moved, "praise the Lord," to Brooklyn.

At Crips headquarters we discovered that last month their leader had had his throat cut by a Harlem crew and that the remaining Crips were gone.

The Savage Nomads were nowhere to be found. Their command center, which was on Gold Organization land, was now part of the moonscape of burned-out buildings and rubble-packed vacant lots. Dispossessed roosters and chickens wandered the streets—a movable feast for the prides of cats and packs of ever-hungry abandoned dogs.

"That leaves the Stoners," I said. "Where they hang?"

"Last I heard," D'Amato thought a moment, "North end, 174th Street and Hoe Avenue." 41 Ida motored down Whitlock Avenue, which paralleled the overhead Bruckner Expressway. Hit men sometimes dumped their victims amid garbage and abandoned cars, in the foreboding darkness under the overpass.

D'Amato spied a mocha-skinned hooker wearing an obscenely short dress and six-inch stiletto heels. She nastystrutted across the boulevard, gave us an eyelash-singeing stare, then moved on, hips waving adieu.

"Wow." D'Amato was bug-eyed. "You see that?"

"I'm a former altar boy. I'd be struck blind."

"She wants me."

"She wants everyone."

D'Amato tapped the horn.

The hooker gave him the finger.

"Maybe I should get her phone number," D'Amato said. "The two of us could bang her like screen doors in a hurricane."

"I don't do threesomes, Vinnie. You know that."

"Not *us*, you idiot." D'Amato swung the RMP into an oncoming lane. Cut back. Hit the accelerator. "Me and the 'beast.' " He grabbed his crotch.

My shoulders sagged and I groaned with remembered boredom. "Oh, yeah. How could I forget the beast?"

"Women don't forget. Oh, no." D'Amato's smile broadened. "I'm not bragging, Beckett. Just telling the truth. Face it. I'm a great lay. And I'm cute." D'Amato honked the horn and screamed at a slow-poke driver to get the fuck out of his way. "Just look at this face. Women see me, they want me. It's a curse I've had to live with all my life. And I'm hung like a T-rex. I got a tongue I could lick a fly off a wall with from six feet."

"And you're modest," I said.

"Physical perfection, matched with deep humility."

"That's it." I smiled tolerantly.

D'Amato switched on the RMP's headlights.

Block after block rolled by. Every crumbling building had a fire escape, and every fire escape window was gated in an attempt to keep the predators out.

D'Amato slowed the police car to avoid scores of children who pranced and splashed in a gushing stream of water, courtesy of an illegally opened fire hydrant. By law, we were supposed to close the hydrant, thereby maintaining the life-saving water pressure in case of a tenement fire.

D'Amato stopped the car. "We should shut that off."

I looked at the children who were shrieking with joy,

momentarily relieved from the mosquito-drenched heat and humidity. I shook my head. 41 Ida drove on.

I checked out the mass of humanity along Faile Street and wondered how the slumlords got away with it: hot-bedding the tenement apartments. Renting the same squalid, un-air conditioned dwelling in eight-hour shifts to three separate immigrant families. Charging each the full rent, of course. The other sixteen hours, the off-shift families had no place to go. Many congregated on the streets, played cards, dominos. A few drank the heat of day away, drowning their poverty and aimless lives in cheap booze, while others resorted to indiscriminate sex and sporadic acts of wanton violence.

D'Amato took a left onto Westchester Avenue and turned north on Southern Boulevard—the intersection was a poor man's version of New Orleans at Mardi Gras.

A scuffle broke out in front of a bodega. Punches were thrown. Passersby laughed at the mayhem. D'Amato slowed the car ready for—no, hoping, for trouble. Seeing us, the combatants wisely dispersed. Resentful stares bombarded our police car from every direction, dogged us.

*Wham!* We both jumped as something struck our RMP roof and bounced off onto the street: an empty liquor bottle. Experience had taught us that there was no chance of catching or even spotting the culprit.

The police car crawled along Southern Boulevard, turned right onto 174th street and made another right. Ghetto blasters assaulted us from a dozen different sources, echoing through the narrow, shadowy canyon called Hoe Avenue.

A junkie-thin hooker saw us, spun and wandered away from an idling double-parked car. The car drove off.

Two teenagers smoking crack ditched their pipes, dropped glassine envelopes, and hurried into a tenement. They'd be up on the roof watching us within seconds.

Several tough guys in a heated argument spotted us and

instantly cooled it—no one in their right mind, not even organized crime figures, wanted trouble with uniformed cops. Unlike movie and TV cops, mouthing off to a real cop could lead to a long hospital stay, not to mention the legal problems and dreaded notoriety. *"The cops don't slap the bad guys around,"* my father always told me, *"the bad guys will be slapping the cops around."*

The RMP continued down the street.

"There," I said. "Stoners."

"Where?" D'Amato said.

I gestured at a half dozen grizzled young black and Hispanic men wearing gang color do-rags, slouched in the shadows against a building stoop, their eyes hostile. They could have been gangsta rap musicians posing for the cover of a CD with a lot of cop killer lyrics. Although none fit Fire Marshal Collyer's description of the Coster Street arsonists, youth gangs often claim hundreds of members across the country.

"That's the leader, Tookie Jones, the fat fuck eating the Devil Dog, talking on the cell phone," D'Amato said.

"Christ," I said, marveling at Tookie's sheer bulk. "He ever miss a meal?"

"Beside stripping buildings, he's into fencing stolen goods, drugs, some prostitution, but mostly strong arms stuff. Collects for the local mob's bookmakers. He's a suspect in at least a dozen assaults and armed robberies."

"Stop the car," I said.

As we exited the car and walked toward the group, we executed an alert sweep of the area, searching for hostiles.

"All right, Stoners," D'Amato said. "Assume the position."

"Aw, man," a Stoner said.

"Why you fuckin' wit us?" another chimed in.

"We didn't do nothin'," a third one griped—the usual inane litany.

"Against the fence," I said. "Now."

Tookie Jones swallowed what was in his mouth, put away his cell phone, nodded for his crew to submit. The gang did their street act; obeyed us, turned and leaned against a fence, but played to the locals with an appropriate amount of grumbling defiance. D'Amato and I patted them down. Found two unopened Devil Dogs, six $10 bags of marijuana which we let them keep.

"Okay," D'Amato said. "Turn around. We're gonna have a pop quiz. Whoever gets the right answer gets a walk. Are you ready?"

Tookie spit on the ground by D'Amato's feet. D'Amato looked at the dark spittle, then at Tookie—the three-hundred-pound gang leader had no idea how close he was to catching a beating.

Chico, another gang member, yawned.

"Jose got six years for attempted murder," D'Amato said. "He also got $10,000 for the attempted hit. If his common-law wife spends $100 per month, how much money will be left when he gets out of prison?"

The gang exchanged uneasy glances. Their expressions said that there was something unusual about this situation and this cop. "Say, what?" Tookie said.

"Morons," D'Amato said. "All right. Listen up. Officer Beckett's got something important to ask you."

I moved forward. "Two white guys used gasoline to start a fire a couple of hours ago." I made eye contact with each gang member. "Down on Coster and Viele."

"We don't know 'em," Chico said.

"All right," I said. "Who does? Gimme a name."

Tookie unwrapped a fresh Devil Dog, stuffed it in his mouth. "Fuck we look like, dawg, 411?"

*Crack.* D'Amato hit Tookie with a stinging face slap.

The un-masticated food shot out of Tookie's mouth. His head snapped back. His recovery was instant. His glare murderous.

"Don't do that again," Tookie said, a threat.

*Crack. Crack.* D'Amato struck with a short, sharp backhand/forehand combination. The fat gang leader staggered. His lip was split, bleeding.

"Watch'er mouth, fatso." *Crack.* D'Amato slapped Tookie harder this time, knowing a slap, used strategically to embarrass a man in public, was more effective than a punch.

People up and down the street were watching. Some peered out of cars, apartment windows. Others observed from fire escapes and roof tops.

"I'd cooperate, I were you," I said, my hand on the butt of my Glock, eyes on Tookie's crew—their body language was submissive, hand movements slow, astutely cautious.

Tookie was defiant. "I don't have to tell you shit."

*Whap.* D'Amato's punch caught Tookie in the solar plexus; his breath roared out. He dropped heavily to one knee.

His crew reacted but wisely held their ground, their eyes riveted on my Glock which was now unholstered, pointing at the ground.

D'Amato grabbed a handful of the gang leader's greasy hair, yanked until their faces were millimeters apart and his spittle sprayed the punk's pock-marked face. "Coster and Viele. Officer Beckett asked for a name."

"Vinnie," I said playing good cop to D'Amato's bad cop. "Back off."

"A name." D'Amato yanked harder.

"Stop," Tookie cried out.

"Easy, Vinnie."

"There's a white guy been hanging around Coster Street," Tookie said. "An outsider, drives a Lincoln."

"A pimpmobile?" I said.

"A plain black Lincoln. You know, a Town Car."

"Good boy." D'Amato released Tookie, left him groveling on he ground. "There's gotta be a thousand black Lincoln Town Cars in the city," D'Amato said to me.

"Not in the South Bronx," I said.

"Straight up, dawg," Tookie said, struggling to his feet, massaging his midsection.

"Describe the guy, Tookie," I said.

"I never seen him."

"Liar." D'Amato shot forward and head-butted Tookie. His nose splattered. Knees buckled. He collapsed onto the building stoop.

I jumped D'Amato from behind, bear-hugged him, dragged him away from the gang and flung him onto a parked car—a head-butt could be lethal, drive nose cartilage into the brain. I wasn't playacting anymore.

"What the hell's wrong with you?" I said.

"*Me?*" D'Amato pushed off the car. "We've been handling mutts the same way for ten years. You're acting like a pansy actor."

I fought to control my outrage. I stuck a warning finger in my partner's face. "Don't hit him again."

"Or what?" D'Amato shoved me.

I shoved back.

"Disgraceful," an old black woman said as she caned past, a disgusted look on her face. "Fine example you two are to the young ones." The old woman used her walking stick to point toward a group of six-to-ten-year-olds who stood fifty feet away in a wide-eyed cluster, watching our every move.

"You making fools of yourselves." The old woman shuffled away, shaking her head.

Embarrassed, we ceased hostilities.

"We were just playing," I said to the children and flashed an awkward smile. They stared back at us, expressionless.

It was then we noticed that dozens of civilians had congregated on the street to watch us. Several cars had stopped in the middle of Hoe Avenue to witness the action.

"Show's over," D'Amato said. "Move on."

People straggled away. The cars crawled off.

"Shit. They beat feet," D'Amato said.

I looked; Tookie and his Stoners were gone.

"Nice going, Vinnie."

"Fuck you," D'Amato said.

We got back into our RMP. I opened my memo book and wrote a watered-down entry about us questioning Tookie and his Stoners, an unnecessary task—no one would care—that also afforded me some much-needed time to calm down and organize my thoughts. I took my time, wrote slowly, reread what I'd written, and reminded myself that arguing with D'Amato had always been pointless, especially when he was right—we *had* been handling mutts the same way for ten years and I *was* acting like a pansy actor: getting soft, losing my edge. Which was yet another compelling reason for me to quit the NYPD that night before I caused myself or someone else to get hurt.

I closed my memo book. "Let's go."

D'Amato started the engine.

I spotted the group of bug-eyed kids watching us from across the street, behind a parked car.

"You broke Tookie's nose," I said. "He's gonna need a doctor." I waved to the children. Several waved back. I couldn't help but smile. "Let's try the hospital."

"What, you saying I'm right?" D'Amato put the car in drive, stepped on the gas. "That what you're saying?"

I sighed. "We gotta do this?"

"C'mon." D'Amato was insistent. "I wanna hear you say it."

"You're right," I said. "Okay? Tookie knows more than he's saying."

"No shit, Colombo."

The radio crackled. *"In the 41 Precinct reports of shots fired."*

We both straightened.

*"Shots fired Hunts Point, Casanova Street and Spofford Avenue in the Black Cat Social Club. That's shots fired Casanova and Spofford. Units responding."*

D'Amato made a squealing right turn. I grabbed the radio and joined the dozen or so sector cars who jammed the airwaves in a frenzy to respond.

"41 Ida on the way," I said.

"*10–4, Ida,*" Central said. "*Use extreme caution.*"

# CHAPTER II

I flipped on the siren. D'Amato stomped down the accelerator. We were at the north end of the precinct and had
to drive at breakneck speed, under the treacherous Southern Boulevard "el" in order to reach Hunts Point and the
Black Cat Social Club. Both of us were grimly aware that
if D'Amato made even a minor error in judgment—struck
a steel el pillar—we had virtually no chance of survival.

I glanced at D'Amato: his eyes were wide with childlike excitement—he loved the "action" of a police chase
or any excuse for high-speed driving.

I braced my feet against the dash. Yanked my seatbelt
extra tight and gripped the car seat with both hands just in
case.

"Get outta the way," D'Amato screamed and steered the
RMP around slower-moving vehicles and into head-on
traffic, playing chicken. Brake. Skid. Gas. Cut back to his
own lane, slicing past the steel el pillars with not a mil-
limeter to spare.

I felt a quick cringe in my stomach, a rush of adrenaline.
The high, that's what racing to a gun battle had always been,
a rush followed by a high: a blessed exhilaration which
numbed fear.

D'Amato slammed on the brakes. Skidded. Swerved to avoid hitting a teenager on roller blades. He jumped a curb. Demolished a cluster of garbage cans. Pedestrians scattered. D'Amato sideswiped an old Buick. Spun out. Regained control. Punched the accelerator and rocketed south.

My fingernails dug deeper into the torn imitation leather seat. D'Amato was howling, slapping the steering wheel, having a blast as shadows from the overhead el slats rippled across the car hood.

D'Amato whipped the steering wheel hard left at Tiffany Street. Raced about six blocks. Fishtailed onto Casanova Street. Eased off the gas and came to an abrupt stop.

I let out the breath trapped in my throat and switched off the siren. Ahead of us five police cars had formed a hood-to-trunk skirmish line twenty-five yards from the front of the mostly abandoned five-story tenement that housed the Black Cat Social Club. Cops crouched behind their cars. Hats on backwards. Guns extended, combat ready. Maybe fifteen of them including footmen. More were arriving by the second.

News vans, a most unusual sight in any high-crime precinct, were also arriving, double and triple parking, their reporters in a frantic race to be the first on air: "Live outside the Black Cat Social Club."

"Gotta be a slow news day," D'Amato commented.

I saw scores of people, like spectators at a sporting event, lining the streets as if they were bulletproof. Youngsters were watching the action from rooftops. Women sat on tenement stoops, some holding infants in their arms. Groups of men loitered on the sidewalks, guzzling cheap wine and beer, waiting, watching, anticipating a Western-style shootout in a place that stank of rotting garbage.

D'Amato tapped the gas, drifted to the curb, and killed the engine. Fire Marshal Collyer, scurrying low along the protective line of police cars, approached us on our RMP's passenger side.

"Whaddaya got?" I said.

"The arsonists from Coster Street."

I grabbed his arm. "You're sure?"

Collyer nodded. "Same description. A patrol car saw them walking down the street, bold as can be, carrying a red container of gas. They saw the cops eyeballing them, pulled a gun and opened fire."

"No reason?" I said. "They just started shooting?"

"Appears that way."

"Let's rush 'em," D'Amato said.

"Can't," Collyer said. "They've got a hostage."

"Gimme a break." D'Amato did an eye roll. "Anyone hangs out in the Black Cat ain't no hostage."

"It's a woman," Collyer said.

D'Amato arched an eyebrow. "What's she look like?"

Collyer glared at him. "Now, what the hell difference does that make?"

"All the difference in the world," D'Amato said.

We opened our doors, slipped out of the RMP, moved to the cover of another car. I looked over the roof to check the situation, spotted Detective Doyle four car lengths down. Doyle was watching me watching him.

"Ain't that Doyle?" D'Amato said. "Doesn't he know he could get hurt out here?"

*Bang! Bang! Bang!* Three quick shots came from the Black Cat's storefront entrance. Cops ducked. Reporters ate black top. Pedestrians ran for cover.

D'Amato yelped as a bullet whizzed by: it was close.

A woman behind us screamed. I turned and saw a man fall to the ground clutching his shoulder, apparently hit by the same bullet that barely missed D'Amato. A police-woman hurried to assist the wounded man.

This was insane: the arsonists were firing indiscriminately into a crowd filled with women and children, but, because the news media was recording the cops' every move, no one was returning fire; they were afraid of killing the hostage and provoking a deadly firefight—not that I blamed the rank-and-file for their lack of action. A street cop makes a questionable decision, even under the most extreme circumstances, and the NYPD brass will usually do the politically expedient thing: suspend, arrest and then prosecute the cop. Yet I was not concerned with consequences. This was my last day on the NYPD.

I peeked over the car hood at the foreboding exterior of the Black Cat Social Club and, all at once, knew what I had to do. Regardless of the consequences, I was gonna be the one to get my hands on the men who'd killed that infant and her mother. I wanted to be the one who looked them in the eye and asked them, Why?

D'Amato squatted beside me, seething. "Those assholes nearly shot me." He glared toward the Black Cat. "What're we gonna do about it?"

I pulled my weapon. "What do you wanna do about it?"

D'Amato's eyes searched mine. "You mean what I think you mean?"

"Fuckin' A."

D'Amato broke into a goofy grin. "Good God," he gushed. "Looks like the old Beckett's back."

We crouched down and moved toward the Black Cat Social Club, crabbed car-cover to car-cover. We ducked behind a gypsy cab, then a delivery van. Cops were screaming at us to pull back, get out of the line of fire. D'Amato gave them the finger. We dashed across the street into an alley which led to the rear of the building.

We moved quickly yet surefootedly through the darkening, garbage-filled alley, leaping over stagnant pools of mosquito-infested water and sidestepping a rotten, discarded mattress which contained a swarming hornet's nest.

I switched on my flashlight, pointed the shaft of light at the building. Cinder blocks sealed the Black Cat's rear exit. There was no way in, but no way out. So much for fire codes.

I raised the flashlight beam. "Check out the second-floor apartments." The windows on the upper floors were covered with thick tin which was nailed to wood-framed borders. "Didn't we read an incident report about the Black Cat being burglarized a few months ago?"

"Yeah," D'Amato said. "The thieves climbed the fire escape, entered a second floor apartment, and chopped a hole in the floor."

We made our way to the building line, jumped up, grabbed the rusty fire escape ladder, pulled it down, climbed up.

I squatted on the second-floor landing. The tin covering the window had three dozen six-penny nails securing it to a two-by-four wooden frame which ran around the perimeter.

"Gimme your knife," I said.

D'Amato handed me a Swiss Army knife. I pried the nails out of the lower right-hand corner of the window and D'Amato helped me peel the tin back. When it was wide enough, we slipped head first into the dark apartment.

The stench of urine, garbage and burned wood came on strong. Muffled country western music emanated from below. I swept the apartment with my flashlight; rats scurried. Then we moved cautiously through the remains of what was once a bedroom, stepping on broken needles and crack vials and ripping through endless spider webs.

We moved past charred bricks and pages of *El Diario* which bore evidence of having been used as toilet paper. The smell of decay was thick in our noses.

A bullhorn sound: an NYPD supervisor had apparently arrived. An authoritative male voice demanded the suspects lay down their arms and surrender immediately. Spotlights shot thin streams of light, like lasers, through the gaps in the tin-covered front windows and throughout the room.

I directed my flashlight beam to the living room. A thick

piece of tin, five by five feet, was nailed onto the wood floor covering a hole. Burglars had indeed hit the Black Cat from up here, probably more than once. I inspected it. It was doable. Pry out the two dozen or so nails, then slide the tin aside just enough to gain access.

I used D'Amato's knife to pry the nails out of the tin sheet. Working together, we quietly slid it aside.

An upsurge of dim light and Willie Nelson flooded the apartment. We holstered our weapons.

Removing our hats, we squatted down on the filthy floor, assumed a prone position, and stuck our heads down though the opening, eyes sweeping the club below like ceiling security cameras.

Beyond stacked cases of beer and plastic palm trees, I spotted the suspects, two white males, crouched behind a makeshift barricade composed of overturned tables and bar stools. They fit the description of the arsonists on Fire Marshal Collyer's report: 19–25 years old, 5'10" tall, thin, stringy blond hair, dressed in jeans, one in a T-shirt, the second shirtless. I could see the lady hostage—a convicted felon I recognized from precinct mug shots—sitting calmly at the bar filing her nails, looking quite bored. The former hooker and identity thief was tall with leg up to Yonkers and massive fake boobs. Definitely D'Amato's style.

The arsonist wearing the T-shirt stuck his right hand down the front of his jeans and began scratching his crotch. I could see a red five-gallon can with GAS written on it on the floor by the barricade. I could not see if anyone else was in the place.

"They're moving up on us," the shirtless one shrieked.

*Bang!* He fired a wild shot at the cops outside.

I heard the commotion on the street, cops yelling for everyone to take cover, shotguns being racked.

A phone rang at the bar.

The female hostage picked up a cordless.

I could only just make out the conversation.

"Mona Love speaking," she said into the phone.

I noted that Mona Love did not act like a hostage, did not appear nervous or frightened.

"They want to speak to whoever's in charge," Mona said to the arsonists.

The one wearing the T-shirt walked over to Mona, took the phone. "Who does?"

Mona yawned. "The cops."

"HOSTAGE'S GOT GREAT tits," D'Amato whispered as we pulled our heads back and pushed to our feet. "Once the lady sees 'the beast',"—he brushed dirt off his uniform, and raked his fingers through his mustache—"she's mine."

"Okay, here's how we play it," I said. "I climb down first, cut to the left. You follow, cut to the right." I pulled my Glock and, out of habit, re-checked that a round was in the chamber. "They get stupid, we take them in a crossfire."

"So, it's me who follows you, *again*, uh?" D'Amato pulled his weapon. "Me Tonto. You the Lone Fucking Ranger. That it?"

I squinted in the darkness, striving to see if there was a smile on D'Amato's face. There wasn't.

"What difference does it make?"

"You've already got your Medal of Honor."

Without saying another word, D'Amato pushed past me and dropped through the hole in the floor. I stood there, flabbergasted—the fool could easily break a leg. I looked down: D'Amato had hit the ground hard and was recovering slowly. I needed to get to him, fast.

I sat at the perimeter of the hole in the floor, scooted off the edge, hung from the splintered sides, let go and made a relatively soft landing—the knee pain was both instant and electric. It was all I could do to stay on my feet and not cry out in anguish. I limped in circles, stifled a guttural gasp and hoped I would not be heard above Willie and the ruckus outside.

It took what seemed like an eternity for the knee pain to subside. I helped D'Amato to his feet. We took a few moments to recoup our strength and then moved stealthily around stacked cases of beer, sleeping cats, and plastic palm trees to the front of the club. D'Amato crept up to the jukebox and pulled the plug. Willie died slowly.

"Police!" D'Amato said, gun pointed. "Freeze or die!"

Mona Love sprung off the barstool and reached for the sky: she did have beautiful breasts.

D'Amato homed his gun in on the two arsonists who sat on the floor by the barricade.

"You two. Lemme see your hands." D'Amato cocked the .38, his finger in the hair-trigger ready to fire. "Now!"

"Easy." I was standing behind D'Amato.

"Fuck easy. It's my collar."

Fortunately for them, the arsonists raised their hands. Making certain not to cross D'Amato's line of fire, I approached the suspects, removed their guns, dragged them to their feet, flung them against a wall, frisked them and found they carried no ID.

"What're your names?" I said.

"Bo," the one in the shirt sniffled.

"Bubba." The shirtless one wiped tears from his eyes.

I realized they were both crying—murderous punks. They disgusted me.

"Well, Bo and Bubba, think things are bad now?" I chuckled for effect. "Wait till the lifers get hold of you two in prison. They don't take kindly to baby killers."

"No!" Bubba wailed. "Ya'll got it wrong."

"We already told the cop on the phone," Bo said. "We didn't mean to kill no children." Their drawls were pure backwoods southern. "Ya'll gotta believe us."

"He told us the building was empty," Bubba said.

I reacted. "Who told you the building was empty?"

"The guy that hired us," Bubba said.

I grabbed him by the arm and spun him around. "Who hired you? What's his name?"

Bubba glared defiantly at the hand clutching his arm. "I ain't sayin' shit without a Jew lawyer."

The phone rang.

Mona answered it. "Hold on," she said. "Officers, I guess it's for you."

I let go of Bubba's arm and accepted the cordless. "Who is this?"

"Captain Ward. Who's this?"

I took a deep breath. "It's me. Beckett."

"Beckett? How the hell did you get in there?"

As I filled in the captain, I considered the prisoners—rednecks who evidently avoided legitimate employment, dentists, and soap and water. Since they appeared to be borderline morons, their claim that they were hired to set the Coster Street fire made total sense. Question was, who had hired them?

Regardless, once we got these hillbillies back to the stationhouse, sans "Jew lawyers" to protect them, they'd tell us everything they knew, one way or another, and all before the end of my last tour.

"Good enough, Beckett," Captain Ward said. "Whaddaya need?"

"Nothing," I said. "We're bringing the prisoners out." I hung up. "You ready, Vinnie?"

D'Amato, a twinkle in his eye, was speaking to Mona, gawking at her breasts. "You're sure you're all right, my dear?"

Mona patted her bouffant hairdo, battered finger-length, fake eyelashes: the poster girl for Hookers-R-Us.

"Thank you, officer," she said, "for your concern."

D'Amato smiled.

Mona smiled.

I wanted to puke. I took out handcuffs.

"No cuffs," D'Amato said.

"What're you nuts?" I said. "We gotta cuff 'em."

"Hey, it's my collar. No cuffs."

I couldn't believe this: handcuffing a prisoner was mandatory. But I didn't want to fight with D'Amato anymore, especially since it was my last tour. And, since the collar was *his*, it was *his* ass on the line—unless, of course, something went wrong. But what could possibly go wrong with dozens of cops waiting for us outside? I put away my cuffs.

"Mind telling me what you're up to?"

"Think about it." D'Amato pulled me aside, lowered his voice. "I got two murder/arson collars here. A damsel in distress. TV cameras are waiting outside."

"Yeah. So?"

"*So*, I toss the prisoners and cuff 'em outside in front of the cameras—think of the drama. My picture will be all over the TV news, the morning papers. I could be awarded another EPD, MD or, hell, the Medal of Valor. Become a security 'expert' on CNN. Maybe a bodyguard for some wealthy Hollywood diva—once I'm in the door, the 'beast' will do the rest." D'Amato unbuttoned his shirt one more button. "Hands up," he said to Bo and Bubba, "laced behind your head."

The prisoners did as ordered.

"They go out first," D'Amato told me. "Then me with the hostage, then you."

"Whatever you say, Vinnie. I just hope you know what you're doing."

"Trust me, Kimosabee." D'Amato tilted his hat rakishly. He gestured to the prisoners with his gun. "Move. Outside."

The prisoners moved to the front door.

"Doll." D'Amato smiled at Mona and arched one eyebrow. "You're with me."

Mona sashayed over and took D'Amato's arm. She was taller than he. "My." She squeezed his bicep. "You're a strong one."

THE YOKELS HADN'T even waited until nightfall like they were instructed, Pete from Queens agonized. He was watching from a tenement doorway across the street from the Black Cat Social Club, seized by a deadly, dark mood. There was no escaping it. No one to shift the blame to, to point the finger at. It was *his* poor judgment that had brought about the disastrous life-and-death drama now unfolding on national television. He'd employed Bo and Bubba Taylor.

Yet the Taylors were the best men he could find on such short notice. And he had personally checked every floor in the building at Coster Street, looked in every apartment. The building *was* empty. How could he know squatters would move in only hours later?

The boss would not be happy.

Pete fumed recalling how the Taylors had literally walked away from the fire scene carrying a red—a freaking *red*—container with G-A-S written on it. The entire neighborhood had seen them.

Once they varied from the plan he should have broken their necks. But a public execution was not the most rational course of action. And his Lincoln was parked in a garage back by the Black Cat so he'd stuck to his original scheme. Was waiting patiently for them outside the club ready to scoop them up, kill them and plant evidence that would implicate them in all the arsons on Gold land. But Bubba, the shirtless one, started firing at the cops.

Suddenly the door to the Black Cat Social Club flew open and fifty cops tensed, crouched behind cars, aimed and cocked their weapons. A breath-holding tension gripped the police ranks. All civilian eyes were on the Black

Cat entrance, many probably hoping whoever came out would make a false move so that the cops would open fire.

Pete scanned the police ranks. Spotted his "contact" looking his way, waiting for instructions. Pete gave him a definite nod.

Pete's stomach sank when he saw Bo and Bubba Taylor exit the Black Cat unmolested, hands up laced behind their heads. And dread filled him when he saw who came out next behind Mona Love: Vinnie D'Amato and Michael Beckett. Of the 40,000-some-odd cops in the city, why the hell did it have to be that Boy Scout, Michael fucking Beckett?

"NIGGER-LOVING JEW REPORTERS," Bubba snarled at the press as videotape whirled and cameras clicked. Both prisoners unlaced their hands, knocked microphones away, shoved reporters. Bubba threw a kick at a video cameraman. Bo stuck his right hand down the front of his jeans and scratched his crotch.

"He's reaching for a gun!" someone yelled.

There was a fusillade of shots.

# CHAPTER 12

D'Amato pushed Mona Love to the ground using his body to shield her. I dove back into the Black Cat Social Club and scrambled for cover behind the arsonists' makeshift barricade. Police bullets strafed the walls of the club, shattering rows of whiskey bottles, pruning the plastic trees, scattering the cats.

As the sounds of gunfire faded, D'Amato sprang to his feet, rushed into the blinding glare of the waiting TV cameras and tripped over the bullet-riddled bodies of Bo and Bubba—there lay his fifteen minutes of fame.

"Why weren't the suspects handcuffed, D'Amato?" Detective Doyle said. "They're supposed to be cuffed."

"Hey, asshole." D'Amato stepped around Bo and Bubba, and got into Doyle's face. "Go fuck yourself."

Doyle bent to search the arsonists' bodies for the guns that were not there. "They're unarmed," Doyle said, incredulous. He glared at D'Amato. "Explain yourself, officer. Why weren't the suspects cuffed?"

"Someone get this prick away from me," D'Amato said.

"Back off, Doyle," I said. "We don't answer to you."

"Yeah?" Doyle said. "We'll see about that."

Without warning, D'Amato lunged, fists pumping.

Doyle responded, doubled D'Amato over with a punch to the stomach. On the way down D'Amato grabbed Doyle's leg, sank his teeth in.

Doyle howled in pain, called D'Amato a "raving psycho" as civilians cheered wildly. Eventually, the both of them were subdued by myself and a bellowing Captain Ward.

An ambulance arrived on the scene and an attendant officially pronounced the arsonists DOA.

Because of the unprecedented news coverage, the Bronx Borough Commander arrived on the scene, asking Captain Ward, "Who saw what gun?" All Ward could do was shrug.

It soon became disturbingly apparent how complicated the investigation would be. Besides having to question an untold number of eyewitnesses, plus over fifty cops, every bullet fired had to be accounted for, collected and matched to a policeman's gun. That meant each cop who had fired a shot had to report to ballistics and test-fire their weapons. The results of the ballistics matches would make known to the brass exactly which cops killed the perpetrators. Those cops would be taken off the street and assigned to desk duty, probably suspended and possibly prosecuted for criminally negligent homicide—the liberal press and the self-serving, publicity-minded Reverend Al Dullard would demand it.

"I declare," Mona Love Scarlet O'Hara'd the Bronx Borough Commander as she lingered outside the Black Cat Social Club. "I owe Officer D'Amato my very life." She fawned all over the grinning D'Amato and turned to allow yet another photographer to snap her photo.

D'Amato aw-shucked. "Just doing my job, Miss Love."

"Call me Mona." She made a production of licking what I'd bet were surgically inflated lips.

"Say, Mona." D'Amato lowered his voice and got all serious. "You like porn movies?"

I couldn't believe what I was hearing.

"Love them," Mona said.

D'Amato did the eyebrow trick again. "You. Me. Porn movies. Whipped cream. Handcuffs. Any questions?"

A reporter stuck a microphone in D'Amato's face.

"How is it possible, officer, that two unarmed suspects, in police custody, were gunned down?"

D'Amato responded as all cops do under similar circumstances: with a puzzled look and a sincere "Duh?"

"SEE IT?" D'AMATO said excitedly as we drove away from Casanova Street on our way back to the 41 Precinct. A series of interrogations and a mountain of paperwork awaited us. "You see Mona pat my ass?"

"What the hell is wrong with you?" I said. "Two suspects in our custody were just killed."

"Yeah, yeah. Did you see her pat my ass?"

I could only shake my head. Although I knew, deep down, D'Amato was as disturbed as I was about the tour's catastrophes, acting like an adolescent letch had always been his way of coping.

For the next few miles I ignored D'Amato and made a concerted effort not to obsess over the Coster Street fire. After all, we'd accomplished what I'd set out to: capture the arsonists. We'd report what Bo and Bubba told us, that they'd been hired to set the fire, and let the fire marshals and detective division take it from there. Bottom line, I was out of it. End of tour, police career, end of story.

I glanced out the RMP window at a group of firemen extinguishing a smoldering car fire, and tried to visualize my life after the NYPD. I decided that I'd take a long vacation, fly down to Key West, sit under a palm tree, soak up the sun, sip rum-runners, and plan my next career move—wouldn't it be nice if Solana Ortiz accompanied me to the Keys?

I thought about how Solana might look in a bathing suit, fantasized about what her lips would taste like, how she made love, wondered if I'd ever find out. But even salacious images of the delectable Solana could not hold my attention. Visions of her dispersed like the Coster Street fire smoke.

"Think the arsonists were telling the truth?" I said.

"About being hired to set the fire?"

"Yeah."

"They confessed to a double homicide," D'Amato said. "Why lie about being hired?"

I eyeballed a collection of rotund $15 hookers—$10 for the trick, $5 for the room—loitering along sidewalks that bordered vacant lots: Gold land.

"I'll bet Tookie Jones hired them," D'Amato said.

"Yeah."

"Or it could've been the guy drives the black Lincoln."

"Yeah."

"Or someone else."

We arrived at the stationhouse, completed Bo and Bubba's posthumous arrest reports and other paperwork that included their statements that they'd been hired to set the Coster Street fire, and dropped it all off with Neary at the clerical office.

Next we endured several short but grueling shooting-related interviews with superior officers—luckily we had not discharged our weapons. It was apparent that we would be disciplined for not following procedure: handcuffing the prisoners while still inside the Black Cat Social Club. That was not my problem. I'd be a happy civilian in less than a half hour.

"Let's go get a beer," D'Amato said once we were in the locker room changing into civilian clothes.

"I'm not in the mood for titty bars."

"Me neither," D'Amato said. "A gang of us are going to J. G. Melon down on Third Avenue."

"All right." I sat on a short wooden bench, slipped off my uniform shoes. "I'll meet you there."

"I'll wait." D'Amato closed and locked his locker.

"I said, I'll meet you there."

"Don't gimme that shit." D'Amato eyed me suspiciously. "What're you up to?"

I reached for my blue jeans and considered telling my partner that I was about to quit the NYPD, then thought better of it. He'd be crestfallen and I didn't want to listen to any objections, especially D'Amato's brand of objections.

"It's personal," I said.

"Fuck does that mean?" D'Amato's eyes were wide. "Since when do you keep things from me?"

"Hey, you wanna wait, be my guest, wait."

"Hurry up, D'Amato," another cop yelled. Several cops had congregated at the top of the locker room stairs, on their way to the bar.

"All right," D'Amato said to me. "I'll meet you there. But you stand me up again, you Irish cocksucker, and I'll rip your fucking arm off and beat you with the bloody end."

"I love you too," I smiled.

"Fuck you," D'Amato said.

I dressed slowly, waited until after D'Amato and his pub posse left the stationhouse, then began the process of cleaning out my locker. I gathered some old memo books and assorted junk and tossed them into a nearby garbage can. From inside my locker door I carefully detached photos of my mother, father, sister Shannon and a rendering of St. Michael the Archangel, patron saint of police officers, and placed them in a leather satchel. As I made a final check of my locker, I saw something in the dark recesses of the top shelf. I reached in, pulled it out.

It was a blue velvet pouch which contained an eight-pointed, star-shaped gold medal suspended from a green ribbon on which were affixed twelve white stars: the police department's Medal of Honor. I'd never worn it, and there was a good reason why. I remembered that night, eight years ago, very well.

*   *   *

I HAD BEEN late for a date with a curvy blonde when I raced into that middle-class apartment building in the Wakefield section of the Bronx, paying virtually no attention to the sounds of approaching fire engine sirens. I rode the elevator to the sixth floor. The adorable seven-year-old girl who answered the bell in apartment 6A informed me that the blonde I'd met the night before in an Irish pub, the woman I had a 7:30 dinner date, with did not live there.

"Apparently," the little girl said gravely, "you've been stood up."

"Are you sure?" I said.

"I'm sure," she said.

"You wouldn't want to go to dinner with me, would you?"

She shrugged. "Where to?"

"McDonald's?"

She looked me over, made a face. "No, thank you."

"Well, in that case, here." I handed the girl the box of French chocolates I'd brought for my date. "Enjoy."

I was heading back to the elevator feeling down about being stood up, when the sheer number and volume of screaming sirens caught my attention. I heard a man yell from somewhere below.

"Fire!"

I heard doors open. Doors close. People speaking in frightened tones and thumping down stairs. I walked over to the stairwell, looked down the six floors, saw no signs of fire, but caught a glimpse of firefighters climbing the stairs. All at once I smelled the faint odor of smoke. I heard a noise, looked toward a hall window. The fire department was deploying one of those accordion, aluminum truck ladders to the building roof.

"Fire drill?" The seven-year-old was standing in the hallway outside her door.

"Yes, better get your mom and dad." I walked down the

hall, knocked on the three other apartment doors—got no answer.

"They're at work," the girl said.

Thinking she meant the people in the other apartments, I said, "Get your mom and dad, hurry."

"They're at work," the girl repeated impatiently.

"You mean, you're alone?"

She nodded and there was sadness in her eyes.

Even if the fire was a minor smoke condition, I had to assume that the situation was serious. That meant I had to take the girl to safety, turn her over to child services, report her parents—I would see to it that they were cited for negligence.

"C'mon," I said, offering my hand. "I'll take you downstairs."

"I can't leave my sister," she said.

*Sister?* I eased the door open, stepped into a cluttered apartment living room, and saw a two-year-old sitting on a blanket in her own filth, empty boxes of cereal and bags of cookies scattered around her.

"Okay," I said. "Help me with your sister."

We wrapped the child in a blanket and I picked her up—the stench of soiled diapers was sickening. I took the girl by the hand, and since elevators can be a trap during fires, we headed to the stairwell.

As we descended, my eyes became increasingly irritated. Breathing became a chore. Oozing, thick black smoke stopped us on the third-floor landing.

"Oh, my," the girl said.

I knocked frantically on several apartment doors, then tried to muscle my way in so we could use the fire escapes, but all the doors were locked. I considered kicking an apartment door in, but then noticed that the doors were metal and attached to steel frames—impossible to force open without tools. Having no other choice, I decided we'd climb back up to the sixth floor, use the fire escape in the girl's apartment, or ascend to the roof and escape using the fire department ladder. But when we started back up, I saw flames licking the fourth-floor railing—the fire was now above us.

*Shit.*

"We're gonna play a game," I said to the seven-year-old, trying to keep the panic out of my voice. "When I count to three, we're gonna take a very deep breath, hold it, and I'm going to carry you down the stairs." The calm in the child's eyes made me feel foolish. She was no stranger to fear.

"All right," she said with practiced resignation. "On the count of three."

I picked her up and covered her and her sister with the blanket. "Keep your face under the blanket," I told the girl, "in case you have to breathe." We counted to three, took a deep breath and a hand grabbed my arm.

"Hold it," a firefighter in full gear, was standing behind us—I was never so glad to see a smoke-eater in my life.

"Not that way," he said. "The fire's everywhere."

He led us back down the hall, used an axe to chop away an apartment door, led us through a bedroom, and used his ax to chop away a fire escape security gate and window.

"I'll take one of the kids," he said.

I looked at the firefighter, he was in full gear, maybe 80 pounds of equipment. "I've got 'em," I said.

"You go first," he said.

I carried the kids out onto the fire escape, got down to the first floor when a burst of thick black smoke enveloped us. The kids started choking. I couldn't breathe or see. I felt for the next ladder rung, it wasn't there. I lost my footing and was suddenly airborne.

I woke hours later in a hospital emergency room. The first thing I saw was my retired police lieutenant father smiling down at me.

"Nice work, lad," he said—funny how Irish Catholic

families are: I shouldn't have been surprised to see my father at my bedside, but I was. We were never close and shared a cold, almost businesslike personal relationship.

"You saved the lives of two children." He flicked on the ER TV: *New York 1 News* reported that I'd been off duty, passing the building, saw the raging inferno and rushed in, to save lives. A news organization videotape showed me, a ghostly vision, climbing down the fire escape all but consumed by ink, black smoke and flames, carrying the two children, then falling onto the pavement, then getting to my feet. "Phoenix rising from the ashes," a reporter commented.

"It didn't happen that way," I rasped through an oxygen mask. I told my father that I wasn't stupid enough to run into a burning building, no matter what. I was there to pick up a date who stood me up, that I'd come upon the kids by accident, simple happenstance. "I was scared shitless. I would've gotten us killed. A firefighter saved us."

"The firefighter's dead." My father patted my arm. Said that the department would most likely benefit from the TV news version of events and advised to keep my big mouth shut.

"You can go to confession," my father whispered as my mother and kid sister Shannon came into the room. "Confess your subterfuge to a priest, but not to the department."

I did just that.

"What's the problem," Father Gorman, a friend from Saint Monica's Church, seemed less concerned then my father had been. "You saved lives."

"Yeah, but don't you see the difference? It's like 9/11. You don't call some poor schnook who was sitting at his desk when the jets hit a hero. It was the cops and firefighters who were *outside*, saw the inferno, knew what they were getting into, that they might not make it out alive. The dead firefighter sacrificed his life to save me and the two kids. He's the hero, not me."

Soon afterward, *I* was awarded the Medal of Honor: *for acts of gallantry and valor performed with knowledge of the risk involved, above and beyond the call of duty.*

To my shame I'd accepted that medal, enjoyed the rewards it afforded me. Sure the firefighter was awarded his own medal—the Mario M. Archer medal—and buried with full honors, but the news people were following me around during the guy's funeral, still touting *me* as the hero.

I'd felt like a fraud ever since.

I dropped the pouch containing the Medal of Honor into the satchel and zipped it up. Somewhere in another aisle a locker slammed closed and two chatty cops walked out of the locker room—the place was all at once church quiet.

I placed the satchel on the floor and realized, for the first time in eight hours, I was totally alone. I sat down on the wooden bench, dropped my face into my hands and tried to deal with what I was feeling.

Fact was, at that moment, although I'd had enough of police work, the revolving-door system of justice and the requisite political bullshit that went along with it, I was no longer as eager as I was at the beginning of the evening to quit the NYPD.

Maybe it was a subconscious desire to do something that entitled me to that Medal of Honor. Maybe it was because, during this tour, my life had changed: a newborn had died in my arms.

Contrary to all police sense, I couldn't help but take the infant and her mother's death personally. I wanted to arrest whoever had hired the dead arsonists Bo and Bubba, be it a youth gang, criminals involved in an unrelated conspiracy, the guy in the Lincoln, a Gold employee. To do that, I'd have to remain a cop a bit longer.

I picked up the satchel, tossed it back into my locker, tripped the lock and headed out to meet D'Amato.

# CHAPTER 13

J. G. Melon, an Upper East Side Irish/American pub, was packed with an eclectic mix of over-served businessmen, cops, firefighters and rowdy flight attendants when I arrived.

The bartender, Kitty Kelly, the daughter of a former FBI Special Agent, flashed a big smile and waved a greeting as I entered.

I spotted D'Amato over by the jukebox drinking a martini, and glad-handing some guys in WRITER'S GUILD OF AMERICA softball uniforms. I bellied up to the bar and ordered a brew.

"Saw D'Amato on the news tonight," Kitty shouted over a U2 song. She thumbed to the HDTV suspended by chains from the ceiling at the front of the bar. "Hell's the matter with him, anyway? Attacking Doyle in public?"

*Good question.* I looked and saw D'Amato making moves on a couple of flight attendants. Heard him loudly recounting *his* animated version of the night's events, making the best of his dubious celebrity status.

Kitty served me a beer. "Slainte."

"Slainte," I toasted.

"Not for nothing," Kitty said, leaning over the bar so as

to be heard. "But D'Amato's a nutcase. If he cracks, he'll crack big time. Don't let him take you down with him."

Kitty's statement gave me pause.

"Excuse me," an attractive blonde said to me. "Can I squeeze in? I want to get a drink."

I stepped away from the crowded bar to allow her access. My eyes drifted down as she spoke her order to Kitty: great ass, long tan legs. I was tempted to strike up a conversation, but the 4–12 tour's horrific events had left me feeling withdrawn, antisocial—I needed the company of cops. Beside, I never had any luck meeting women in bars, and I couldn't take being shot down.

I sipped my beer, watched D'Amato compete with a WGA softball player for the attentions of a blowsy flight attendant, and wondered whatever possessed me to team up with him in the first place. But then I recalled, I had had little choice.


WE HAD FIRST become acquainted while recruits in the New York City Police Academy. Before joining the force, I had been in the Navy, a ship's cook and hand-to-hand combat instructor aboard various warships. D'Amato tended bar in the Kew Gardens section of Queens. We both excelled during our six months' training in the academy.

Upon graduation, I was assigned, thanks to my father's influence, to the low-crime 52nd Precinct on Webster Avenue in the Bronx. D'Amato's father—a violence-prone police sergeant who was credited with starting the Harlem riots by throwing the first punch and firing the first shot—made certain that D'Amato was assigned to another low-crime precinct, the 50th in the Riverdale section of the Bronx. But those choice assignments were to be short-lived.

I was working my first set of 4–12 tours, walking a quiet, snow-covered foot post when I responded to a "calls for help" run assigned to me over a portable radio. I rushed to the address, a five-floor walkup, and was directed by alarmed elderly neighbors to the second floor. There I discovered an open apartment door and a seventeen-year-old boy standing over two bloody bodies: his father and mother.

"I want a lawyer," was all the teenage killer said as he dropped a blood-covered carving knife. I placed him under arrest, read him his rights, cuffed him, and radioed for backup, all the while fighting the revulsion of witnessing my first murder scene.

Thick, dark blood matted both victims, the floors and walls. Oozing defensive wounds were visible on the man's and woman's forearms. I determined with a shiver that the couple had fought hard for their lives—I blessed myself, said a prayer for them. And for the first time I experienced the unsettling aura that is associated with recent violent death. Smelled the dank sweat and blood-laden air.

It would not be my last time.

As police cars arrived on the scene, I took some solace in the fact that this would be my first class A felony arrest, or so I thought. A detective named Robert Doyle would change that.

I thought Doyle was a model of a cop when I first laid eyes on him, entering the crime scene. Not a perfectly coiffed salt-and-pepper hair—in those days—was out of place. A midnight blue chesterfield overcoat was draped, cape-like, over a charcoal gray business suit. The fashionable getup was in stark contrast to the surreal, blood-splattered murder scene.

As is the norm, the responding detective took charge of the investigation. Doyle asked me, a rookie, to guard the apartment, "just until the lab technicians arrive," while he did me the favor of escorting my prisoner to the station-house. But what Doyle did was transport my prisoner straight to Central Booking, steal the homicide arrest, the glory, and ten hours of overtime pay.

"He did it for the overtime pay," a fat beat cop whispered to me the following afternoon during the 4–12 roll call. I had arrived at the stationhouse early, searching for Doyle, furious about him stealing my collar, complaining to anyone who'd listen.

"He's got some kind of problem at home," the fat beat cop continued. "Sick wife, I think. He never talks about it. Works more overtime than anyone I know."

I didn't want to hear it.

"Johnston," the roll call sergeant called out.

"Here."

"Stewart."

"Here."

"Doyle."

I jumped up from my chair, turned and located the detective, who was standing against a wall behind me.

"Doyle." I pointed an accusing finger. "You stole my homicide collar."

The roll call sergeant stopped short. All fifty cops in the muster room turned to look at Doyle. A few cops snickered. Someone grumbled, "Doyle's a pussy." The air crackled with pre-combat anticipation.

"I will not dignify your preposterous allegation with a reply, rookie," Doyle said. "Back off, if you know what's good for you."

I rushed Doyle—he threw a punch. I blocked it and landed a blow that bounced him off the muster board. Several cops broke up the brawl.

The roll call sergeant wrote us both up for fighting. The 52nd Precinct's captain docked us each two days' pay and told us we would be transferred.

D'Amato, for his part, was racing home from a night of cavorting and drinking when a Chevy sped up alongside his car and cut him off. Furious, D'Amato accelerated, overtook the guy, and was giving him the finger when he saw a gun pointing at him. D'Amato drew his own revolver and fired, hitting the Chevy door. The Chevy's driver swerved and slammed against a concrete guard rail, leaving a spectacular shower of sparks. He skidded to a stop on the parkway shoulder.

D'Amato stopped a few feet behind the Chevy and bolted out of his car, gun in hand. He identified himself as a police officer and ordered the driver of the Chevy to exit his car. The driver, shot in the left buttock, struggled out and flipped open a shield case. D'Amato saw the badge and moaned. The Chevy's driver was a drunk off-duty DEA agent.

Because the two cops stuck to a bizarre story about an accidental gun discharge, and because drunken cops don't press charges against other drunken cops, D'Amato's only discipline was a transfer.

So D'Amato, Doyle and I were all dumped into the worst precinct in the city, the 41st in the Bronx, an unsupervised dumping ground for head cases, drunks, and those with acute disciplinary problems. Cops there were aggressive, violence-prone.

The roll call man in the 41st thought it would be a hoot to team up police academy mates, D'Amato and me, and assign us to an RMP in the most violent sector in the precinct, sector Ida.

REMEMBERING THE PAST with a frown, I swallowed some beer and watched the now tipsy D'Amato work his charm on the flight attendants. He had focused on a boozy, jiggling piece of eye candy.

"Do I know you?" D'Amato said.

"No," the flight attendant said.

"Do you know me?" D'Amato said.

"No."

"Ever see me in here before?" D'Amato said.

"No."

"Then how do you know it's me?"

I'd heard that lame routine countless times, but it still made me chuckle. In retrospect, the 41 roll call man had been right. Working with D'Amato had been a hoot and not just because he could be entertaining. Although he had freaked me out once by drunkenly placing a gun to his head and daring me to dare him to pull the trigger—I brought an abrupt end to that surreal situation by accusing him of being a self-centered idiot. Told him if he pulled the trigger I'd be buried in paperwork for the next month. He apologized and put the gun away.

That craziness worked both ways, though. I'd also witnessed D'Amato face down gun-wielding felons. Dive into the path of an out-of-control car to save a small boy. Talk jumpers off of roof tops. Deliver babies. Treat heart attack, stroke and crime victims with heartfelt compassion.

I'd once tried to analyze the friendship we'd developed as a result of our association. But for me, dissecting relationships of any kind was difficult. I take my friends at face value. So all I came away with was that D'Amato was a good cop, a decent human being. He was consistent in his eccentricities, and he made me laugh.

"Hey, Beckett. C'mere," D'Amato yelled down the bar.

Kitty handed me my second brew. "He's a mess, again," she said. "Keep a leash on him."

I took my beer and moseyed over to D'Amato, trying to gauge his frame of mind as I approached.

"Here he is." D'Amato put his arm around me. "Ladies, say hey to my partner, Michael Beckett. Handsome son of a bitch, ain't he?" The flight attendants smiled politely. None made eye contact. They seemed to be more interested in a couple of prosperous looking older gentlemen who were seated at a nearby table flirting with them.

"Beckett is a TV star," D'Amato said.

"Really?" The flight attendant D'Amato was interested in focused on me. "What show?"

"*Law & Order*," D'Amato said.

"I only worked a couple of months on the show," I said. "A featured role."

"I'm a part-time actress," the flight attendant said. "Studied drama in college, but I can't seem to get a break in this town."

Her smile was enticing.

"Maybe you could help me out?" she said.

*Uh, oh.* I knew where this was going. Even though D'Amato was married, he reacted badly to competition. In his mind, he'd seen the flight attendant first, God help any guy who tried to muscle in on him.

"Honestly, I'm not in a position to help anyone."

"How did you land the part on the show?" she said.

"Vinnie can tell you all about it." I excused myself, went to the men's room, and made certain to avoid D'Amato and his flight attendant on the way back to the bar.

"Thanks, partner," D'Amato said, standing next to me not five minutes later. "You're a piece a work, you know that?" He was slurring his words.

I glanced to the back of the restaurant. D'Amato's flight attendant was schmoozing one of the older rich guys.

"What're you talking about?" I said.

"You knew I was interested in that broad. You hit on her anyway."

"Bullshit."

"Yeah? Why'd you bring up being an actor, working on *Law & Order*?"

"You brought up *Law & Order*—"

"'Cause you would have. It's all you talk about. Your fucking claim to fame."

I shook my head. Fact was I rarely talked about the TV show, but I didn't feel like arguing with a drunk.

"Kitty," D'Amato called out. "Another martini."

"I don't think so," Kitty said.

"What?" D'Amato was incredulous. "You cutting me off?"

"How 'bout a cup of coffee?" Kitty said.

"Fuck that."

"Time to go home, Vinnie," I said.

"Home to what: a fat bitch who hasn't slept with me in over a year?"

"Lower your voice," I said.

I hated when D'Amato lambasted his wife. True, Doreen was no beauty queen—she'd let her appearance go—but she was a sweet girl, a good mother and, as the daughter of a retired cop, a perfect match for D'Amato.

D'Amato looked into his empty glass, looked at Kitty, and then at me. "Let me ask you something, Beckett, and be honest with me." D'Amato put his glass on the bar. "You really think you're better than we are—" He gestured to some other 41 cops. "Don't you?"

I was stunned by the assertion. "No, I don't. Where do you get this crazy shit from?"

"Crazy?" D'Amato was getting louder. "I'll show you crazy." He stuck a finger in my face. "How'd you like a punch in the mouth."

I pushed off the bar, planted my feet. "I wouldn't try it, partner."

J. G. Melon went silent. Everyone was looking at us. A couple of the 41 cops hurried over and stood behind D'Amato ready to restrain him if he started swinging— his volatility was legend.

"Hey!" Kitty the bartender said. "Out." She took D'Amato's empty martini glass off the bar and pointed to the door. "Get him outta here, Beckett. I mean it."

"C'mon, Vinnie." I took D'Amato by the arm.

"Get off." D'Amato ripped his arm from my grip, shoved

me away. He dug into his pocket and threw some money on the bar. "You ain't better than me, Beckett. You ain't better than anybody."

I watched speechless as D'Amato pushed several patrons aside on his way out the door.

# CHAPTER 14

To say the broadcast of the 5:30 A.M. edition of *New York 1 News* infuriated R. J. Gold would be an understatement. The arson in his building at Coster Street had caused the horrifying deaths of a teenage mother and her infant—that was bad enough. Then the arsonists—two rednecks by the looks of their mug shots on TV—were gunned down by police in a headline-grabbing hail of bullets. As a result, his competitors, men like Donald Trump, Larry Silverstein, and the Fisher Brothers were watching his every move. Fire marshals, police detectives, parasitic investigative reporters were out in force snooping around, asking questions. Soon they'd be checking land deeds, building permits, plans and trade union contracts—so much for discretion. Gold would be forced to lean heavily on every newspaper publisher, reporter, union official, top cop and politician in his database in order to suppress an inquisition.

Gold lay back on his king-size bed in his palatial bedroom atop Gold Tower and began doctor-recommended breathing exercises in an effort to relax and control his temper. He breathed in deeply, exhaled slowly. Commanded his toes, legs, torso, arms and fingers to relax. As his anger subsided, a vague, shameful awareness replaced it.

The senseless deaths of the girl, infant and the two arsonists were bad enough. But, even worse, was a police officer he'd seen among the swarm of blue uniforms at the shooting scene outside the Black Cat Social Club. Michael Beckett was right in the thick of this mess.

The first time Gold had met Michael Beckett was at the insistence of a blond bombshell he'd picked up in front of the Sherry Netherland Hotel. Janet Roth, a former Ms. Hawaiian Tropic, said her ex-boyfriend was a Bronx police officer, that they were still close friends, and that she wanted Gold to meet him—bottom line, Janet wanted her cop friend's approval.

Although Gold had misgivings about becoming acquainted with some rough-around-the-edges street cop, meeting him was requisite to getting close to Janet. He asked Janet for Beckett's phone number and called that very day.

Much to Gold's amusement, Beckett turned out to be charismatic, articulate. He wore expensive business suits, had the look and bearing of a young Wall Street power broker—which gave Gold an idea: befriend Beckett and exploit him in social situations as a decoy. The ruse worked better than anticipated. Beckett, enamored of the billionaire lifestyle, soon became a Gold groupie and willing "beard." As a result, Gold and Janet enjoyed a torrid affair without Gold's wife ever finding out.

The problem was, although Gold felt he knew Beckett pretty well, he could never figure out how he'd react to a given situation, or why. For example: when asked, Beckett had no problem employing NYPD computers illegally on Gold's behalf, using his badge to quash a Gold employee's minor drug arrests, another's first time DUI. But when Gold's eighteen-year-old nephew was arrested and charged with a bullshit assault, date rape, Beckett flatly refused to intervene. Beckett, as it turned out, possessed a unique sense of values, which caused Gold to look upon him as a potential "loose cannon." If he became involved in the

Coster Street arson investigation, stumbled upon anything incriminating, there was no predicting the results.

Gold stared at the winged cherubs painted on the ceiling over his bed, then looked at his eighteen-carat-gold, diamond-studded, Piaget wristwatch. It was 5:45. He kicked back the silk bedsheet, rocked up from his canopied bed, and landed on the thick white carpet. He wondered if Beckett was the type of man to hold a grudge. Was he still angry about how Gold had treated Janet Roth?

Gold moved past the floor-to-ceiling windows facing Central Park feeling uneasy in the disquieting semi-darkness. Then he recalled that his wife Helga and his two daughters were still in Paris shopping.

Gold walked past a façade of fake Greek columns with gold leaf dripping from the molding, to an antique French bureau. On top sat silver-framed photographs of Helga and his daughters. Gold pressed his index finger to his lips, touched the girls' photos, looked at Helga's and could not help but smile at the young face beaming back at him.

"Rakishly romantic," was how he'd once overheard Helga describe him to a group of wine-giddy girlfriends. She said that, because of his longish brown hair, silver-blue eyes, pouty lips, and—in those days—pronounced jawline that she found him "leading man handsome." Helga was twenty years old at the time, gushing with a virginal effervescent spirit. Not any longer. Gold had taken the greatest pleasure perverting her—cajoling her into sexual liaisons with him and other women, thoroughly eroding the very things that had attracted him to her. He loathed himself for corrupting her. Loathed her for allowing it. Studying the winsome young face, he felt an emptiness, a sense of loss. Thanks to him, the Helga of today was a guileful, perfumed monster.

They had not been intimate in years.

Gold moved to the bathroom, a large mirrored black onyx and brass chamber, washed his hands, dropped his

XXL boxer shorts and gave his six-foot-two-inch frame the once-over—ugh. He detested his soft, pear-shaped body. But he hated exercise more. God, he had to lose some weight. He grabbed the thick roll of blubber around his midsection. Maybe it was time for another round of lipo-suction.

Gold reached into the medicine cabinet, pulled out a bottle of diet pills, popped several into his mouth and swallowed them with a sanitary paper cup full of cold water. He crushed the paper cup, dropped it into a wastebas-ket, and realized he felt lonely in his thirty-million-dollar palace in the sky. He had slept alone again last night.

Gold showered, shaved, dressed hurriedly and slipped a handful of diet pills into his pants pocket. He pressed an intercom button and announced, "I'll dine in the kitchen."

Again Gold washed his hands, then, whistling an ob-scure show tune, he headed to a winding staircase which would take him down to the first floor of his triplex apartment.

Gold descended into the living room, which he proudly claimed was the largest in New York, eighty feet long, cov-ered with honey-hued marble. The walls were bedecked with art, a collection, if he owned it outright, worth over $20 million.

Gold trudged through the dining room with its two-story windows facing west on Fifth Avenue and north along Central Park. A grand crystal chandelier illuminated a gilt-edged table surrounded by high-backed chairs, cov-ered with pure white Italian leather and trimmed in gold.

Gold stopped by the apartment's front door, sixteen panels of solid bronze resembling the gateway to an an-cient Mayan tomb, and found his copies of the *Wall Street Journal,* the *New York Times*, the *New York Daily News* and the *New York Post* stacked on a foyer table. TEEN MOTHER AND INFANT KILLED IN SOUTH BRONX ARSON read one headline. The shootout at the Black Cat Social Club was the headline on another.

Gold entered the kitchen, a vast stainless steel affair of Sub-Zero appliances, and sat on a stool at a marble counter—it was too quiet. He missed the chaos of breakfast with Helga and the girls.

"Top of the morning to you, Mr. Gold," a stone-faced Irish maid said. She served Gold four McDonald's Sausage McMuffins on a solid silver platter—he had them delivered daily—and a glass filled with Dr. Brown's cream soda.

Gold buried his face in the tabloid news story that dramatized the arson and subsequent shootout at the Black Cat Social Club. He glanced at the many news photos, spotted Michael Beckett and his wild-man partner, a rather entertaining rooster of a man with crazy eyes, Vinnie Something, in a group of cops.

Gold finished his breakfast, washed his hands, and checked his Piaget; 6:30 A.M. It was time for work.

Gold made his way from his penthouse, escorted by two armed bodyguards, via a secret passage, down four floors to the Gold Organization executive offices.

Gold's bodyguards peeled off to their security posts by the elevators as Gold pushed through a set of plate-glass doors. He moved through the beige-carpeted, burl-trimmed reception area—the statuesque brunette receptionist would arrive at nine—and passed the gleaming billboard-size bronze letters which spelled out GOLD ORGANIZATION.

Gold's executive assistant, Norma, a middle-aged brunette, offered her boss a stack of messages as he strode by her desk.

Gold paused, snatched the pink pile and scanned them impatiently. He stopped at one, read it, then held it up for comment. "Pete?"

"He said he'll be here this morning," Norma said.

"Today's schedule on my desk?" Gold's face twitched.

"Not yet."

"Get Tomo Nagasue on the phone."

"It's rather early for Tomo, R .J."

"Just do it," Gold snapped. He performed a face-shoulder-face twitch and strode into his office.

Norma picked up a phone, dialed an extension and whispered a warning, "He's taking diet pills again."

Gold moved behind his gull-winged, Brazilian rosewood desk. His gigantic private office, carpeted with a rich beige and brown wool, was enclosed on three sides by floor-to-ceiling windows. Scale models of Gold's yacht, Puma helicopter, private 727, and Gold Airlines 767 jet rested on display pedestals on the south side of the room. In the middle of the office, where he always showcased his most current building project, atop a large rectangular table stood an elaborately detailed scale model of a mammoth, ten-square-city-block construction project. The gold plate affixed to the table was inscribed GOLD BRONX CITY.

Gold walked over to the mock-up, reached under the table and switched on the model's overhead spotlights.

Norma stuck her head in the office. "Tomo Nagasue."

Gold walked to his desk, picked up his phone.

"You know what time it is, R. J.?" Nagasue, the Gold Organization's chief financial officer, spoke with a Japanese accent.

"Talk to me."

The CFO yawned. "It's more bad news, I'm afraid."

Gold took a deep breath, exhaled. "Let's hear it."

"First off, the banks are threatening to force us into bankruptcy unless you agree to hire a corporate overseer, one of their choosing. His mandate will be to trim the excess from the Gold Organization operations. Assist your creditors in selling off all your, what they consider, cash-consuming properties. Including the jet, yacht, helicopters and the airline. Second, they want to place you on a spending allowance. They intended to limit your personal expenses to $550,000 a month."

"And if I capitulate?"

"The banks will grant you an $85 million bridge loan and agree to allow you to forgo interest payments on $3 billion in loans for five years. For their generosity the banks will, in effect, control the Gold Organization."

"They're bluffing," Gold said.

"Doubtful."

"Listen carefully." Gold's voice was icy calm. "You tell the banks that if they will not agree to restructure my debt so I maintain control of my empire, I will file for bankruptcy." Gold hung up.

He took a few steps back, circled the scale model of Gold Bronx City and reveled in the genius of his scheme.

Although he'd mortgaged all his assets and was, in reality, not only flat broke but in debt for billions, he felt that the banks could not possibly permit a Gold Organization bankruptcy. His debts were so enormous that the results would be catastrophic: the banks themselves would fail along with him. It amused Gold to think those pinstriped fools who were attempting to seize control of his empire were at his mercy.

So much for his immediate cash-crunch problem.

Gold reached under the table and, using remote control, realigned the overhead pin-light which illuminated the name Gold on the tallest of the miniature skyscrapers.

Although the high-crime borough of the Bronx was not Gold's first choice in which to build—Donald Trump had outmaneuvered him for the more desirable Penn Central train yards on Manhattan's Upper West Side—revitalizing the Bronx would be a monumental achievement. Single-handedly he would shepherd the rebirth of that squalid borough. An ambitious, some said impossible project.

Gold planned to provide underground parking, state-of-the-art security, Olympic-sized swimming pools, first-class health clubs, playgrounds and parks, gourmet grocery stores, half a dozen ethnic and theme restaurants, private limos and other transportation to Manhattan. And with the Gold Organization name attached to the development, he was convinced the public would rush to buy. Especially after he leaked to the press that a consortium of Japanese business-men had—thanks to Tomo Nagasue—placed in escrow binders totaling $150 million for advance condominium purchases. That was providing the Gold Organization be-gan construction within the next twenty-four hours, thereby assuring millions in government loan guarantees. Which meant, thanks to the Coster Street debacle, relocating the tenants in only one or two remaining buildings. Not a prob-lem. Unless someone like Trump, the feds, fire marshals, the NYPD, or some incorruptible investigative news reporter stumbled onto his scheme. And then there was the wild card; Michael Beckett.

Gold picked up a miniature figure of a uniformed police officer walking a beat in front of the southernmost Gold Bronx City tower and studied it. He could not permit his old friend Beckett to interfere and cause a deal-breaking construction delay—not that the NYPD was in a position to do any real harm. After all the arsonists were dead. Case closed. Any incriminating evidence they might uncover would be circumstantial, take time to investigate and would then have to be handed over to the Bronx District Attor-ney.

Gold owned the DA.

Gold looked closer at the tiny cop, frowned, dropped it on the carpet and crushed it under his size-thirteen shoe.

# CHAPTER 15

Zeke Taylor nearly screamed when he saw his brothers shot down by a firing squad of cops that morning on the TV news. Nearly screamed but didn't.

Zeke had just finished a Riker's Island, Men's House of Detention breakfast—bologna sandwich with a mayonnaise-like substance on stale white bread. He was standing with his back to a peeling wall in the inmate "lounge" feeling positively depressed about life in general, and wondering why none of the prison's "homo"-sexual inmates had made a pass at him. Not that he ever entertained any perverse desires. But homosexuals had been bothering him all his life: while in the Mississippi chain gang he beat the living hell out of more than one sissy for making improper advances. Zeke was pondering why the homos no longer found him attractive when a buck-nigger with a TV remote happened to switch on the 6:00 A.M. edition of the news.

Zeke heard his brothers' names, saw old mug shots of them flash on the TV. "Arsonists," the news anchor called Bo and Bubba. "Murderers."

Zeke was trying to figure what in the hell the talking head was yapping about when the station played his brothers' execution in slow motion. Zeke blinked several times as Bo and Bubba's faces flexed into painful contortions and bullets ripped into their bodies. Zeke gasped, choked back tears, a sign of weakness to the ever-watchful predatory prison population. He told himself that it couldn't be *his* little brothers on national TV, it couldn't be. What had the dumb asses gotten themselves into?

Zeke heard the news anchor say something about a burned building and the death of a teenage mother and her infant. Then the station played more videotape and Zeke saw familiar faces in front of the Black Cat Social Club.

There were the cops he'd seen in the 41st Precinct clerical office. Zeke remembered that they'd all been in the office when he was being processed. They'd been discussing . . . a fire.

Bubba and Bo must have set that fire. But why? Zeke couldn't understand it. He'd left them on their own for a few hours and they go and commit arson, a double murder, and then get themselves killed in the process.

"Got a match?" an obviously gay prisoner said to Zeke. Zeke evil-eyed the fruitcake, told him to get lost: at least he hadn't lost his manly appeal.

Zeke stepped over to a barred window that overlooked LaGuardia Airport, squinted into the rising sun and mustered up his dark powers of positive thinking. He decided that he had to get out of jail. Find out what had happened. Deal with whoever it was that killed his little brothers.

# CHAPTER 16

Solana Ortiz woke a little before seven the following morning with Michael Beckett on her mind: the way he looked when he got out of the police car in front of the 41st Precinct, the pained expression on his face, his blood-stained uniform.

Following the rude cop Schultz's suggestion, Solana had headed home—stopping only to say good-bye to yet more neighbors who were moving out—booted up her computer and typed "license plate check" into Google. She was astonished by the number of hits: 2,770. She clicked the first link which launched her to a Web site called Net-Snoop. Net-Snoop claimed: *Use Your Computer to Investigate Anyone! Most Complete Investigative Site on the Internet! Used by Professional Investigators Since 1995! Net-Snoop allows you to investigate anyone by permitting access to public record databases in every state and county: credit reports, criminal and driving records, civil court records, birth, marriage and divorce records. The information available on this Web site will blow your mind!*

Solana charged $29.95 to her credit card and discovered that Net-Snoop was a fraud. Instead of granting her instant access to the public information databases, she was supplied with the names of detective agencies who charged additional fees or directed to government offices where you could unearth the information yourself. Net-Snoop also suggested subterfuge to acquire semi-public information, like automobile registration information, and supplied its subscribers with dozens of scripted examples.

Although Solana felt she'd been hoodwinked by Net-Snoop, she had learned that it was relatively easy to investigate a person's life, and that the amount of sensitive personal information available to anyone who knew where to look was mind-boggling—the implications were dire.

Solana rose from bed, stretched, padded to the kitchen, microwaved a cup of tap water, and dropped in an herbal tea bag. She reached into the Gucci-knockoff shoulder bag and took out the piece of paper with Beckett's phone number. She unfolded it, studied his penmanship—Tina, who considered herself an expert on all things male, called Beckett's cursive "sensitive yet dominant." Solana crushed the piece of paper and tossed it in the kitchen trash.

Solana sipped her tea, walked into the living room, said, "*Te amo*" to a photo of her deceased mother. She picked up the phone and dialed the *Law & Order* studio, left a message on her boss's answering service that she was in bed with a fever, and taking a sick day off—Tina was already in the loop. Solana had phoned her last evening, told her about Pete from Queens following her and her experience at the police station.

"I'm gonna call in sick tomorrow," she told Tina. "Go to the courthouse, check public records, see what I can find out about Pete."

"Why?" Tina said. "What good will that do you?"

"I'll feel less helpless," Solana said. "He knows me. I wanna know something about him—knowledge is power," she added quoting from the Net-Snoop home page.

"What if he finds out?" Tina said.

"He won't," Solana said with less confidence then was in her voice. "Checking public records is like looking someone up in a phonebook—there's no way he'd know."

"If you say so," Tina said. "Be careful."

Solana dressed in an inconspicuous, loose-fitting tank top, baggy jeans, New York Yankee baseball cap, no makeup, and then carefully positioned the hat pin along with fruit and crackers in her shoulder bag. She stepped to her computer, assembled the printed results of the Net-Snoop Web search.

Solana slipped on a pair of sunglasses and made her way to the Hunts Point subway station. Destination: New York State Department of Motor Vehicles in lower Manhattan.

Stepping around sleeping derelicts and garbage cans overturned and ravaged by packs of hungry dogs, breathing in the ghetto's disagreeable odors, she found herself wishing she had known about public information years ago. She would have investigated her first and only serious boyfriend, the son of a transit worker she met while a junior in high school. Her mother had strongly disapproved. The handsome Latino youth sported gaudy jewelry, wore the latest hip-hop clothes, said he loved her, stole her heart and her virginity, and dumped her for another girl a few months later. His extensive criminal record came to light after he was arrested for exposing himself to female shoppers along Southern Boulevard. She had not permitted a man to get close to her since—not that she was a prude. She'd had affairs with reckless men, damaged, careless men. But she allowed no one to touch her heart.

Solana exchanged passing pleasantries with Carmen, a career waitress and fervent *Law & Order* fan who was standing outside of her restaurant chain smoking.

"*Cuál es nuevo en el* Law & Order?" Carmen said through a thick cloud of smoke. She was always asking about the show's gossip and yet-to-be-broadcast story lines.

"*Nada.*" Solana dropped into the subway, passed a couple of heavily armed, narrow-eyed Transit cops stationed by the token booth. She swiped her Metro Card, pushed through the turnstile, and was passing the newsstand when she saw the headline: TEEN MOTHER, INFANT KILLED IN SOUTH BRONX ARSON.

Solana wedged through the crowd of commuters, snatched a paper from the pile, paid the newsstand attendant, and paged to the article. The fire had taken place at Coster Street and Viele Avenue last evening. *Last evening.* Solana recalled hearing distant sirens, even smelling smoke. But sirens and fires were the norm in the 'hood. Plus her neighbors who were moving out had made quite a racket. And she'd had her stereo on, listening to her mother's Julio Iglesias CDs while she surfed the net. Solana opened the newspaper and read the entire article.

According to the newspaper, the tenement where the unidentified homeless teenage girl and her infant had been killed had been set ablaze by building strippers intent on pilfering valuable copper wire and various fixtures. Bo and Bubba Taylor, the two perpetrators, were apprehended but later gunned down while in police custody.

"Cold-blooded murder," the ACLU was quoted as calling the shooting of the unarmed Taylor brothers by police. "A monumental police blunder." The mayor vowed sweeping changes in the police department's deadly physical force guidelines. The same mayor had promised the same sweeping changes five years ago after the police murdered Solana's unarmed sixteen-year-old neighbor. Yet, it appeared, cops were still executing unarmed men.

As her train thundered into the station, Solana considered the fact that yet another building had been destroyed by arson. But this time a teenage girl and her infant were dead and the arsonists apprehended. Solana pushed into the packed subway car, and reflected that perhaps her instincts were wrong about Pete from Queens. Maybe he was not responsible for the fires.

Solana walked into the offices of the New York State Department of Motor Vehicles a half hour later.

Using one of the suggested scripts from the Net-Snoop Web site, Solana explained to a heavyset male clerk that her car had been damaged by a hit-and-run driver. She said, "His plate number is 542-PVC."

"File a police report?" The clerk's eyes were fixed on Solana's breasts. "You need to file an accident report before I can give you that information."

"I have the report right here," Solana lied, thinking quickly. She dug through her shoulder bag. "I don't believe this." She feigned frustration. "I must have left it home."

"I can't help you," the clerk said.

Tears welled in Solana's eyes. "Please," she said in Spanish. "I'll have to take the subway all the way back to the Bronx, take another day off from work—"

"That's too bad." Yet the clerk was leering at her, clearly interested. "Sorry."

Solana leaned forward, giving the lecherous old bastard a better view of her breasts. "Please?"

The clerk smiled, clearly pleased. "What was that plate number again?"

Solana repeated it.

The clerk entered the plate number into a computer. Moments later he handed Solana a copy of the Lincoln's registration. The Lincoln was registered to Peter Costello, 103-22 Main Street, Flushing, Queens, New York.

Solana walked a few blocks south, entered the County Clerk's office, and told a clerk she wanted to find some-one's birth certificate. She was directed to a stack of log books, found "C" and began her search. Solana located two Pete Costellos in Pete's apparent age range, but only one at 103-22 Main Street. Pete from Queens had appar-ently resided in the same Flushing location all his life.

Solana accessed a microfilm copy of Pete's birth certificate and discovered his parents had applied for a Social Security number at birth—luckily for Solana. According to the Net-Snoop Web site, a birth date and Social Security number are essential to any background investigation. Solana wrote down the information and noted that at four pounds, the six-foot-four-inch muscle-bulging Pete had been an underweight baby.

Using Pete's birth date and Social Security number, Solana investigated Pete's criminal history by checking criminal conviction records. She had to fill out forms, pay a filing fee. The results were negative. But a clerk told Solana that those results were for "convictions" only and did not include arrests. He said, "Theoretically, a person could be arrested a dozen times, but if he was not convicted of a crime, those arrest records are not available to the public. Also, if a person was arrested and convicted as a juvenile offender, those criminal records may not be available."

Next Solana checked if Pete was a defendant or complainant in any federal or state civil law suits, checked if he had any tax liens, judgments. All were negative. She even investigated Pete's property records statewide. The home he lived in was apparently owned by his mother. Pete owned no property in New York State.

Solana had spent her time searching through dusty record books, computer databases and eye-straining microfilm, dealing with lecherous and/or predominantly apathetic clerks, spent fee money she could not afford, and had little to show for it.

Brooding, Solana left the county clerk's office, moped toward the subway station, and took some solace in the fact that she hadn't involved Michael Beckett. If she had told him about her instincts regarding Pete from Queens, he probably would have thought her an utter fool.

Solana descended into the subway station, still puzzled

by the fact that Pete's public record was nearly nonexistent. She wondered if it was that way by design; could someone manipulate their public record? Wondered if there was something she'd missed.

She entered the uptown train, found a seat, and, while making sure to avoid eye-contact with other passengers, read the various subway posters. In between ads for cosmetic dentists and ambulance-chasing lawyers was an ad asking people to support the New York Public Library. *The public library*. Solana remembered reading on Net-Snoop that the newspaper and magazine databases at the library were a prime source of information.

Solana made her way to the main branch of the New York Public Library, a monumental structure at 42nd Street and Fifth Avenue. She passed the two massive sculpted lions guarding the entranceway, climbed the endless series of granite stairs to the entrance, and wove through a group of toothy Asian tourists snapping pictures.

She entered through the main doors and climbed yet more stairs to the third floor. There she signed the computer access log and was directed to an unoccupied computer work station.

Once settled at the computer, she toggled to the library's newspaper databases, typed in the name Peter Costello and hit the enter key.

"PETER COSTELLO in 2 titles," appeared on the screen. Solana scanned the list:

1. Loan Shark Linked to Murder.
2. R. J. Gold Names Decorated Former Military Police Officer as Security Chief.

Solana read the articles.

Read about organized crime.

Read about R. J. Gold.

# CHAPTER 17

Pete from Queens entered the cavernous lobby of Gold Tower, lumbered across the marble floor and scanned the bustling six-story atrium. The overpriced boutiques were doing a brisk business. Waiting lines snaked outside the restaurants. Tour groups posed for pictures at the base of the magnificent eighty-foot waterfall.

Pete checked to see that the security staff were at their assigned posts, positioned at every entrance with orders to discourage "undesirables." In addition, armed patrols policed the building's external perimeter—loitering of any kind was not tolerated on the sidewalks around Gold Tower.

"Looking good," Pete said to a pretty, crisp female security officer as he moved past her. She flinched at the very sight of him.

Pete entered the elevator marked PRIVATE and touched the button that read GOLD EXECUTIVE OFFICES. The door swished closed.

Inside, the elevator was mirrored, floor to ceiling, the overhead, diffused light designedly flattering. Pete checked his reflection, scowled. He was aware that his Lurch-like appearance sometimes alarmed people. An asset when he was in the military, or when he needed to be tough: a detriment when it came to approaching women, like the Puerto Rican beauty Solana Ortiz, whom he had saved from a pack of vicious dogs. Even women who worked for him—the pretty security guard for example—were put off. Working eighty hours a week didn't help his social life either. And he had grown tired of hookers.

Pete stepped off the elevator, turned right through plate glass doors that read GOLD ORGANIZATION, and passed two Gold bodyguards who came to soft attention. He graced the gorgeous receptionist with a passing leer, pushed through a second set of glass doors and stopped at Norma's desk.

"He in?"

"That's debatable," Norma said.

Tomo Nagasue, Gold's CFO and attorney, stepped out of his office. "If you leave now, Pete," Nagasue said, "he'll never know you were here."

Pete looked at the diminutive CFO. "Don't tell me."

Nagasue flexed his face. "Diet pills. Again."

Pete sat heavily on Norma's desk, mind racing in an effort to conjure an excuse to put the meeting off. His first instinct was to turn and run. "How bad is he, really?"

Nagasue glanced toward Gold's open door. "Bonkers." He took Pete by the arm, led him off to the side—a fox steering a grizzly bear—and spoke in a whisper: "Remember what we discussed last month?"

"Last month?"

"I'll refresh your memory." Nagasue had to look up at Pete. "R. J. is losing it. Making one bad business decision after another. It's only a matter of time before word gets out about his drug problem. The banks will smell blood, attack like sharks, take over, kill the Gold Bronx City project—the Japanese investors will not be happy."

The former MP shifted uneasily. He looked toward Gold's office door: Nagasue was talking mutiny, a coup d'état.

"We shouldn't be talking about this," Pete said.

"Then don't talk," Nagasue said. "Listen. I can't do this without you—you've been his security chief for years. You know where the bodies are buried."

"Mr. Gold's been good to me."

"And he's been good to me too, but that was yesterday. He's not the same person."

"I know, but—"

"Look, just keep in mind, if the banks take over, the Yakuza will lose their investment. They may hold us somehow responsible. It's not beyond them to extract revenge. Think about that."

"Norma?" Gold yelled from inside his office. "Pete here?"

Pete looked at Norma who looked at Nagasue who looked at Pete.

"That Pete's cologne I smell?" Gold said. "Norma?"

"Yes, Mr. Gold," Norma called back. She looked at Pete, shrugged, mouthed the words, *"Sorry, Pete."*

"Try not to upset him." Nagasue gave Pete an encouraging pat on the back. "We'll talk later."

Pete straightened his tie, squared his shoulders and marched into Gold's office rethinking his decade-old decision to wear Napoleon cologne exclusively.

Gold was leaving his lavatory, frantically toweling off his hands.

"Morning, Mr. Gold." Pete tried a smile.

Gold, gnawing at a hangnail, motioned for Pete to sit in an overstuffed, burgundy leather chair. He yanked open a drawer, pulled out eight-by-ten head shots of three beautiful women and spread them across his desk for Pete's inspection.

"You believe it, Pete? Beautiful, aren't they?" Gold's pupils were dilated. "Which one is best? Which one is a ten?"

Pete had been through this drill before and not just on diet pill days. He leaned forward, dutifully studied the pictures, waiting for the hint he knew Gold would eventually give him. Gold had already made his choice.

"They're all beautiful, Boss."

Gold beamed. "Yeah. Can you believe it, Pete? And they're all in love with me." Twitch.

*Bullshit.* Pete lowered his eyes to the three beautiful faces before him, and pondered, yet again, what in the hell was wrong with R. J. Gold?

"This one," Gold pointed to the brunette in the middle photo, "is the Penthouse Pet of the year. She's fantastic. Unbelievable body. And that one," pointing to a blonde, "is this year's Miss Georgia Peach. Plays basketball, acts, sings, dances. Fabulous tits." He pointed to an Asian. "She won a silver medal for gymnastics in the Olympics. They say she can suck a football though a garden hose."

Pete's chuckle sounded more like a rhinoceros snort. "I'd crawl over broken glass for your leftovers, Mr. Gold," he said in mock admiration.

"Can you believe it, Pete? They're all in love with me. They call at least ten times a day asking for a date."

"That's 'cause they have good taste, Boss."

Gold's grand piano smile was blinding. "Which one should I take out tonight?"

Pete focused on the photos waiting for the clue.

Gold hummed a few bars of "Georgia On My Mind."

That was it. The clue.

"Miss Georgia Peach," Pete said.

"Miss Georgia Peach it is." Gold's smile was goofy. He swept the photos back into his desk drawer. "You want a soda or something, Pete?—Norma!"

Norma walked in. "Yes, R. J.?"

"Get Pete some—Pete?"

"Nothing. Thank you."

Gold checked the time. "You can bring my next appointment in when they get here."

Norma backed out of the room, closed the door.

"So," Gold said. "How's it going in the Bronx?"

"Going good," Pete said.

The hand Gold slammed down on his desk sounded like a gunshot. Pete startled. Gold bolted to his feet, face now flushed with rage.

"Good?" Gold screamed. "You call causing the deaths of four people *good*?" Gold came out from behind his desk and did a caged-lion pace. "Last night was a disaster. A fucking disaster." He wrung his hands. "And whose bright idea was it to hire those, those criminals?"

"That building was empty," Pete explained. "I watched the last tenant move out the day before."

"It wasn't empty, Pete."

"I checked every floor."

"It wasn't empty!"

"Yes, Boss." Pete hung his head. "It was an honest mistake."

"That cost the lives of an innocent teenage girl and her infant." Gold faced the windows that overlooked Central Park. His voice was all at once flat, far off. "I'd scrap the entire Gold Bronx City project today, this minute, if it would bring that mother and baby back."

"I feel terrible about that," Pete said, and he meant it. He knew that Gold, the father of two young girls, would obsess over the dead children. But he also knew what concerned Gold most—the bottom line.

"We're on schedule, Mr. Gold. The arsonists are dead. Nothing can be traced back to you."

Gold turned to face Pete. "How many occupied buildings are left?"

"One," Pete said.

"Just so there are no misunderstandings: I'd appreciate it if you'd empty that building without killing anyone."

"Yes, Mr. Gold."

"All right." Gold switched gears, walked over to the Gold Bronx City model. "Fantastic, isn't it."

"That it is, Mr. Gold." Pete was genuinely awed by the enormity of the project. "It really is."

"You see our old friend Michael Beckett?" Gold said offhandedly.

"I, er, was about to mention it. Saw him yesterday at the Coster Street fire. Later at the Black Cat Social Club."

"I saw him on the news." Twitch. "And his partner, the amusing one with the crazy eyes, Vinnie—?"

"D'Amato," Pete said.

"Right, Vinnie D'Amato." Shrug. Twitch. Shrug. "Beckett or D'Amato see you?" Gold said.

"No, sir."

"Good." Gold gnawed at the hangnail. "You think they know anything?"

Pete considered the question. The Taylors *could* have confessed everything to Beckett and D'Amato while inside the Black Cat Social Club, but he doubted it. There wasn't enough time. As for Mona Love, she would never talk. His police contact would alert him if she did. And Mona knew the consequences.

"They don't know a thing, Boss."

"I don't trust Beckett," Gold said. "His perceptions of right and wrong are sometimes naïve. If he gets suspicious, stumbles onto anything, he may cause trouble."

"How?" Pete chuckled. "The police commissioner's your friend."

"He could go to the newspapers—"

"No newspaper's gonna take you on—"

"Bring in the FBI."

Pete scrunched his face. "Beckett that motivated?"

"Never underestimate the determination of a principled man," Gold said, "especially one who carries a badge and a gun."

Pete stroked his chin, evaluating what had just been said.

He'd first met Beckett after taking the job with the Gold

Organization and, as a matter of due diligence, had checked him out. Beckett had a reputation on the police force as a hard case but likable, a straight shooter who was not beyond compromise. He apparently enforced the law selectively, never hassled gamblers, drug addicts, or prostitutes on his beat. Instead he focused on violent felons and sexual predators, those he judged to be an imminent danger to the community. And in dealing with those criminals, Beckett was not beyond taking the law into his own hands.

If Beckett did discover the Gold Bronx City arson conspiracy, he might simply ignore the facts and choose not to get involved—who cared about vacant buildings being incinerated?—or even ask for a piece of the action, a silence-insuring cash incentive. But if Beckett connected the Taylor brothers to him and Gold and the Coster Street deaths, there was no telling what he'd do.

"I'll take care of Beckett, Boss."

Norma knocked. "Your 11:00 A.M. is here, R. J." She led Nagasue and several assorted staffers into the office.

"Find Beckett, Pete," Gold said as the staffers filed in. "Go to his apartment. Take him to lunch, dinner, whatever. Get him laid. Buy him a thousand beers, but find out if he knows anything."

"Done." Pete got up to leave the office.

"Pete."

Pete stopped. "Yes, sir?"

"You'd do anything for me, right, Pete?"

Pete glanced around at the staffers, Gold's audience. He hated it when the boss showed off. "Yes, Mr. Gold."

"You'd kill for me, right, Pete?"

"Yes, Mr. Gold."

"You'd kill for me, Pete?"

"Yes, Boss."

"You're sure you'd kill for me?"

"Yes, Mr. Gold. I'd kill for you."

# CHAPTER 18

Solana Ortiz did not know what specifically set her off when she arrived home from investigating Pete from Queens: a fleeting memory, a familiar scent, the fact she was forced to negotiate around yet another fly-by-night moving company relocating more of her neighbors. But as she climbed the front stoop and walked into the vestibule of her tenement residence, her eyes brimmed with tears and her heart filled with grief. She missed her mother terribly.

Solana moved across the lobby hall, heard the Ayalas up in 3B arguing, as usual. The Rubios' German shepherd up in 5A was barking. A loud TV blasting a Yankee game could be heard coming from the Browns' in 2C—childhood sounds she knew she'd miss.

Solana had been born an only child in that woebegone, five-floor walkup located at 1123 Manida Street, apartment 1C—a cramped one-bedroom, no air conditioning—twenty-three years ago. She never knew her father.

Her mother, a religious Puerto Rican immigrant, eked out a living cleaning other people's homes during the day and scrubbing floors at night in a downtown office building. She worked tirelessly, abandoned personal comforts to provide her daughter with a Catholic school education. That was why Solana's mother neglected the mole that developed on her back. It was small at first, nothing to be concerned with. She had no health insurance and doctors cost money. The melanoma had taken her life almost thirteen months ago.

Devastated by the loss, Solana immersed herself in her final year of college. She stopped socializing and dating—her primary goals: finish school, then secure a job that paid well enough for her to move out of the Bronx—seven miles south and a universe apart—to the ultra-fashionable Upper East Side of Manhattan.

Solana graduated with honors and, thanks to an endorsement from her English professor, whose wife worked as a director on *Law & Order*, she landed a coveted, albeit low-paying, apprentice writer's position.

Despite a college loan and other financial obligations, Solana calculated that she could relocate to a Manhattan roommate situation within three months. But with the current wave of arson it seemed that fate might play a hand.

Solana unlocked her apartment front door, closed and triple-locked it behind her. She walked into her kitchen, slipped off her shoulder bag, and hung it on the back of a chair. She checked the time on her mother's black Felix the Cat clock that had hung above the stove for as long as she could remember, its tail a pendulum, large round eyes rolling left with each tick, right with every tock.

Solana sniffled and used the sleeve of her T-shirt to wipe the tears from her cheeks. She opened the refrigerator, removed a carafe of iced tea, poured herself a glass, and drifted into the living room.

The embarrassingly common velvet Jesus Christ mural, that her mother had purchased just before her death from a furtive street vendor who convinced her it was a rare religious work of art, hung in a prominent position above the threadbare couch. Solana never told her mother that she hated it. Her eyes swept the cluttered room.

Solana considered which charity she would donate her mother's possessions to when she finally made her big move to Manhattan: thirty-year-old cheap but meticulously maintained and spotlessly clean furnishings. Other than a few precious keepsakes—photographs of her and her mother, and some worthless, sentimental hand-me-down jewelry—she wanted none of it. She planned to purchase all new furnishings for her future digs, an attempt to purge all memories of her life in the ghetto.

Solana's phone rang.

"Wasssup, hoe?" Tina said; kids were shrieking in the background, dogs barked, a computer game blared.

Solana wondered how Tina did it; working a full time job, rising three kids, taking care of a shiftless husband.

"*Nada*," Solana said. "Everything okay at work?"

"No problems. What'd you find out?"

Solana told Tina that she was able to establish Pete's identity and home address, but that the search of his public records was fruitless.

"Then I went to the public library," she said. And told Tina about the newspaper articles she'd copied. That the first clipping had both shocked and frightened her.

"Pete was a suspect in the disappearance of an organized crime associate who was in debt to a loan shark." She said police investigators claimed that Pete Costello was the last person to have seen Mario Vitelli, Sr. alive. With no hard evidence of foul play—a body—no one was ever prosecuted.

"Another article," Solana said, "reported that the Gold Organization had engaged a decorated, former military (Army) policeman, Pete Costello, as their director of corporate security."

"The same Pete Costello?"

"There's a picture."

"For real?" Tina said. "What're you gonna do?"

"Hide."

"Girl, you've gotta get outta there."

"This is my home, Tina. Besides, I've got nowhere to go."

"You know I'd let you stay with me—" Sounds of mayhem in the background. "But with my husband, the kids, the dogs, cats, birds—"

"I'll be fine."

"Look," Tina said. "Michael Beckett goes gaga every time you walk into a room—I've seen it. I mean, he gave you his phone number. Call him. Ask for his help. Worst he can do is tell you no."

Solana fiddled with her hair. "I don't know—"

"What's your problem?" Tina said, growing exasperated. "People on the set say he's a good guy. I mean, you gotta trust someone."

Solana's mind raced. "Maybe you're right, Tina." She reached into the kitchen garbage and salvaged the crushed piece of paper with Michael Beckett's phone number on it. "Maybe you're right."

## CHAPTER 19

The telephone rang in my second-floor walkup apartment.

I dawned from layers of beer-sodden sleep and forced one eye open. Recalled with a start that the horror of last evening had not been a dream. An infant had died in my arms and its teenage mother had burned to death in a tenement fire; the chill of reality settled in.

*Damned phone*.

I knew I should rise and shine, locate the leader of the Stoners, Tookie Jones, find out once and for all if he hired the DOA arsonists, Bo and Bubba Taylor. If not, force him to tell me what else he knew about the mystery man who drove the black Lincoln Town Car.

And I figured I'd better start planning for life after the arson/murder investigation was closed and I resigned from the police department. Maybe I should skip the Key West trip and explore the possibility of a career in show business—although common sense told me my prospects were poor. Making a living as a performer was almost certainly a pipe dream. Being an actor in the first place had been something I did on the spur of the moment.

I had spotted the "open call" audition advertisement for

*Law & Order* in a local newspaper. Responded to the ad as a lark, telling no one for fear of being ridiculed. It seemed like an intriguing adventure, plus a great way to meet women.

I had arrived at the casting office at the appointed date and time, stood in line on a Manhattan street for hours along with hundreds of other wannabe actors. Eventually I was led into the office, handed a script and asked to "cold read" with an experienced actress. Having never acted before, or even considered it—artistic talents were not nurtured in an Irish Catholic police family—I flubbed lines and missed cues. I couldn't have been more astounded when I landed the part.

The first weeks of shooting were nervous ones for me. Having no idea if I even *could* act, I was stiff, forgot my lines and could not retain even simple directions.

To my surprise, the director and other actors had taken my lack of experience in stride. Finally, one day, something "clicked." In truth, I was frustrated, embarrassed. I stopped *trying* to act and reverted to being me. After a few takes the director and other actors applauded.

My phone stopped ringing. I rolled over onto my back, rocked up and out of my king-sized bed, was feeling biting line-of-duty aches and pains when the twelve-gauge headache struck. "Jesus, Mary and Joseph." I bit back a gasping scream. I was dizzy. My mouth tasted like I'd been sucking on a fetid bar rag. I hadn't felt this horrid in five years, the week I'd spent in Dublin, drinking with a group of Gardai—Irish cops.

I trudged across the gleaming parquet floor, headed to the shower, turned on the water, stepped into the stall, and shuddered awake. After a good fifteen minutes, I dried off, walked into my kitchen, filled a glass with cold water—I was dehydrated. As I gulped down glass after glass, I noticed that, even with a dreadful hangover, my hands were rock steady. D'Amato's frequently shook uncontrollably.

I found an ice pack, filled it, and realized my stomach was churning. I had not eaten a thing last night and I'd slept half the day. I pressed the ice pack to my temple, walked into my bedroom, reached for the portable phone, dialed a local deli and ordered some food, a bagel and coffee.

I then phoned the 41st Precinct, asked the desk sergeant if they'd recovered the woman in the red dress from the Coster Street fire. He said they had and that her body was at the Medical Examiner's office. I phoned the ME, asked if they were able to identify the body. The answer was a bored no.

I saw the flashing message light on my answering machine and remembered someone had called and woken me. I touched the playback button, cocked an ear.

The message was from Solana Ortiz.

"I'M SO GLAD you returned my call, Michael," Solana said.

"Oh?" The sound of her voice had a soothing effect that diminished my hangover. I sat up in bed and the ice pack slipped off my head. "You go to work today?"

"No."

"'Cause you left me a Bronx phone number."

"I'm home."

"Where's that?"

"Manida Street and Viele Avenue."

Hunts Point, the ghetto—that surprised me. I had pictured Solana living with a rich boyfriend in an Upper East Side penthouse. "What's up?"

"I need to talk to you, Michael."

"Anytime. I told you that."

Solana said, "Is today convenient?"

I chinned the phone. "Today?"

"Soon as possible."

I took personal stock. In addition to the on-the-job injuries I'd sustained last night, my kidneys hurt, my head was tender, my eyes burned. I didn't even know if I'd be able to keep down my yet-to-be-delivered food. "Well, I gotta be at work at four. Wanna tell me what it's about?"

"The South Bronx fires."

I sprang to my feet. "What about the fires?"

She paused before saying, "It's too involved to go into on the phone. There're some newspaper articles I copied this morning at the library. I need to see you. I'll come down to the city."

"All right." I glanced at the bedside digital clock. "How's one hour at P. J. Clarke's, 55th Street and Third Avenue?"

"I'll be there," she said and hung up.

My mind churned with possibilities.

I replayed Solana's message, wrote down her phone number and entered it into an Internet reverse phone directory. Solana lived at 1123 Manida Street.

I surfed to an online map and located the Manida Street address. Solana lived on the southern end of Gold Organization land, not far from the Coster Street fire.

The lobby buzzer nearly put me on the ceiling. The shrill sound stabbed my brain—it had to be my food delivery. I lurched to the front door and hit the "talk" button on the intercom panel.

"Yes?" There was no answer. "Who is it?" I listened closely for a long thirty seconds, could swear I heard someone breathing, but nothing else. Creepy.

A sudden sharp knock on my front door made me jump.

"Yeah?" I peered through the front door's security peep hole, saw nothing but darkness. Strange. Had the neighbor's kids been fooling with the hall lights again?

"Who is it?"

Still no answer.

Someone was playing games.

I was in no mood.

I slipped on a pair of jeans and a T-shirt. Grabbed my

off-duty weapon from a closet shelf. Snapped the door lock to the left. Yanked it open. Pointed the gun.

"Hey, pencil neck." A dark figure, big as a sasquatch and reeking of Napoleon cologne, was offering a white paper bag with a BAGEL-RAMA logo on it.

"What's the gun for?" The Sasquatch stepped into the light. "What, you gonna shoot an old friend?"

"Pete." I accepted the bagel bag. "What're you doing here?" I stepped back allowing Pete Costello—everyone called him Pete from Queens—to enter, closed and locked the door behind him.

"Heard you were in a big shootout up in the Bronx last night," Pete said. "Thought I'd stop by to make sure you were all right. Hey, this is one beautiful apartment." Pete was looking around. "What, you hire a professional decorator?"

I shook my head. "An old girlfriend helped me out— you made a special trip?"

"Yeah." Pete smiled—not a pretty sight. "That's it. Ran into your delivery guy in the lobby. Saw him push your apartment bell. Thought I'd surprise you."

"That you did." I regarded my visitor suspiciously. "Question is, why?"

"Whaddya mean, why? Can't a guy visit an old friend?"

I had never thought of the former military cop as an old friend. I put my gun away.

"Thanks for coming, Pete." We shook hands—the ex-MP's grip was vise-like. "Grab a chair," I said. "Take your jacket off. You gotta be dying wearing a suit in this heat."

Pete loosened his tie, unbuttoned his jacket but kept it on. He remained standing. "So, you all right?"

"A few bumps and bruises." I pulled the bagel out of the bag, unwrapped it and noticed that my right hand now stank of Pete's cologne. I flipped the top off the steaming coffee container. "You're looking fit, Pete. Still working out?"

"Doing martial arts. Some power-lifting. And you?"

"Still boxing," I said. "You want half a bagel? We can split the coffee."

"No, thanks."

The coffee was steaming hot. I took a cautious sip. "How much I owe you?"

"Nothing. It's on me."

"Thanks." I sat at the kitchen table and ate hungrily.

Pete wandered around my one-bedroom apartment. He glanced at a wall-mounted landscape photo of Cavan, Ireland, my father's birthplace. He studied photos of the four warships I served on during my time in the Navy. Looked at Waterford Crystal-framed photos of my family that were on display in a custom-built wall unit: my kid sister, Shannon, and me at a St. Patrick's Day parade, a portrait of my father in police uniform, my mother in her wedding dress.

"Nice family."

"Not during a full moon," I said.

Pete laughed a little. "I got no brothers or sisters." Pete walked to the window, eased aside the designer drapes, and gazed down onto East 77th Street.

I ate and pondered the almost ludicrous irony of the situation. Here I was about to investigate an arson and double homicide on Gold land, and its Director of Corporate Security was standing in my living room. Happenstance? I doubted that. But if R. J. Gold wanted to know the status of the official investigation, he'd call the police commissioner. So what did Pete want from me?

"So, what's up, Pete?"

Pete turned to face me. "This and that. You know, the boss keeps me busy."

I watched Pete as he folded his arms across his massive chest, then stuffed his porterhouse hands in his pockets and fidgeted with some loose change. Pete was a man with something on his mind.

"Sit down, why don't you. You're making me nervous."

Pete obliged. Sat across from me at the kitchen table. "Kinda bagel is that?"

"Poppy seed. You gonna stare at me while I eat?"

"Sorry." Pete got up, sat on my leather couch, picked up a remote and clicked on the wall mounted, big-screen HDTV. Two fat trailer-trash blondes were fighting it out on *Jerry Springer*. The audience chanted, "Jerry. Jerry. Jerry."

"Say, you like working on *Law & Order*?"

"Sure."

"I watched an episode. So'd the boss. He said you were great."

"No shit?"

"Know what else he said? He said if he ever got that TV show about his casino off the ground, you know, the one ABC's been after him to do for years, he'd want you to play a role."

I stopped eating. "He sent you, didn't he?"

"The boss? No."

"C'mon, Pete. I've know you since you started working for R. J. We've had a few beers together. That's all. You've never stopped by my place before."

"Exactly. That's why I'm here now."

"To check on my health."

"Right."

"I can't tell you how deeply moved I am."

Pete chuckled. "That's a good one."

"Yeah, I'm a regular Seinfeld." I continued to eat.

"Say, Beckett," Pete finally said.

"I'm right here, Pete."

"I gotta talk to you about something."

"Last night's fire," I said. "Right?"

"What fire?" Pete said with a straight face.

"The one on the front page of the *Post*."

"Oh, that fire." Pete's expression turned grim. "A terrible tragedy. The boss is beside himself."

"We all are," I said.

Pete seemed to be considering that fact. "Well, I don't wanna talk about the fire."

"What then?"

"Miss Hawaiian Tropic."

"Janet Roth?" That was a surprise. "I'm listening."

"The boss feels really bad about the disagreement you guys had over that girl."

"He could've picked up the phone," I said.

"He's stubborn."

I ate the last bite of bagel.

"Look, all I'm saying is, the boss is looking to make peace." Pete slipped an envelope out of his suit pocket, reached over and handed it to me.

"What's this?"

"A ticket to Saturday's Red Sox-Yankees game. The boss wants you to be his guest. Sit in Steinbrenner's box. Like old times."

I was taken aback. Was Pete's visit a sincere attempt by Gold to revive our friendship? Did Gold truly wish to be pals again?

"Tell R. J. I'll try to be there." I stood, signaling that the discussion was over. "I hate to be rude, but I gotta shave, meet a lady over at P. J. Clarke's."

"Yeah? How about that. I'm going to Clarke's too."

"Really?" *Another coincidence.*

"I'll wait for you." Pete settled back on the couch, picked up the remote, started channel surfing. "We'll take my car. Have a few beers," Pete said. "Talk till your date shows up."

"All right—talk about what, Pete?"

Pete shrugged. "This and that."

# CHAPTER 20

"Loser!" Doreen D'Amato screamed into her sleeping husband's ear. D'Amato bolted upright in bed. His face was sleep-lined, hair a sweat-matted mess, eyes crusted, bloodshot.

"Where am I?"

Doreen flung the shirt D'Amato had worn last night in his face. He pulled it away, glanced at it. There was lipstick on the collar.

"I can explain," D'Amato said, his breath a vile memento of the booze and cannabis he'd consumed last night.

"Don't bother." Doreen circled the bed. The floral tent-sized house dress she wore did little to conceal the fact that she'd gained another ten pounds.

"I've had it. You hear me, Vinnie?" Doreen pounded her fist into a beefy palm. "This is the last time I tolerate you staying out all night with whores, getting drunk." She pointed a chocolate-smeared index finger at him. "Next time, I'm taking the kids and leaving you." Doreen waddled out and slammed the bedroom door. Paint chips flew every which way and speckled the carpet.

"You ain't taking my daughters!" D'Amato yelled after her. "Warthog!" He fell back onto the king-size bed feeling stale and woolen-mouthed, his skull weighed down by stone. He placed a pillow over his face in an attempt to keep the afternoon sun out, and tried to recall last night.

He remembered having words with Beckett—the self-absorbed asshole—in J. G. Melon. Then Kitty, the bartender had refused to serve him another martini and thrown him out. He recalled hailing a cab on Third Avenue and—wait a minute. D'Amato grabbed his shirt, sniffed it, smiled: Mona Love's perfume.

He'd gone to Mona's place, knocked on her door. She was home, glad to see him. She'd invited him into her red velvet abode. They drank beer, smoked pot. He recalled dancing with Mona, whipping out "the beast" but couldn't remember if they'd been intimate. And try as he might, he couldn't remember when he left Mona's apartment, how he got home, or at what time.

"Loser!" Doreen shrieked from the other side of the bedroom door. A moment later D'Amato heard the front door open, then slam shut; the fat bitch was losing her mind.

D'Amato wished his wife would leave him like she'd been threatening to do for years. He'd take the kids, rent them a small apartment close to the city and as far from Doreen as possible. Then he wouldn't have to answer to anyone, like Beckett. He'd be able to come and go as he pleased, meet new women, party all night every night if he wanted to. Spend some quality time with his new main squeeze, Mona.

Seen from a helicopter, D'Amato's A-frame house was indistinguishable from all the others in Long Island's Massapequa Shores. Actually, the "shores" had recently been bulldozed. The little manmade lake was gone. No longer could D'Amato stand at its banks, surrounded by scrub pine, far from the shattered South Bronx, and cast for fish he knew were not there. The lake had been labeled polluted so the greedy landlord could bury it, and he did just that— buried it to get rid of it, make it seem it never existed. Then he cut down the last of the scrub pines and put up more houses just like D'Amato's: fifty more, but he did not strike "shores" from the sign—twice D'Amato had put a bullet though it.

The bedroom door flew open and D'Amato's three- and five-year-old daughters ran into the room and leapt on the bed.

"Daddy. Daddy. Daddy."

D'Amato hid under the covers, an attempt at saving the girls from his noxious breath.

"Mommy's outside," the five-year-old said.

"She's crying," the three-year-old said.

"Mommy's always crying," D'Amato said.

"What did you do, Daddy?"

"Nothing, sweetie. Daddy is perfect."

"Mommy doesn't think so."

"Oh, yes she does. She just forgets sometimes—why aren't you girls out playing?"

"We wanna ask you something, Daddy," the older child said. "Stop hiding." She pulled at the bedsheet but D'Amato held fast.

"Ask what?"

"Take us to Disney World?"

"Ask your mother."

"She said ask you."

"All right." D'Amato peeked out from under the covers. "If you promise to be very quiet, and leave daddy alone for the next hour, I'll take you to Disney World."

"When?" the older child said.

"Next week."

"Hurray!" his daughters said in unison. "Hurray!" They jumped up and down on the bed, the jarring movement raked D'Amato's brain, scrambled his stomach.

"Stop jumping, please."

The girls calmed down, giggling.

"Now, go outside and play."

"We love you, Daddy." The girls leapt off the bed and raced out of the room.

"Close the door," D'Amato said, but the girls were already out of earshot. D'Amato couldn't help smiling. His daughters were the center of his world.

D'Amato got out of bed, walked across the chilly, air-conditioned room and closed the door. He reached for the portable phone, dialed the 41 Precinct and asked to be connected to roll call.

"Roll call," a man said.

"D'Amato here."

"Hey, Vinnie, how'ya doing?"

"Great—look, how much vacation time I got left?"

"Lemme check."

D'Amato could hear the click of computer keys.

"Five days."

"I need the next set of tours off."

"Next week, all five days?"

"I got no choice," D'Amato said. "It's Disneyland time again."

"No problem, Vinnie. I'll fill out the request. Come by and sign it when you have the time. Anything else?"

D'Amato's eyes settled on a recent photo of him and Beckett amid a pile of junk atop his dresser. It'd been taken about six months ago at the police department pistol range out in Rodman's Neck in the Bronx. As usual Beckett and he had qualified as expert marksmen.

"D'Amato," the roll call man said. "You there?"

"Look, this is off the record," D'Amato said. "I don't wanna partner with Beckett anymore."

"You're shitting me," roll call said. "I thought you guys were best friends."

"We were," D'Amato said. "Anyone available to switch sector cars?"

"No one that I know of. You have someone in mind?"

"I'll work with anyone," D'Amato said.

"Destiny Jones is looking for a partner."

"Fuck that."

"You kiddin'? She's a babe."

D'Amato hesitated. She *was* beautiful. "No way I work with a woman."

"I might be able to get you a fixer guarding prisoners at the hospital."

"I gotta be on the street."

"Hey, wait a minute." The roll call guy hit more computer keys. "You know Fitzpatrick and Grabowski in sector Henry? Grabowski retires in two weeks."

D'Amato thought it over. Fitzpatrick had been dumped into the 41 Precinct from a narcotics detail because of a drinking problem. But he was good guy, a good cop. And he didn't live far from D'Amato, they could carpool to work. "I'll take it."

"You got it," the roll call guy said.

D'Amato hung up the phone, checked the time, and headed to the shower.

# CHAPTER 21

"Driver, *please* turn on the air conditioner." Solana Ortiz was feeling claustrophobic behind a Plexiglas partition in the rear of a grimy, coffin-small gypsy cab.

The Chinese driver shrugged. "No English."

Solana heaved a resigned sigh. Such is life when you are a South Bronx resident and are forced to engage gypsy cabs: illegal, unregulated taxis not subject to the stringent rules that govern the city's licensed yellow cabs. But the drivers of yellow cabs, afraid for their lives, did not cruise the South Bronx in search of fares.

Solana noticed the driver had a small fan mounted on the dashboard, blowing directly on him. *He* was cool and comfortable.

"The air conditioner." She tapped on the Plexiglas partition, pointed at the dashboard air conditioning controls, fanned herself with a hand in an attempt to communicate the fact she was sweltering. "I'm suffocating back here."

Again the driver shrugged. "No English. Speak Chinese. Moo shu pork. Szechuan dumplings. General Tso's chicken—"

"Great," Solana said. "Just great."

The cab slowed to a crawl in heavy traffic. Sweat appeared on Solana's neck, meandered down her chest and disappeared in the valley of her bosom. She reached to roll the cab's windows fully down, to let in more air. But both window handles were missing. Solana fought to control her exasperation, sat back and checked the time. She was running late, only about ten more blocks to Third Avenue and 55th Street, P. J. Clarke's.

Michael Beckett would already be there, waiting.

"Gentleman" is the word Tina used to describe Beckett. Solana had to admit, on the surface, it was an accurate description. Unlike other cops she'd seen in action—the aggressive ones who exhibited disdain for minorities, routinely brutalizing her neighbors—Beckett was laid-back and polite—at least that's how he acted on the set of *Law & Order*.

Solana was confident she had enough street smarts to see though Beckett's act, and what she saw disturbed her—something scary, maybe even dangerous beneath all that easy charm. And something else she could not yet define.

Solana wondered how Beckett would react once he read the two newspaper articles, and she told him of her theory, that the man in the stories, Pete Costello, director of security Gold Organization, was involved in the South Bronx arsons. Would he patronize her, treat her with condescension, or be the concerned, accommodating gentleman he pretended to be?

Solana smoothed down her clingy cotton dress, adjusted the scooped V-neck top and pulled a small compact from her shoulder bag, checked her makeup, and wondered what Michael Beckett thought of her appearance. She gazed out the window and saw an attractive couple groping each other in an ATM doorway. She thought about the fact that she hadn't been with a man in the thirteen months since her mother died. She wondered if Beckett had a steady girlfriend. Probably. A man who looked like him didn't have to spend many nights alone.

The gypsy cab rolled to a stop in standstill traffic. Horns honked. Drivers cursed.

"Can't believe this traffic," the driver commented in perfect English.

"Thought you didn't speak English?"

The driver smiled stupidly in the rearview mirror.

Solana would have slugged him if she could. "I'm getting out here."

The cab pulled to the curb. The driver told Solana how much she owed him. She handed him the exact change.

The driver counted it. "Hey, you forget tip."

Solana smiled thinly. "No English." She opened the cab door, got out, and slammed it shut behind her.

# CHAPTER 22

Pete from Queens and I entered P. J. Clarke's through the 55th Street side door. I took a deep breath and reveled in the cold-as-a-meat-locker air conditioning, the mouthwatering aroma of grilling hamburgers, the soaring Sinatra music.

"Nice car, Pete," I said. I slipped on the navy blue blazer I'd been carrying, hoping that Solana would like the way it looked with my light blue polo shirt and off-white linen slacks. "It's a Lincoln Town Car, right?"

"Good for two hundred thousand miles," Pete said. "If you take care of it."

I checked out the bar. The old-fashioned Irish saloon was packed, as usual, with suits swilling drinks, jabbering about sports, politics, and the stock market. Several senior corporate executive types sitting at checkercloth-covered tables gave Pete a double-take marveling at his size. Pete nodded pleasantly. He was accustomed to such scrutiny.

I led the way and settled at a spot at the head of the bar where I could easily observe both of the pub's entrances: 55th Street and the Third Avenue main entrance. Pete ordered a beer. I ordered a club soda with lime.

"You drive your Lincoln to R. J.'s property up in the Bronx much?" I said.

"All the time," Pete said. "Why?"

"No reason." I glanced left, then right. "Can't believe I'm in a bar after last night." The bartender served our drinks. I set a foot on the brass foot rail, picked up my club soda and gulped down half the glass. The coldness took my breath away. "Christ, that's good."

"Where'd you go last night?" Pete sipped his beer.

"J. G. Melon with D'Amato." My eyes, on autopilot, swept the bar. I recognized a Bronx bookmaker standing up front, under the big wall clock, in hunched conversation with two men who looked like central casting wise-guys. In the center of the bar, a hooker worked two out-of-town businessmen.

"How do you work with that nutcase D'Amato?" Pete said.

"Sometimes I wonder."

Pete shook his head. "He's dangerous."

I almost laughed. "Look who's talking."

"I work at it," Pete said in all seriousness. "D'Amato doesn't." Pete set his elbows on the bar. "Since you brought up last night's fire, what do you hear?"

"The arsonists are very dead."

"Yeah." Pete chuckled. "I saw the papers. The boss feels terrible about that woman and her kid. Just terrible."

"So you said."

"At least the firebugs got what was coming to them."

I watched Pete slug back his beer.

"Level with me, Pete," I said. "The Gold Organization planning to renovate those old building, or build a whole new project?"

"Renovate." Pete's brow furrowed. "Why?"

My eyes were trained on the bar's Third Avenue entrance. Solana should be walking in at any moment. "There's a theory that R. J. has been planning to build a major new development on that site all along. Maybe he's not all that unhappy about the fires."

Pete pushed off the bar angrily. "That's bullshit."

The bartender and several patrons reacted.

"Take it easy," I said.

"Whose dumb ass theory is that?"

"Some fire marshal's." I swallowed more club soda, sucked on the lime. "A car like yours sticks out in the ghetto." I signaled for another soda. "You know?"

"You got something to say, Beckett, say it."

I smiled. "What're you getting upset about?" My drink came. "Relax, Pete, have another cold one."

Pete's cell phone rang. "Pete speaking." He stuck a finger in his ear, an attempt at blocking out the jukebox music. "I can't hear. Hold on." He tapped my shoulder. "Be right back." Pete slipped out the 55th Street door.

Just then Clarke's Third Avenue door swung open. Solana Ortiz breezed in, cotton dress swirling, sweat glistening on bare tan shoulders; lips red, heels high. The Bronx bookmaker and the wise-guys saw her, halted midconversation, and leered.

"Solana." I waved.

Her face lit up and her eyes grew bright.

Solana worked her way through the crowd and extended her hand as she approached. "Hello, Michael."

"Hi, Solana." I took her hand, pulled her close, kissed her once on each cheek. "Drink?"

"Yes. Pinot Grigio."

I ordered.

Solana placed a shoulder bag on the floor by her feet, then used a gentle head-flip gesture to swing her hair from her face—I found that erotic. Then again, I found her very existence erotic.

"Love your dress."

"Thank you." She looked around. "Place is crowded."

"As always." I sipped my soda. "First time here?"

"I've been a few times with girlfriends. They say it's a great place to meet eligible men." Solana made a face. "I don't do well meeting men in bars."

"I hear ya."

A group of businessmen on their way to the back room wedged by, forcing Solana closer to me.

"You smell like April rain," I said.

Solana's eyes glistened. "Is that good?"

"Oh, yeah."

The bartender set Solana's wine on the bar. She tasted it. Her expression indicated that it was pretty good.

"So, what about the Bronx fires?" I said, getting right to it.

"Is there somewhere quiet we can talk?"

"Sure," I said. "I'll get us a table in the back room in a minute. Gotta say good-bye to a guy I know first."

"I'm back." The voice came from out of nowhere.

Solana, still smiling, looked over my shoulder. All expression on her face ceased. The blood drained from her face. She seemed to stop breathing.

"Solana, are you all right?" I said.

"Well, hello there, Solana," Pete said.

I turned to include him. "You know each other?"

"We've met," Pete said.

Solana dropped her wine glass.

It shattered on the cold, cracked tile floor.

# CHAPTER 23

It was 8:32 P.M. when Detective Robert Doyle parked a derelict Chevy in front of the 19th police precinct on Manhattan's East 67th Street. The automobile was one of hundreds of official "undercover" vehicles—as obvious as a flashing blue-and-white—that the city employed in a laughable effort to deceive lawbreakers.

Doyle got out, slipped on a pair of dark sunglasses, lit a smoke, and moseyed west, slicing through the smothering nighttime humidity and heat. He loosened his tie, slipped off his silk suit jacket and, after casually scanning the streets behind him in search of a tail, turned left down Fifth Avenue toward Central Park South.

Doyle negotiated his way around well-to-do couples emerging from limousines, entering hotels on the east side of Fifth Avenue. He dodged speeding cars and horse-drawn hansom cabs as he hurried across 59th Street, then west crossing Fifth Avenue.

Doyle flicked his cigarette into the street as he drew abreast of the main entrance to the Plaza Hotel. He spun around, again checking to see if he was being followed. But he spied no sudden movement into the shelter of a doorway, no face masked by a newspaper to hide identity, nobody bending down to tie a shoelace.

Doyle climbed the hotel steps and pushed through a revolving door. He labored through thick wool carpet and super-cool air and felt a chill. He slipped on his jacket and checked out the busy baroque lobby.

Dozens of Chanel-suited, silk-draped guests were milling about, looking suitably burdened by affluence. Doyle walked past reception and stopped in front of a lobby jewelry boutique. Pretending to look at watches, he used the plate glass display window as a mirror to study the faces behind him. He saw no one suspicious.

Doyle continued down the corridor, turned right through a group of name-tagged senior citizens, past the Palm Court restaurant.

Just short of a lower-level retail store, by the men's room, Doyle approached an inconspicuous mahogany door gold-stenciled PRIVATE. He punched a security code on the door's numeric key pad, yanked it open, and took one last slow look around before slipping through the opening.

Doyle descended several levels of recently painted gray cement stairs and walked through the Plaza's basement. He moved past locker rooms and a few employees: kitchen workers, porters, bellhops, none of whom acknowledged his presence in any way.

He continued into the bowels of the building, through the hum of giant generators, past boilers with their faint smell of coal gas, until he reached the far end of the basement. There he stepped onto an open service elevator. He pressed the up button. A loud pedestrian warning bell sounded. Doyle smashed it with the butt of his hand. It clanged a final time as it hit the lift's corrugated steel floor.

The elevator broke ground, and its steel doors parted. Doyle inhaled a sickening lungful of idling delivery truck exhaust as he stepped onto the sidewalk at the rear of the hotel. He coughed out the fumes, looked around, saw normal nighttime activities.

Doyle walked across the street and entered the rear of the Avon building. He legged through the deserted lobby and alighted on the West 57th Street side. He fired up another smoke and carefully scanned the street.

An attractive woman in a business suit, apparently waiting for someone, looked his way, made eye contact, smiled. Doyle felt his heart flutter, blood rush throughout his body. But he forced himself to turn away. He was very married.

A building perimeter security guard making his rounds nodded a greeting as he walked by. A beggar, hat in hand, approached pleading for a handout. Doyle handed the bum some pocket change, then dumped his cigarette. He walked out onto 57th Street, flagged down a yellow cab going west, and got in.

"Where to?" the driver asked.

"Right on Sixth Avenue. Left on 59th. Left on Eleventh Avenue. Left on 46th. Left on Madison."

The driver looked at Doyle in his rearview mirror. "I need a destination for my trip sheet." His accent was Middle Eastern.

Doyle glanced at the hack license displayed on the dashboard, read the driver's name. "What you need, Mohamed," he flashed his detective shield, "is to drive the car." As the taxi pulled away, Doyle peered out the rear window.

FIFTEEN MINUTES LATER Doyle directed the cab to stop on Fifth Avenue, only a few blocks away from where he had originally hailed it. He handed the driver the fare along with an appropriate tip, left the cab, and hurried into an upscale clothing emporium adjoining Gold Tower.

Doyle made his way through the crowded stately establishment, ducked under a velvet EMPLOYEES ONLY rope that was strung across the bottom of a narrow spiral staircase. He climbed to the mezzanine offices.

An impeccably dressed senior salesman was busy at a rich mahogany desk. He noticed Doyle and, without a word, gathered some papers, stood and headed down the same stairs the detective had just climbed. Doyle moved to the salesman's desk, picked up a phone and dialed a number. It was answered on the first ring.

"This is Doyle."

A voice said, "Stand by."

Doyle heard a sound, turned and saw an oak panel on the wall across the mezzanine retract: a secret passage. He walked across the floor and stepped through the opening. The panel swooshed closed behind him.

Doyle moved cautiously through a cool, bare, well-lit concrete corridor which contained scattered residue from its construction crew: crushed cigarette packs, stained cardboard coffee containers, soda cans. He walked the fifty feet or so to a dead end and another wood panel swooshed open.

Pete from Queens said, "Follow me."

Doyle accompanied Pete up a stairwell, down a meandering corridor, and into an ornate vestibule.

"We're not going to your office?" Doyle said.

"No."

Ten paces later Pete pressed the up button on an elevator panel. An elevator opened. Doyle and Pete stepped in. Pete pressed the large oval button marked EXECUTIVE OFFICES. The elevator doors closed.

Doyle checked his appearance in the elevator mirrors, fiddled with his silk tie, ran his fingers through his red-brown hair. He followed Pete out of the elevator and through an elegant reception area. Doyle noted that even at that time of night the place was busy, staffed with fashionable, absurdly beautiful young people. The resulting ambiance was sexy, glamorous.

Pete pushed through a second set of doors where they were greeted by an attractive middle-aged woman.

"Detective Doyle, I presume." The woman rose from behind an orderly desk, extended her hand and shook his firmly. "I'm Norma."

"My pleasure," Doyle said.

"I'll tell Mr. Gold you are here."

Doyle watched Norma walk off; she must have been a beauty in her youth. He turned to Pete. "I'm meeting *the* Mr. Gold?"

Pete nodded. "R. J. Gold, CEO, Gold Organization."

Doyle looked toward the door Norma had walked through and felt a rush of excitement—he was about to meet one of richest, most powerful men in the country; shake his hand, engage in a face-to-face conversation. Who knew where this introduction could lead?

Doyle recalled the recent conversation in the 41 Precinct clerical office—sure he'd heard the rumors that Beckett and D'Amato had once palled around with R. J. Gold. But he had assumed that they'd probably been moonlighting, performing some low-level security work for the organization, and that the two street cops were exaggerating their importance—D'Amato was notorious for absurd embellishments. Doyle had to admit that he felt envious when he'd heard the facts. I mean, he could see a man like R. J. Gold befriending *him*; a cultivated, urbane First Grade detective. But cretins like Beckett and D'Amato?

"Now, listen up, Doyle." Pete leaned against Norma's desk. "Mr. Gold doesn't shake hands."

Doyle looked at him. "Why is that?"

"Germs."

"Ah." Doyle said. "Prudent."

"You will address him as Mr. Gold. Sit when you're told. Speak only when spoken to. Take coffee if he offers it."

"I abhor coffee."

"You love it now. And remember, Mr. Gold doesn't

wanna be your friend. He doesn't give a shit what you've gotta say about anybody or anything. Keep your opinions to yourself. Got it?"

Doyle felt somehow deflated. "I understand."

Norma reappeared. "Mr. Gold will see you now."

As they entered Gold's private office, the first thing Doyle noticed was the shimmering view of the nighttime Manhattan skyline. Then he saw the ship, helicopter, and airline models. In the middle of the gigantic, modern office was a huge scale mock-up of Gold Bronx City.

"Fantastic, isn't it?" R. J. Gold said, coming out from behind his desk. Doyle regarded the mogul, his cop eyes taking the usual, practiced, flickering inventory: tailoring, fabric, tie, jewelry, hands and fingernails—Gold bit his nails—shoe shine, haircut, all subtle clues to status.

Gold was over six feet, rather jowly and, although he was losing his hair, handsome in that over-groomed rich man's way. Doyle decided that the custom suit probably hid a gone-to-pot physique.

"Yes," Doyle agreed. "Impressive scale model."

Gold moved to the plastic replica of his pet project. "Gold City will be the most colossal residential development in the country. It'll make Co-op City look small time. Right, Pete?"

"Right, Mr. Gold."

"Damned right." Gold sat on the edge of his desk. "Pete tells me you've been a great help to us up in the Bronx." He pointed Doyle to a chair.

Doyle nodded thanks to Pete as he sat.

"You want anything?" Gold asked Doyle. "Coffee?"

"Please don't go to any trouble, Mr. Gold."

"Norma! Get Mr. Doyle coffee."

"Coming," Norma called out.

"So," Gold said. "How long have you been a police detective?"

"Twenty-nine years."

"That's fantastic. You must enjoy it."

"I did when I was younger. These day I look forward to putting in my thirty; I retire next year."

"Make sure you let us know when you do," Gold said. "There'll always be room for a man like you in the Gold Organization. Right, Pete?"

"Right, boss."

Norma walked in, handed Doyle his coffee, turned and walked out.

Gold said, "Pete tells me you did a great job at the Black Cat Social Club. A great job. Screaming 'Gun!' was pure genius."

Doyle kept his mouth shut. The truth was that the nod Pete had given him while out front of the Black Cat Social Club had only served to confuse him. What on earth did Pete expect him to do in front of scores of cops, eyewitnesses and a national television audience? When he saw the arsonists emerge from the Black Cat and one of them reach down his pants, he shouted, "He's reaching for a gun" *only* because the dolt could very well have been doing just that. He'd had no idea that the other cops would panic and start a deadly shooting frenzy.

"I suppose it worked out for the best," Doyle said. "The arsonists were a liability."

"Hear him, Pete? Uh? 'They were a liability.'" Gold applauded. "I love this man. I tell you, *I* know genius. And it was genius. Pure genius."

Doyle's lips twisted into a humble grin.

"But imagine," Gold said gravely, his manner changing with the ease of a repentant TV evangelist. "Those two arsonists killing a poor innocent child and her infant." He shivered with revulsion. "It was never supposed to happen that way. It was the arsonists' fault and they got what they deserved."

Doyle's head bobbed in obsequious agreement, impressed by the ease with which Gold explained away his compliance in arson and murder.

"I asked to meet with you because I have a very important assignment I'd like to offer you," Gold said.

Doyle resettled himself in his chair.

"I won't bore you with details, but if I don't start demolition, break ground on Gold City by tomorrow, I'll lose crucial government loan guarantees. Then, as a result, the project's core investors. I can't let that happen."

Doyle readily agreed. "Understood."

"Problem is, the scrutiny we're under because of those tragic deaths is unprecedented. I mean, everyone from the feds, the newspapers, even my competitors are watching. As a result I can't even start demolition until every building on the Gold Bronx City site is vacant. That's where you come in."

Doyle leaned forward.

"What I need you to do," Gold said, "is convince some, I'll call them 'inflexible,' tenants to move from the last occupied building on the site."

"Only one tenant, Mr. Gold," Pete injected, coming away from the door. "The five other families relocated earlier today."

"Good work, Pete. Got that, Robert?—may I call you Robert?"

"Of course, Mr. Gold."

"One tenant." Gold snapped his fingers. "Address?"

"1123 Manida Street," Pete said. "Apartment 1C."

Gold reacted. "That the woman you told me about?"

"Yes, boss, it is."

Gold's focus shifted back to Doyle. "Normally, if we had more time, which we don't," Gold said, "Pete would handle things. However, Pete has informed me of an extraordinary issue. Pete?"

"The tenant in 1C, Solana Ortiz," Pete said, "is acquainted with Michael Beckett."

*Beckett*: the man was like a bad penny. "Acquainted," Doyle said. "How?"

Pete told how he became aware of the Beckett-Ortiz connection earlier that day; the incident at P. J. Clarke's. "I followed up," Pete said. "Checked her out. Solana makes her living as a writer on *Law & Order*—that's where they met. I've got a solid source on the show, a teamster who's no fan of Beckett's. His opinion: Solana and Beckett are not close."

Gold folded his arms across his chest. "Should we be concerned about this, Robert?"

Doyle shrugged. "If this woman and Beckett are not close," he said, "I don't see any cause for concern."

"Good. Now the question is . . ." Gold's eyes were penetrating. "Can I count on you?"

Doyle considered the question. "Did I understand you correctly: you intend this person—"

"Ortiz," Pete said. "Solana Ortiz."

"You want her removed from the premises tonight?"

"By midnight," Gold said. "That a problem?"

"Yes." Doyle leaned forward, placed his coffee on a table. "I'm assuming you offered to buy her out?"

"She accepted the same under-the-table deal I told Pete to offer all the other tenants to vacate," Gold said. "Ten thousand dollars."

"She's a shrewd one," Pete chimed in. "Took our money. Now she's stalling, holding us up for more."

Doyle shrugged. "So? You have no choice. Pay her."

"She's being unreasonable," Pete said.

"And there's no time left to negotiate," Gold said. "Understand, if even one tenant occupies even one apartment in one building one minute after midnight, my competitors, the feds, the newspapers, hell, everyone will know. Which will mean Gold Bronx City is dead."

Doyle thought a moment. "Mr. Gold, I don't see how I can possibly be of help—"

Gold's raised hand stopped him. "You ever hear of Helmut Krauss?"

Doyle thought about it. "I don't believe I have."

"He's a neurologist," Gold said. "Based at Boston General. World's foremost expert on amyotrophic lateral sclerosis: Lou Gehrig's disease. Doctor Krauss is a good friend of mine." Gold grinned self-importantly.

Doyle digested the information.

"With your permission," Gold said, "I'd like to set up an appointment for your wife. A consultation and complete examination to start."

"How do you know about my wife?"

"Does it matter?"

Doyle glanced at Pete.

"No," Gold said. "What matters is your wife obtaining the finest medical care that money can buy."

"I would imagine," Doyle said, "that Krauss's fees are beyond my means."

"Not any longer, Robert. Not any longer."

"What are you saying?" Doyle searched Gold's face. "You would extend yourself for me?" There was an appropriate amount of skepticism in the detective's voice.

"I already have." Gold pulled a fat envelope from his suit jacket pocket, handed it to Doyle. "That's just a small token of my appreciation."

Doyle opened the envelope and examined the contents. It was stuffed with $100 bills.

"You do this for me, Robert, and it's just the beginning." Gold stood and guided Doyle to the door. "I'm a man who believes in loyalty. Friendships. Right, Pete?"

"Right. Mr. Gold."

"A man does the right thing by me, and we're friends for life. That's the kind of guy I am. Right, Pete?"

Pete scowled, his expression betraying the fact that he did not like the way Gold was cozying up to Doyle.

"Now remember, Robert," Gold said. "Get the Ortiz woman out of apartment 1C by midnight." He patted Doyle's back as he ushered him out the door. "And then, sometime soon, we'll sit down, have dinner and discuss your future with the Gold Organization."

# CHAPTER 24

I left D'Amato curbside, sitting in the RMP, listening to the radio. I stepped through a South Bronx greasy-spoon's front door—a known Tookie Jones hangout—and grabbed a passing busboy.

"Tookie been in?"

The busboy, a pimple-faced, frightened adolescent, shook his head.

"Any Stoners?"

Another head shake.

I made my way through the dinner crowd to the take-out counter by a noisy air conditioner.

"Hey, Carmen," I said to a rumpled, chunky waitress working behind the counter. "I phoned in an order to go: two bacon cheeseburgers, two diet cokes."

Carmen's face lit up. "Tell me," she said as she came toward me, wiping sweat from her thick brow with a soiled dish towel. "Is Jack McCoy as intense in person as he is on TV?"

Carmen was referring to Sam Waterston, the actor who played the Assistant District Attorney on *Law & Order*.

"I never got to meet him."

"When you do," Carmen's Cheshire Cat smile revealed

a single gold tooth, "tell him he can put his shoes under my bed anytime."

"I'm sure he'll be flattered." I never quite figured out how to react to people like Carmen: a *Law & Order* enthusiast who acted as though the show's characters were real.

"Are you allowed to tell me what happens in your future episodes?" Carmen said.

I leaned over the counter and whispered in Carmen's hairy ear. "Detective Stone gets shot."

"Killed?" Carmen said, shocked.

"They haven't decided yet."

"They can't kill Detective Stone off that quickly. His story line has too much potential."

"Really." I almost laughed. "I think you're on the money. Why not write an e-mail to the producers. Better yet, start an e-mail campaign."

Carmen beamed. "I think I will."

My cell phone rang and I hurried to answer, hoping it was Solana returning my calls—she had flabbergasted me by dropping her drink and running out of P. J. Clarke's. I'd followed her out, tried to stop her, ask what the problem was. But she'd looked at me with hatred in her eyes, brushed me aside, hailed a cab, and sped away.

"You have a problem with her?" I asked Pete when I walked back into the bar.

"No," Pete had said, acting as surprised as I at Solana's seemingly irrational behavior. "I met her only once, spent about three minutes with her."

"Hello," I said into the phone.

"Pickles," D'Amato said. "Don't forget the pickles."

I hung up, asked Carmen to add pickles to our order, and considered phoning Solana once again. But I had already left her several messages.

Carmen handed me the bill and a plastic bag which contained our order. "Enjoy, 'Detective Stone.'"

Outside, the heat and humidity forced me to gasp for

my next breath. I was edging through a group of pedestrians, toward the RMP, when I heard D'Amato yell a warning: "Behind you."

I turned and found myself facing a pack of dogs led by a black Rottweiler. I stood still, all too aware that my right hand, my gun hand, held a bag of food.

D'Amato called out. "That's Lobo." He jumped out of the RMP, his hand wrapped about the butt of his gun. "Be careful."

I recalled the precinct scuttlebutt—Lobo was a silent attack dog rumored to have torn apart other animals: dogs, cats, rats. No humans. Yet.

As a veteran of many encounters with ferocious attack dogs, I found myself planning what to do: if doggy diplomacy failed, I could offer my left arm and pull my weapon with my right hand. Then I noticed that the mangy animal was missing an eye and that mosquitoes were buzzing around a thick scab on his head—this dog had been recently mistreated. I reached out a cautious, probing hand.

"Hey, big fella."

The Rottweiler bared its teeth.

"Good Lobo," I said in a soothing voice.

The Rottweiler stopped.

"Nice Lobo."

Lobo looked at me the way dogs do, cocking its thick canine head this way and that, trying to figure me out, friend or foe.

"Hungry, Lobo?" I tried. "You hungry, boy?" I held out the bag of burgers, shook it. "This what you want?" The Rottweiler dropped its head, eased into a submissive stance, began to wag his tail and prance closer—he understood. I took a chance, reached down and petted the dog, being careful not to upset the head wound. Lobo began to rub against my trousers—the old submissive, lovable dog routine.

"You like burgers, boy? Sure you do."

"No," D'Amato called out. "Not the burgers."

Lobo began to slobber and wag his stubby tail with such force he could hardly stand. I reached into the bag, unwrapped a burger and offered it to him. The dog seized the offering without so much as nipping my fingers. He dropped to the hot pavement at my feet and devoured his meal.

"Good Lobo." I unwrapped the second burger and threw it to the pack. The dogs went into a wild feeding frenzy fighting each other for every scrap of meat.

"That's a good boy." I gave the Rottweiler a final pat as I moved to the RMP.

"Good thing I ain't starving, dickhead," D'Amato said.

I slid into the car, handed D'Amato his Diet Coke and a small plastic bag. "Here're your pickles."

"Very funny." D'Amato scowled. "I never did like you."

I opened the glove compartment searching for something to clean the dog smell from my hands.

"What's the story with Tookie?"

"Not around."

"Think he's gone underground?"

The dog pack loped up the street, snarling and snapping at each other until they turned down Whitlock Avenue, heading to the Hunts Point piers. All but Lobo. He padded over to the RMP and sat gazing imploringly. I rolled the window all the way down, reached out and Lobo licked and sniffed my hand, recording my scent. I knew I'd made a new friend.

"Hey, Beckett," D'Amato said. "What am I, talking to a fucking wall. How 'bout telling me what's going on."

As I patted Lobo on the head, I told D'Amato about Solana—explained she was a 41 Precinct resident and a writer on *Law & Order*—calling me saying she had information on the South Bronx fires. Told him about Pete from Queens's unprecedented visit to my apartment delivering an olive branch on behalf of R. J. Gold. That Pete drove a black Lincoln Town Car and what transpired later between me, Pete and Solana at P. J. Clarke's.

"Now," I said, "Solana's not returning my calls."

"Why'd she run out?"

I shrugged. "She took one look at Pete—"

"So they know each other?"

"Pete said he met her once."

D'Amato gave me a sideways glance. "So, you think Pete's Lincoln's the one Tookie mentioned?"

"Yeah, I do."

"Doesn't mean he started any fires."

"Right," I said. "It doesn't."

"I mean, Pete's got every right to be on Gold land—"

"Yeah. He does."

The radio crackled in the background. Central was holding sixty jobs in the 41 Precinct.

"And I can see why Pete visited you," D'Amato said. "I mean, the Yankee tickets were probably an excuse, but we work the precinct. He wouldn't be doing his job if he didn't pump you for information. Agreed?"

"Agreed."

"So we don't wanna go around making any wild allegations." D'Amato looked at me. "We don't wanna fuck with R. J. Gold."

"Not if we can help it."

"Gold pals out with the mayor, the police commissioner, the DA. We piss him off and he gets us fired, you've got other options—you're a goddamned actor. Me? I got no options. Being a cop's all I ever wanted. It's my life."

"I know, Vinnie." I did not wish to discuss it any further. "I know."

"You do, huh?" D'Amato took a moment. "How far you wanna take this?"

"All the way," I said. "You got a problem with that?"

"I got a problem with everything you do lately."

"I got that impression last night."

"About last night—"

"Forget it," I said.

"I ain't forgetting anything," D'Amato said. "Look, I don't want you to be the last to know—I called roll call today and asked to be reassigned. I'm gonna be working with Fitzpatrick next month in sector Henry."

I have to admit I was shocked: D'Amato was dumping *me*. Although his antics last night in J. G. Melon had greatly disturbed me, I'd conveniently chosen to chalk it up to the job's pressures and the fact he was drunk. After all, it wasn't the first time D'Amato had acted irrationally while intox. And I guess I didn't want to deal with the only other explanation, the fact that my partner resented me.

"I understand," I said not really meaning it. "Change is good."

"No hard feelings?" D'Amato said, offering his hand.

"None," I said and shook.

D'Amato slipped the car in gear. "You think that woman, Solana, really knows something about the arsons?"

"Only one way to find out."

"Where she live?"

"Manida Street out in Hunts Point."

D'Amato eased from the curb, hit the gas and made a left heading toward Solana's residence. He slowed to watch a reed-thin teenage boy ramble down the avenue, glancing into parked cars looking for something to steal. The teen saw us looking, ducked into an alley, and disappeared.

The radio crackled. "*41 Ida.*"

"Damn it." I picked up the radio. "41 Ida."

"*You available, Ida?*"

I hesitated. Thought about telling central we were not available, come up with some excuse; say we were breaking up a dispute, or dealing with a vehicle accident. I wanted to drive to Solana's place forthwith, knock on her door, ask her what she knew about the fires, why she ran out of P. J. Clarke's.

"Look." D'Amato gestured across the street.

Police officers Ryan and McShane were sitting in their RMP, watching us, listening for our response to the radio call.

"We'll find piss in our lockers tonight we don't take that call—maybe worse."

D'Amato was right. Solana would have to wait.

"41 Ida available," I said.

*"Past robbery, 37 Bryant Avenue."*

"10–4, central."

# CHAPTER 25

Solana used her body weight to close and lock an over-stuffed suitcase. She glanced around the bedroom and figured it would take all night to rummage through and pack the remainder of her personal belongings. One trip in a gypsy cab would be sufficient to move her, once and forever, out of her mother's Bronx apartment.

After twenty-five years, one trip.

Solana carried the suitcase across the floor, then phoned a local gypsy cab service and told them to pick her up tomorrow morning at seven A.M. She planned to travel to the *Law & Order* studios in Manhattan, stow her gear in wardrobe. Begin her search for a Manhattan apartment after work—after seeing Pete from Queens in the company of Michael Beckett, she was afraid to remain in the South Bronx.

Solana picked up the copies of the newspaper articles that she intended to share with Michael Beckett, ripped them in half and tossed them into growing piles of leave-behind junk. She looked at her mother's velvet Jesus, which gazed down upon her in silent lampoon piety. Grief bubbled up in her throat. She dropped to her knees, leaned her elbows on the couch, clasped her hands in prayer, and took stock of her emotions: she felt utterly alone and vulnerable. She vacillated between self-pity, frustration at her lack of options, and a growing, all-encompassing wave of despair.

The knock on Solana's apartment door startled her. She was not expecting anyone—it was probably Michael Beckett. He'd already left a half dozen messages on her answering machine. Thank goodness she hadn't given him her cell number.

Rising, Solana tiptoed across the living room and peered out her front door peephole. She saw a man in a suit, a stranger.

"Yes?"

The man held a gold NYPD shield up for her to see.

"Detective Doyle, 41 Squad. May I speak to you a moment?"

*Now what?* Although cops canvassing apartments for witnesses to robberies or other violent incidents were common in the 'hood, as a seasoned ghetto resident Solana was suspicious of everyone.

"Just a moment." She left the chain lock on, opened her door three inches, braced her foot against so it couldn't be pushed in, and spoke through the crack. "What do you want?"

Detective Doyle smiled pleasantly. "Got a report of suspicious men prowling the building."

He was a rather attractive, albeit overfed, older man. Impeccably dressed. The crudely dyed reddish-brown hair was bizarre.

"Have you seen or heard anything suspicious?"

"In this neighborhood?" Solana laughed. "Every day of my life."

"Yeah. Well." Doyle put his shield away. "Look, I don't mean to alarm you. But it appears that you are the last remaining tenant in this building."

Solana fixed him with a perplexed stare. "But the Ayalas up in 3B? The Rubios in 5A?"

"I just checked." Doyle shrugged

"But they were here yesterday," Solana said. "At least I think they were."

"They fled," Doyle said, "by the look of things."

"Fled?" Solana felt the first twinges of panic. "I was planning to move out myself tomorrow morning, 7 A.M."

"Tomorrow? Look, junkies are already beginning to squat in some of the vacant apartments." He thumbed toward upstairs. "In my opinion, it's not safe for you to stay here tonight."

*Not safe to stay here?*

"If I were you," Doyle counseled with the concerned warmth of a protective big brother, "I'd pack up your family. Sleep at a friend's house tonight. Maybe a hotel. Come back tomorrow during daylight hours and retrieve your possessions."

"I live alone."

"Alone? Even more reason to—"

Solana shook her head. "I grew up in this neighborhood. I'll be all right."

"Look, miss, there is no more neighborhood. I don't mean to be pushy, but I'm a two-hundred-pound cop, I carry a gun, and there's no way *I'd* stay here tonight."

The detective's statement gave Solana pause. She knew all too well that there were marauding predators and degenerates in the ghetto. If any one of them discovered she was alone in an abandoned building. . . . She pursed her lips, tried to think of some friends who'd allow her to spend the night. Thought about phoning Tina—no, Tina was not an option.

"Most of my friends lived on this block. They're gone." Solana shrugged in embarrassment. "I can't afford a hotel."

Doyle leaned against the door jamb. "I'm not supposed to tell you this, but the police department has an emergency fund. You know, a safety net for cases similar to yours."

"Like welfare?"

"More Red Cross. How it works is, I check you into a hotel, and the police department reimburses me."

Solana's eyes narrowed with suspicion. Was this detective a dirty old letch attempting to lure her to a hotel room under false pretenses? Or perhaps some strange new breed of cop: kind, sympathetic, compassionate. Or could he be part of a some plot to extricate her from the building tonight—she *was* the last remaining tenant.

"Look. Since you're only one person, I believe I can convince the department to cover you for a few days, a week even, until you find a new place to live." His hands opened in appeal. "Can't do better than that."

Solana thought over the offer. She had to admit the detective *seemed* sincere. His offer *sounded* reasonable, even wise. And she did not wish to remain the lone tenant in an empty building overnight.

"Which hotel?"

Doyle smiled. "The department has a special deal with the Milford Plaza down on Eighth Avenue."

Solana knew the place; a class "c" hotel but it was clean and she could walk to work. She removed the chain lock and opened the door. "Would you like to come in and wait?"

That's when a familiar, distinct scent reached her. A man's cologne. Napoleon. Strong. Expensive—Pete Costello's cologne. Solana heard heavy footsteps, looked and saw a giant shadow move across the hallway wall—and gasped. Her hand shot to her mouth, eyes wide with comprehension.

"Something wrong?" Doyle took a step across the threshold. Solana shoved him back. He stumbled into the hallway. Fell against a pitted wall.

Solana heaved her weight against the door. Slammed and locked it. "You're one of them. You son of a bitch!"

Doyle pounded on the door once, hard. "Look, miss." He sounded like he was speaking through clenched teeth.

"I'm only trying to do something nice. Pack a bag like a nice girl and I'll take you to a hotel."

Solana felt a tremor of rage in her throat. Knew at that instant that they were determined to oust her from her apartment, tonight. "I'm calling 911." That's when Solana heard a series of thundering footfalls move rapidly away from her apartment and down the stairs.

"Don't be foolish." Doyle's voice was now gentle, so clear that he sounded as if he were in the room. "The ten thousand you accepted is all you'll receive. They will not, I repeat, will *not* renegotiate."

"What are you talking about?"

"The money to buy you out of your lease," Doyle said. "Don't lie to me. I know you accepted it."

"I never received money from anyone." Solana tried a laugh. "Not even an offer."

Doyle was silent for a long moment. "Pack a bag," he said. "Do it now. I'll be downstairs waiting."

She heard him walk casually away.

Solana fell against the door trembling, her mind swirled. She raced into the kitchen, picked up the phone and dialed 911.

"*Operator 205 speaking. What is the location of the emergency?*"

"I live at 1123 Manida—"

*Click.*

"Hello?" Solana jiggled the receiver. "Hello?" Dead air. She hung up. Rechecked for a dial tone. There was none. A lump of ice formed in her chest. Someone had cut her phone line.

Solana dashed into the kitchen, found her purse, dumped the contents, but her cell phone was not there. She tore through piles of paper, tossed old clothing aside, and overturned boxes overflowing with leave-behind junk— where the hell had she put her cell phone?

# CHAPTER 26

Pete from Queens ripped the entire telephone circuit box from the basement wall and smashed it on the cement floor.

Eighty years of dust rose in torrents.

Doyle waved his hands to clear breathing and vision space as he legged down the stairs and stepped into the dimly lit room. The place was heavy with the smell of garbage and coal gas.

"Told you so," Pete said.

Doyle tracked Pete's voice, squinted through the gloom in an effort to locate him.

Pete was standing across the room, by an antiquated oil burner, shrouded in murky darkness, the telephone circuit box splintered at his feet.

"What's the point?" Doyle said. "She'll only use her cell phone."

"Yeah?" Pete's expression said he hadn't thought of that. "So, let her."

"You didn't pay her the ten grand, did you, Pete?"

No response.

"Did you pay any of them?"

"I'd mind my business," Pete said, "if I were you."

"Correct me if I'm wrong. You were supposed to buy tenants out of their leases. Empty the buildings, then set the fires." Doyle could feel Pete's eyes boring into him. "But what you did was employ physical intimidation to frighten people away."

"You can't prove a thing."

"Nor do I intend to." Doyle meant it. He was part of the criminal conspiracy, in too deep. "How much money did you pocket? I'm curious."

"Curiosity killed the cop." Pete stepped forward.

Doyle saw a plastic five-gallon can of gasoline in Pete's right hand. In his left was an arson instrument: matches rolled around an unlit cigarette.

"You're not serious?" Doyle was incredulous; was this guy for real? "Look, she said she's leaving in the morning."

"Midnight's the deadline," Pete said. "You know that."

"Who's gonna know the difference?"

"I ain't taking any chances." Pete put the arson instrument in his pocket then unscrewed the gas can top. "Tomorrow this time bulldozers will have already leveled the whole block. There'll be nothing left."

Doyle's mind raced.

What a fool he'd been.

In the beginning, all he was recruited to do was derail any pertinent arson investigations. Blame the fires on the youth gang strippers. Simple enough. Hell, the abandoned buildings eventually became havens for junkies, giant rats and wild dogs. He was doing the city a favor. But then yesterday's fiasco: the girl and her infant killed. The two arsonists shot to death on national television. And now this—to stand by and watch Pete set fire to an occupied building. For Doyle, a man who had dedicated his life to police work, such an act was incomprehensible.

Yet if he stopped Pete, and therefore became responsible for Gold losing his Gold Bronx City government loan guarantees and core investors, Gold would undoubtedly renege on his promise concerning Dr. Helmut Krauss. His wife would surely die from Lou Gehrig's disease, little by little, day by day, slowly, torturously.

Doyle caught a whiff of gasoline. Felt full-blown panic. It was up to *him* who would live, who would die: his beloved wife or Solana Ortiz. He felt a tightness in his chest. A terrible sorrow raked his heart.

"Put the gas can down," Doyle said.

Pete didn't even bother to glance at the detective. "You heard the boss."

"Fuck the boss."

Pete stopped. Looked.

Doyle was pointing a gun at him.

"Turn around," Doyle said. "Put the gas can down. Show me your hands."

Pete obeyed. "You know, of course, what this means?"

"That you are walking out that door." Doyle stepped back clearing a path. "And you're to keep walking and not come back. Anything, and I mean *anything* happens to the Ortiz woman I'll look for you."

"Your wife's only chance is Doctor Krauss," Pete said. "I know it. You know it."

"Move." Doyle motioned with his gun.

"Think about what you're doing. Sacrificing your wife's life for the life of a stranger. That doesn't make sense."

"Move." Doyle's voice was unwavering. "I won't say it again." The ensuing silence was palpable.

Pete heaved a monstrous sigh. Walked toward the exit. Past Doyle. Spun. Kicked. Doyle's gun flew from his hand.

Doyle responded instantly. Attacked. Threw a series of digging lefts and rights at Pete's midsection. Slugged away like an out-of-shape fighter working a heavy bag. And with the same results. Pete, unfazed, had not even bothered to defend himself.

Doyle lowered his bruised hands, exhausted.

"Who do you think you're dealing with?" Pete clamped a vise-grip hand around the detective's throat, strangling him. "That's R. J. Gold *himself* giving the orders. He owns everyone. The governor. The mayor. The police commissioner. Me and you." Pete emphasized the point by slamming Doyle against a cement wall. "There're Mafia dons standing in line begging to do him favors." Pete released Doyle. He crumpled to the filthy floor gulping air.

"You'll do as you're told," Pete said. "Or burn with Solana Ortiz."

It took a few hacking moments before Doyle managed to rasp: "It's premeditated murder."

Pete laughed a little. "Hey, me? I got a heart like a whale. I don't wanna see anything happen to Solana. I got a thing for her. Another time, place, she and me? Well, who knows? But it ain't my call." Pete bent down, picked up Doyle's gun, dumped the clip and handed it back.

"I'll get her out," Doyle said.

Pete looked down at him. "Give it up."

"I mean it. She'll be out tonight."

"All right." Pete picked up the gas container. "Get her out before midnight."

"That gives me less than an hour." Doyle struggled to push himself up to one knee. "I'll need more time."

"Midnight." Pete spread the gasoline on the basement floor. "Then the building burns."

# CHAPTER 27

I pushed the end button on my cell phone, leaned against the RMP trunk, and cursed the evening's heat and heavy work load. I knew now that I should have taken the tour off so I could investigate the Coster Street fire uninterrupted. As it was, the summer heat and humidity had helped to fuel a mini crime wave, and as a result, the entire 41 Precinct had been inundated with radio runs. We had had no time to stop by Solana's apartment. And now a telephone company recording was reporting that her home phone was out of order. I did not know her cell phone number.

An el train roared overhead, its wheels emitting a shrill, ear-piercing screech as it rounded the turn off Westchester Avenue and onto the tracks that ran along Southern Boulevard. The sound alerted me to the headache forming behind my eyes. I massaged the bridge of my nose and realized that, at this rate, it would be well after midnight by the time we signed out. Too late to go knocking on Solana's door. I put my cell phone away, stepped back into the RMP.

"10–4, central," D'Amato said, acknowledging a radio run, our twenty-third of the tour.

"What'd we get?" I said.

"A dispute at the PR Bodega."

I looked at the store to my right, the PR Bodega. The store was dark, closed and locked. "Place closed an hour ago."

"No shit, Dick Tracy." D'Amato depressed the accelerator, eased the car from the curb as the police radio droned in the background.

"I'm gonna take tomorrow off," I said. "Track down Tookie Jones. Go see Solana. You with me?"

"Can't. I got no vacation days left. Taking the next set of tours off. Kids wanna got to Disneyland."

I sipped a warm Diet Coke, glanced out the window and spotted the level-3 sexual predator and drug dealer Juan Langlois, cruising the neighborhood in search of a pubescent victim, no doubt offering drugs for sex—the hair on the back of my neck stood up. There was a time not too long ago when I wouldn't have been able to stop myself from rousting Juan. But even if I locked him up for possession of drugs, the courts would only let him go with a slap on the wrist—there was simply no point. Besides I wanted my last arrest to be whoever was responsible for the Coster Street fire.

I turned my attention back to D'Amato, wondered if he was telling the truth about his lack of vacation days, taking his daughters to Disneyland, or was this his way of distancing himself from me and the arson investigation.

*"Central to 41 Mary. K."*

*"41 Mary."*

*"41 Mary, got a series of calls at 1123 Manida Street. An hysterical woman in apartment 1C claims someone's attempting to evict her from her apartment. Now I got a call of a gas leak at the same address. Fire department already on the scene."*

*"41 Mary. 10-4."*

I picked up the radio. "41 Ida to Central."

*"Go ahead, Ida."*

"The dispute at the PR Bodega is unfounded. 41 Ida is also responding to the gas leak at 1123 Manida Street."

*"10-4, Ida."*

D'Amato looked at me.

"It's Solana's building." I switched on the lights and siren. "Step on it."

MANIDA STREET WAS awash with clear, cool water gushing from several open fire hydrants when we arrived. Pulsing lights and sirens had drawn a multitude of spectators from the surrounding area. A fire truck sealed off one end of the dark, ravaged street. 41 Mary had used their RMP to block traffic on the opposite end. Several firefighters had grabbed wrenches from their rigs and were rushing to shut off the hydrants, chasing away the foulmouthed, sweltering kids who'd opened them, frantic to rebuild the critical water pressure—just in case. D'Amato nosed our RMP to the curb behind a gas company truck.

A fire department chief, speaking into a bullhorn, was urging all civilians to leave the area.

No one budged.

I looked toward 1123 Manida Street and saw a couple of firefighters jostling Solana down the tenement's front stoop—by the way she was acting, they must have forced her to evacuate her apartment.

"Solana," I called out.

Solana reacted, looked in my direction, grabbed a suitcase from one of the firefighters, barked something at him, and stalked away.

*What the hell?*

I started after her, circled around a collection of scabrous Hunts Point hookers, leapt over a river of rushing water, sidestepped a group of drooling pill-heads, then scurried over a parked police car hood and blocked her path. Solana reared to a stop.

"Talk to me," I said. "Why'd you run out on me today at P. J. Clarke's?"

"Get out of my way," Solana said.

"No." I didn't budge. "Tell me why."

Solana gritted her teeth. "You think I'm stupid?" She tried to push past me.

"What do you know about the fires?" I grabbed her arm. "You're not going anywhere until you tell me what you know."

"Take your hands off me."

"Police brutality," a man shouted. I looked and saw that a group of rum-swilling Hispanic men were watching the altercation: a white cop accosting an Hispanic woman.

"Leave her alone," a man said.

"Fuck off, *pendejo*!" another guy said.

I let go of Solana's arm.

She turned her back and hurried off.

I had no choice but to let her go.

Watching Solana walk away, I was hit with a sinking feeling. I knew that, even if I could talk her into telling me what she knew about the fires, the possibility of ever getting close to her was lost. And I'd probably never know the reason why.

"I take it that was Solana." D'Amato was at my side, his eyes riveted to Solana's derriere. "You never told me she was hot."

"What's the story on the gas leak?"

"Intentional," D'Amato said. "The gas company guys said there's fresh wrench marks on the old gas pipe. And the basement stinks of gasoline. So does the stairwell. The place is a fucking time bomb."

I looked down the block at one of the still open hydrants; the water no longer gushed, it trickled. The precipitous drop in water pressure would be disastrous in the event of a fire.

The bullhorn reactivated. The fire chief was now ordering everyone to leave the block, immediately.

I turned and saw Solana enter a gypsy cab and head south.

"Hey, look," D'Amato said.

Detective Doyle was exiting Solana's building. He wove inconspicuously though a group of firefighters, crossed the street, stepped into an unmarked car, started the engine, and drove away.

"What's that prima donna doing investigating a common gas leak?" D'Amato said.

"Hey." It was Fire Marshal Collyer speaking. "You guys got a minute?"

The three of us crossed the street and then settled into our RMP. The fire truck that had been blocking Manida Street eased forward, swung right and stopped in front of Solana's building. Once the water pressure was restored, they would pull hoses, wash down the basement, and dilute the gasoline thereby decreasing the danger of an explosion or fire.

D'Amato started the engine, backed up, took the fire truck's place and cut off Manida Street.

"Whaddya got," I said.

"The Gold Organization had to file plans with the New York City Building Department and apply for certain permits in order to renovate the tenements on this ten-block area," Collyer said from the back seat.

I gazed distractedly down Manida Street and saw McShane and Ryan's RMP come to a stop at the opposite corner. They exited their car and assisted the fire department, forcing the straggling and/or obstinate pedestrians to a safe distance.

"You listening?" Collyer said.

"Yeah," I said. "So, did they file?"

"They did."

"Then all you'd have to do is check what type of plans were filed, along with what type of permits were applied for. Right?"

"Right."

"Don't keep us in suspense," I said. "I know you checked."

"They filed the correct plans," Collyer said, "and applied for the appropriate permits for the renovation of the existing structures."

I turned around and looked at the fire marshal. Pulsing fire department truck lights strobed his shiny, freckled face.

"That shoots your forcible eviction theory to hell," I said. "No?"

Collyer shook his head. "In New York City you gotta book labor, steelworkers, electricians, plumbers and the like, months, sometimes years in advance and file plans with the Building Contractors Association of New York. The Gold Organization did just that. But a confidential source told me that there's an alternative, secret set of plans for an entirely different project, at the same location. And not for a piddly renovation. It's for a mega-development, one of the largest residential projects ever undertaken in New York State."

D'Amato and I exchanged a glance.

"But that doesn't make sense," D'Amato said. "In the end all the contracts and building department permits would be public record."

"If a fire guts 1123," Collyer said, "all they have to do is update the secret set of plans, make 'em look like they were only just filed."

"Gut 1123?" D'Amato scoffed. "With fifty firefighters standing around?"

"All it'll take is a spark," Collyer said.

"So Gold's been planning to build all along," I said.

"Doesn't prove anyone in his organization is involved in arson," D'Amato said.

"Affirmative," Collyer said.

"So all you've got is a theory," D'Amato said.

"And one hell of a motive," Collyer said.

"Anything tie Gold to the Coster Street fire?" I said.

"No," Collyer said, "nothing."

"You convinced strippers were behind it?"

"I'm not convinced of anything," Collyer said.

"But everything points to strippers," D'Amato said.

"Or to someone who wants us to *think* it was strippers," Collyer said.

"Tookie Jones doesn't confess," D'Amato said, "we may never know who hired the Taylor brothers."

D'Amato was right—but somebody somewhere knew. Maybe it was going to take me pulling the old bull in a china shop routine, ask provocative questions, make accusations, piss people off, push until someone pushed back—I honestly didn't know what else to do. "All right," I said, "I'll look into the Gold angle."

Collyer leaned forward. "Look, Beckett, you know as well as I do, these construction associations and unions are mobbed up *and* they're in bed with the Gold Organization. We're talking organized crime muscle plus the best legal expertise money can buy."

I knew what Collyer said was correct, to an extent. Like anyone in the construction industry, the Gold Organization was forced to deal with certain elements of organized crime: it was the price of doing business in New York City. I had once asked Gold how he dealt with mob shakedowns: no-show jobs, tariffs on equipment and supplies. Gold stated that he simply "paid the freight" and passed the costs onto his commercial and residential tenants.

"And don't forget," Collyer continued, "even if by some miracle you did put an arson/murder case together, uncovered evidence that proved someone in the Gold organization, maybe even Gold himself was complicit, who're you gonna give the information to? Not Doyle, I hope."

I shook my head. "Captain Ward."

"Ward's a good man. But who's gonna prosecute?" Collyer said. "Not the Bronx DA. Gold put him in office."

"I could give the info to a few ambitious sleazebag reporters," I said. "No shortage of them around."

"I doubt any mainstream newspaper would take on Gold."

"Then I'll go to the feds," I said.

"There's more," Collyer said. "You aware the arson investigations are about to be closed?"

I couldn't believe what I was hearing. "Who's closing it?"

"Doyle."

"Fucking Doyle," D'Amato said.

"He insists he has enough evidence to tie the Taylor brothers to about six fires, including the East Bay Avenue and Coster Street arsons."

"Does he?" D'Amato said.

"Circumstantial evidence?" Collyer said. "Probably."

"Two girls are dead." I looked directly at Collyer. "We can't let whoever's responsible get away with it, even if it's R. J. Gold himself."

"Whoa," Collyer sat back. "Look, Beckett. I ain't gonna risk a thirty-year pension going up against a five-thousand-pound gorilla like R. J. Gold. There're no odds in it."

"He's right," D'Amato said.

"I got a wife, school-age children."

"That makes two of us," D'Amato said.

"I'm gonna do my job," Collyer said. "File my report. Turn what I got over to my supervisor. He wants to hand it off to the NYPD or take it any further, that's his call."

"He's right again," D'Amato said. "Let the system work. See what happens."

I had to admit, Collyer and D'Amato had a valid point.

But there was no way I was gonna stick around long enough to see *if* the system worked—which with Doyle involved was doubtful.

"I'll handle it," I said.

D'Amato threw up his hands. "There you go, the Lone fucking Ranger again."

"Are you out of your mind?" Collyer said. "You *know* R. J. Gold. He could destroy you on a whim. Plus, I hate to point out the obvious, but you're nothing but a lowlife Bronx beat cop—no offense. What the hell you expect to accomplish?"

We heard someone shout. Looked and saw a half-dozen firefighters racing from Solana's building, screaming for everyone to move back.

That was followed by a low, flat "boom." Bright blue flames shot out from the basement windows. Scorched the sidewalk. Licked the front and sides of the building.

"Holy shit," D'Amato said.

Firefighters raced to the closest hydrant. They attached a hose, turned on the water, then gestured frantically, helplessly—not enough water pressure.

Spectators began congregating, reveling at the intensity of the rapidly spreading inferno. Cops and firemen did their best to keep them back. Within moments 1123 Manida was engulfed in flames.

"Hey!" an angry voice said.

We looked and saw McShane and Ryan standing in front of our RMP, glaring at us.

"You fucking assholes need a special invitation?" McShane said. "Get your asses out here and give us a hand."

"You don't punch that prick out soon," D'Amato said as we exited our RMP, "I will."

# CHAPTER 28

Two armed Gold Organization security men were standing outside Gold Tower, leaning against a wall, casually smoking cigarettes, when I exited a yellow cab on Fifth Avenue the following morning. I shrugged into a silk, charcoal gray suit jacket, adjusted the gun on my waistband, and looked up the entire sixty-eight-floor height of Gold Tower as Fire Marshal Collyer's words reverberated in my brain: "There're no odds going up against a five-thousand-pound gorilla like R. J. Gold."

A doorman, dressed like a Buckingham Palace guard, smiled mechanically and said, "Welcome to Gold Tower," as I walked past him and through the revolving doors.

The dazzling six-story atrium was bustling with over-wrought child-laden tourists, frantic shoppers and camera-ready sightseers. I made my way to the elevator banks, breathed in the atrium's faint, familiar bouquet and felt a sense of déja vu. I'd walked across that gleaming marble floor countless times.

"Can I help you?" a fire-hydrant-thick security guard, standing at a small podium-high desk said as I approached the roped-off elevators. There was a time when I personally knew every member of Gold's security team. Not any longer.

"I'm here to see R. J. Gold."

"Name?" The guard picked up some sort of appointment/security sign-in sheet.

"I don't have an appointment."

He put down the sheet. "You need an appointment to see Mr. Gold, sir."

"Call Norma," I said. "Tell her Michael Beckett's here."

The guard looked me over; my designer shoes, suit and tie, evidently deciding if I was for real, or some whack-job. He picked up a desk phone, punched in a four-digit number, and spoke in hushed tones. When he hung up he said, "I need to see some ID."

I flashed my shield and NYPD ID card.

The guard focused on my ID card. He wrote my name on the sign-in sheet, then handed me his pen. "Sign here, please."

I signed and handed him back his pen.

"You armed, Officer Beckett?"

"No," I said, not about to surrender my weapon to a twelve-dollar-an-hour rent-a-cop. "I'm not."

"This is private property," the guard said. "Unauthorized weapons are not permitted."

"Good policy," I said.

For a moment, the guard looked as if he was about to challenge me. Then he moved aside. I stepped into the elevator and pushed the Executive Offices button.

My plan—if you could call it that—was to drop in on Gold under the guise of thanking him for the Yankee-Boston baseball tickets, talk about old times. Ease into the subject of the South Bronx fires, make a few provocative statements, see where things went from there.

What I couldn't do was be specific; make accusations, accuse Pete of hiring the Taylor brothers to burn down Gold's Coster Street building, accuse him, and therefore

Gold, of conspiracy and murder—which would be utterly counterproductive. R. J. would toss me out of his
office. Guilty or not he'd call out his legal team, circle
the wagons.

I stepped off the elevator, walked past two more armed
security guards and into the Gold Organization's executive
offices. The reception area was basically as I remembered.
Although all the furnishings had been upgraded, the glaring morning sun still poured in, gracing the space with a
cheery albeit unforgiving light. A stunning brunette receptionist looked up from her desk, saw me, and said, "Go
right in, Mr. Beckett. Mr. Gold is expecting you."

Norma greeted me as I pushed through the next set of
glass doors, with a warm smile and a kiss on each cheek.

"So good to see you again, Michael," Norma said like
she meant it—I knew she didn't. She had never approved
of Gold befriending a common street cop.

"Hello, Norma." I hugged her, glanced over her shoulder to the sea of desks which were staffed by young, beautiful women. It was good to see that R. J. hadn't changed his
hiring policy; the place looked more like a model agency
then a business office.

"When're you going to quit this popsicle stand," I
said, "and run off with me? We could be in Bermuda by
evening."

"Oh, you dirty young man," Norma said. "If I thought
for a moment that you meant it—" She slipped from my
clutches. "You can go right in." She thumbed toward
Gold's office. "You know the way."

I heard a child's voice as I entered Gold's inner sanc-
tum. The first thing I noticed was that Gold, sitting behind
his football-field-size desk, had gained about twenty
pounds. None of it muscle. His face was bloated, neck
thick. Then I noticed a Japanese man in a suit sitting on an
overstuffed chair facing Gold: Tomo Nagasue, an attorney
and Gold's CFO.

"I throw-did up, Daddy." Seven-year-old Faye Gold's voice was loud and clear over the speaker phone.

"I'm sorry, Little Faye," Gold said. "Are you feeling better now, honey?" Gold saw me enter and motioned for me to come in and sit by Nagasue.

The CFO glanced at me as I sat in a chair beside him and gestured a vague greeting with a cup of coffee.

"No." Little Faye sighed theatrically.

"What's wrong?"

"My stomach's broke-did."

Gold chuckled. "What broke-did your stomach this time, baby. Tell Daddy the truth."

"Mommy said it was the candy. But it wasn't, Daddy. It wasn't."

Nagasue laughed.

My eyes slid to the CFO—his slight build and self-effacing demeanor belied the fact he was a tough corporate executive who excelled in the cutthroat world of international law.

"What was it than?" Gold asked Faye.

"I don't know."

Gold winked at me. "Daddy has to go now, Faye. Put Lauren on the phone."

"Lauren's not here."

"Put Mommy on the phone."

"Mommy's not here."

As I listened distractedly to Gold's conversation, I sat back and crossed my legs. I had to admit, on one hand it felt good being back in the clubby luxury of Gold's private office, yet I felt a sense of loss and longing for the old days. I recalled that, beside the occasional impromptu after-work cocktail parties I'd attended, I'd sat precisely where I was sitting, watching Gold carpet-putt as he hammered out million-dollar deals. And then there was the endless string of celebrities that I'd met as they passed through Gold's door, hat in hand. Everyone from former presidents of the United States, religious leaders, to Hollywood madams. They all wanted something from Gold.

I glanced around the familiar room feeling ill at ease, every bit the outsider. The same scale models of Gold's ships, planes, helicopters and other toys were still scattered around the place. Pictures of his family still adorned the wall beside his desk, although a few new ones had been added. And then I noticed that the display table where Gold always kept a detailed scale model of his most current building project was not there. Deep carpet indentations indicated that something had recently been on display.

"Where's Lauren and Mommy?" Gold said.

"Fighting," Faye said.

"About what?"

"They're always fighting, Daddy."

"All right, baby," Gold said. "Tell Mommy and Lauren to call Daddy later. Will you do that for Daddy?"

"Oh, all right."

"Daddy loves you, Faye."

"Yes, I know," Faye said and hung up.

Gold abruptly shifted gears as he hung up on his end. "Ever think of having a family, Michael?"

The CFO regarded me appraisingly.

"Yeah," I said. "More as I get older."

"You should. You'd be a great father. A great father." Gold gestured to his CFO. "You remember Tomo Nagasue."

"Sure." I reached to shake Nagasue's soft, delicate hand. "Good to see you."

"The artiste with a gun," Nagasue said with a hint of sarcasm. "We heard you were performing on *Law & Order*."

"I was." I looked at Gold. "How's the family?"

"Great. Lauren's thirteen. Thinks Helga and I are fascists. Faye's seven and already showing signs of independence, pulling away. She won't allow me to hold her hand in public. I can't kiss her anymore in front of her friends. She gets embarrassed."

No one spoke for a long moment.

"So, Michael." Gold came out from behind his desk, patted me on the back, and actually shook my hand—he rarely shook hands. "You look great," Gold said. "Just great. You coming to Saturday's Yankee game? We'll have an early dinner afterwards at Peter Luger, like old times."

"I wouldn't miss it." Peter Luger steak house, as Gold knew, was one of my favorite restaurants.

"You want something to drink?" Gold said.

I said I didn't.

"So, tell me," Gold said, "what do you guys think about the Yankee pitching staff?"

"Unbeatable," Nagasue spoke up. "If they can stay injury free, which is doubtful."

"What do you think, Michael?" Gold said.

I paused for a moment, wanting to get the words right. "There are those in the department who think your director of security, Pete Costello, forcibly evicted some tenants from your South Bronx buildings."

"What?" Gold appeared genuinely shocked.

I leaned forward, spoke as if divulging sensitive information. "I'm aware of some evidence that suggests he may have been involved in arson."

"Whoa," Nagasue said.

"I don't believe it," Gold said.

"Involved, how?" Nagasue said.

I put on my best game face. "A witness places him at the scene of at least one arson."

Gold exchanged looks with his CFO. "Pete's supposed to be on the property. You saying someone actually saw him start a fire?"

I nodded. "That's what I heard, yes."

"But why in heaven's name?" Gold said.

I bit back the answer. I didn't want Gold to know that I knew about the two sets of building plans, the fact he was the *only* person who stood to benefit from the forcible evictions and arson—not yet anyway. "That's still being investigated."

"I thought you were still a uniformed beat cop," Nagasue said. "Have you been assigned to the detective division?"

"I'm still in uniform."

"Then by whose authority are you here?" Nagasue said.

"No one's. I came as a courtesy." I looked at Gold. "We go back a ways, R. J. I didn't want you to be blindsided."

Nagasue looked at Gold. "This conversation is over."

Gold's raised hand silenced his CFO. "According to my sources at the newspapers, the evidence suggest the dead arsonists were responsible for the fires on my land."

"That's also being investigated." I paused for effect, sat back and braced for one of Gold's famous temper tantrums. But he remained cool, composed. Not at all what I expected.

I heard a noise, looked and saw several Gold security men mustering hurriedly outside the office. The timing of that show of force suggested to me our conversation was being monitored.

Gold rose from his chair, walked over to a window, peered out. I came up behind him. The view was panoramic, majestic. Rainclouds were skirting the city fifty miles to the north.

"There anything you wanna tell me, R. J.?"

"Remember the fun we used to have, Michael? A party every night. Wine. Women. Song—and women."

I gazed down at a horrific traffic jam that stretched as far as the eye could see along Fifth Avenue. "I remember."

"Life's more complicated now." Gold fiddled with the scale model of his yacht. "Look, I'll check into this thing with Pete. If he, or *anyone* in my organization, is involved in *any* illegal activities, I swear on the lives of my children, I'll personally turn them over to the Bronx District Attorney—that satisfy you, Michael?"

I gaped at Gold. His normal MO was to answer any and all challenges with loud, obscenity-laced fits of rage. I hadn't expect him to be cooperative, act reasonably.

I glanced at the security team standing in a straight line outside Gold's office, noted that several more men had joined them, and decided not to push Gold any further.

"You'll keep me posted?" I said lamely. "Tell me what you find out?"

"Of course," Gold said and slapped me on the back. "Look, I've been thinking," he said. "You remember how ABC's been after me to do a TV series based on my casino? They wanna call it *Gold Plaza*—a *Love Boat* type show. Each week they'd have different guest stars play lovelorn gamblers who come to my casino and find adventure and true love. What do you think?"

"I always thought it was a great idea," I said.

"I told you, R. J.," Nagasue said. "Everyone loves romance."

We sat around Gold's office and spent the next ten minutes discussing the TV series, *Gold Plaza*—Gold did all the talking. Bottom line: he said that ABC was willing to finance the entire project *and* willing to grant him final script and cast approval.

"My opinion," Gold said, "which is the only one that counts—is: you've got the right look, Michael. And, lets face it, you wouldn't have been on *Law & Order* if you didn't have talent."

"Right look for what?" I said.

"I'd like to cast you as the casino manager," Gold said. "A pivotal co-starring role. Would you like that?"

"I'd love it—are you serious?"

"As a heart attack—of course, you'd have to quit the police department. That a problem?"

"Not in the least."

Norma came into the room and told Gold that the executives from Citibank were waiting in reception.

"I'll be right with them," Gold said.

That was my cue to exit. I rose from my chair. "Good seeing you again, Tomo." I shook Nagasue's hand.

"We'll finish talking about *Gold Plaza* on Saturday," Gold said, "at the Yankee game." He came out from behind his desk, again shook my hand again, and walked me to the door.

GOLD'S SMILE COLLAPSED the moment Beckett left the office.

"Get in here, Pete," Gold said.

"What was that all about?" Nagasue said.

"He's delusional." Gold looked up at a fiber optic surveillance thread. "Pete, I said, get in here."

"No, he's not," Nagasue said. "Make no mistake, if anyone in this organization is implicated in a criminal conspiracy, the consequences will be nothing short of catastrophic."

"What're you, a lawyer with ethics?"

Pete walked in. "Yes, Boss?"

Gold raised a hand to silence Pete. He did not wish to speak in front of Nagasue. "That's all for now," Gold said to Nagasue.

It took a moment for the dismissal, a slight, to sink in. Nagasue slammed his coffee cup down and stalked, red-faced, out of the room.

"You heard?" Gold said after Nagasue was out of earshot.

"Yes, sir," Pete said.

"Is it true?"

Pete shook his head. Except for the Taylor brothers debacle, he did his own dirty work. No one had ever seen him actually start a fire. "Beckett's bluffing."

"Did you forcibly evict anyone, Pete?"

"Only the Ortiz women," Pete said with a straight face.

"Don't bullshit me, Pete."

"Every single tenant, *except* the Ortiz woman, took the money and ran."

Gold looked at Pete for a long moment. He sat behind his desk, reached into a drawer, pulled out a form letter and slid it across to Pete. "Sign it."

"What is it?" Pete said.

"Your letter of resignation; a formality." Gold filled in Pete's full name and the date, then signed his own name at the bottom. "We'll need it on file in case this whole mess blows up in our faces."

"You saying that's a possibility?"

"Anything's possible." Gold used his teeth to tear off a hangnail, spat. "Even if Beckett got lucky, gets someone's ear, it should only be a matter of damage control."

Pete took a moment to let the implications of Gold's words sink in. "You know," Pete said, "it's a dangerous job, being a cop in this city."

"What's that supposed to mean?" Gold shot to his feet, began pacing. "I don't want Beckett hurt."

"He has to be neutralized."

"Destroy his credibility, then."

Pete mulled that one over. "We've got a dozen newspaper reporters on the payroll."

"No. That will take too long. I want that sanctimonious prick accused of 'official misconduct.' Or 'conduct unbecoming a police officer.' Something that will get him suspended from the police department immediately."

"I'll handle it." Pete headed for the door.

"Pete." Gold pointed to the letter of resignation.

Pete walked back to the desk, plucked a Mont Blanc pen from his suit jacket pocket, signed the letter and handed it back to Gold.

"And remember, I don't want Beckett hurt."

"No matter what?" Pete said.

"Unless absolutely necessary. He's a royal pain in the ass, but he's not the bad guy here."

"If he's not, who is?"

"We are, Pete." Gold picked at a hangnail. "I am loath to admit it. But we are."

# CHAPTER 29

I walked out of Gold's office, rode the elevator down to the atrium lobby, left Gold Tower and walked south en route to the *Law & Order* studio. Whether she liked it or not, I intended to have a tête-à-tête with Solana Ortiz.

I loosened my tie as I moved hurriedly through the humid air and pedestrian traffic along Fifth Avenue. I gawked at a group of fabulous-looking businesswomen as I hailed a yellow cab.

"Chelsea Piers," I told the driver. As we drove across West 57th Street, I mulled over my visit with R. J. Gold.

The only thing I learned was that Gold had gained some weight, he'd matured emotionally, learned to control his temper. Tomo Nagasue was still his CFO—the "alleged" pipeline to the Yakuza?—and that D'Amato had been right. I *was* holding a grudge. I resented the smug, controlling son of a bitch Gold more then I ever imagined.

Gold had summarily dumped me after our argument over my ex-girlfriend Janet. Spitefully cut me off from the high life which he'd introduced me to and to which I'd quickly grown accustomed. When Gold stopped phoning, the hangers-on who solicited my company merely because I was one of Gold's cronies also stopped phoning. The year-round torrent of invitations to café society affairs gradually stopped. I'd experienced a period of withdrawal, loss and hard feelings.

Yet now Gold was soliciting my friendship once again, offering to take me to sporting events, dinners, co-star me in a primetime TV project he controlled—which led me to believe that I'd stumbled onto something. Implicating Pete must've hit home. Gold must think I know more than I do. He thinks he can buy me off.

The cab stopped in front of the Chelsea Piers. I paid the driver, stepped out, and noticed a dark sedan motor by; the driver and passenger were the same two security guards I'd seen smoking cigarettes outside Gold Tower.

I walked into the TV studio's busy lobby, signed in with security, and made my way to the *Law & Order* sound stage. I moved down a long corridor, exchanged greetings with people I knew, and glanced into the wardrobe room. Solana's suitcase was on the floor alongside a sofa. She must have made her way to the studio last night, slept on the couch.

"Michael Beckett."

I turned and found myself face to face with one of *Law & Order*'s directors.

"You did a first-class job the other day," he said. "The rushes look good."

"Thanks," I said. "I appreciate that."

"We'll be seeing you," he said and moved on.

I watched the director walk away, wondering if the "we'll be seeing you" was just an expression or an assurance of work to come. I continued to the end of the corridor and stepped through a sound stage door.

The sound stage was alive with activity. I crossed as inconspicuously as I could; the thick-necked, ex-con teamster shot me a hard look. I returned the gesture.

I climbed the metal stairs and stopped just outside the

mezzanine production office. Through the glass partition I could see half a dozen production assistants scurrying about. Solana was seated at a computer, probably working on a script.

I knocked on the office door, opened it, stuck my head in. Several of the PAs glanced absently at me. One heavy-set girl, Tina Roe, winked and waved hello.

"Do you have a moment, Solana?" I said.

Solana looked up and did a double-take. Surprise and anger alternated on her face. Although I was gambling that she didn't want to make a scene, I had the distinct impression that she was about to tell me to go to hell, call security and have me thrown out.

"Go," Tina urged. "I'll cover the phones. Go."

Solana exchanged looks with Tina, then she pushed away from her desk, stood and walked toward me.

"Yes?" Solana crossed her arms across her chest, all attitude. "What is it you want?"

I stepped outside the office and held the door open for her. Reluctantly, she followed.

"What do you know about the fires?"

Solana shifted her weight, made a face, her expression a study in incredulity. "I think your friend Pete Costello is responsible."

"You think?" I wanted to tell her that Pete was not a friend but that could wait. "Any proof?"

"I saw him exit a building on East Bay Avenue," Solana said, "that burned to the ground a few minutes later."

I stopped myself from telling her how easily Pete could explain that away. Not only did he have the right to be on Gold property, but it would be her word against his. "All right. Anything else?"

Solana told me about some newspaper articles she'd discovered at the public library. About Pete's past association with organized crime. The fact he was once a murder suspect.

My jaw dropped.

"You didn't know?" Solana said.

I shook my head. "No, I didn't."

"You're a cop. How could you *not* know?" Solana turned to re-enter the office.

"One more thing," I said.

Solana stopped.

"Last night, after you left your building—"

Solana gasped. "My apartment?"

"I'm afraid there's nothing left."

Solana's eyes glazed over and she seemed to withdraw within herself. "I expected it," she said, "but I thought I had a few days—there were things I left behind, mementos."

"I'm sorry." I reached to console her.

"Don't," she said, pulling away, keeping me at arm's length.

"Hey!" the thick-necked teamster was watching us from the sound stage floor below. "He bothering you?"

Solana looked down at the teamster, looked at me. "No."

"You sure?" the teamster said.

Solana nodded.

I gave the teamster the finger.

Solana leaned against a wall. Tears appeared in her eyes and rolled down her cheek.

"Anything I can do?" I said.

She shook her head. "I'm so alone."

"Don't say that. You're not alone." Cautiously, I stroked her shoulder. This time she did not shrink away.

"I'm here for you," I said, all the while thinking about other things I wanted to say: *I'll protect you. I'm crazy about you.* But being close to her put my stomach in knots. And I knew this was not the time or place. "I mean it. I'm here if you need me."

Solana's dark eyes settled on my face. I saw a small smile curl at the corners of her mouth, and something like gratitude in her eyes.

"I don't know why," she said, "but I believe you."

"That's a start."

"Start to what?"

I couldn't stop what happened next—I leaned close and kissed her lightly on the lips. Her eyes locked on mine and she kissed me back.

I did my blushing best to hide the fact that, for a split second, my heart stopped beating. "Promise you'll call me if you need anything?" I said and thought I must've sounded like a lovesick teenager.

"I promise." Solana turned to re-enter the production office then stopped. "Oh, you know a Detective Doyle?"

"Sure."

"He knocked on my door last night," Solana said. "Tried to talk me into vacating my apartment."

"That makes sense, what with the gas leak."

"No." Solana shook her head. "Before the gas leak."

"Before—?"

"He was insistent. Offered to put me up in a hotel."

I have to admit I was puzzled. What was Doyle up to?

"There was someone with him," Solana said.

"Who?" I said.

"Your friend Pete."

"You saw Doyle with Pete?"

"Not exactly."

"I don't understand."

"Look, I know this will sound crazy—"

"Go on."

"I could smell him," Solana said. "Smell Pete's cologne."

SOLANA'S KISS LINGERED as I watched her enter the production office and walk over to her co-worker Tina's desk. Solana said something to Tina. Tina looked at me, smiled and gave me the thumbs-up sign. I waved appreciatively and climbed down to the sound stage floor.

I brushed roughly passed the thick-necked teamster,

my aggressiveness daring him to utter a fucking word—
he didn't.

I headed to a rear exit—giving the slip to the Gold Organization security men who were following me—thinking
about Detective Doyle. What was his connection to Pete
Costello? I took out my cell phone, and searched my phone
book for the number of a pal of mine who worked at the
NYPD's Organized Crime Control Bureau; OCCB.

# CHAPTER 30

As Vinnie D'Amato switched off an *I Love Lucy* rerun, a demon voice told him to kill his wife. He bounded from the plastic-covered sofa, and walked into his cluttered bedroom.

*The gun,* the voice said.

Atop the dresser, amid a pile of junk, he found his off-duty .38 revolver and picked it up.

*The gun,* the voice repeated. *Kill her.*

D'Amato lowered his weapon, pulled on a pair of worn blue jeans and a T-shirt bearing a likeness of the once majestic Twin Towers and went outside. He leapt from his back stoop, galloped across his brief, unkempt lawn, stepped over an array of rusting lawn tools, crept up behind Doreen and said:

"Repeat after me: 'The beast lives.'"

Doreen startled.

D'Amato hated the unconcerned roll of flab around her middle, the pink plastic curlers in her hair. She dared to ignore him and continue digging a hole in which to plant a rose bush, stepping on the long shovel head, using her ample weight to slice into the rocky earth.

"I ain't playin', loser," she said. "So get lost."

D'Amato gazed skyward. He opened his arms as if to importune a deity. "Whatever happened to the sweet girl I married?"

"You're kidding me." Doreen spoke as if to a halfwit. "Right?"

*Man, she was asking for it.*

"Down on your knees, sow," D'Amato said, knowing he could never do this to Catherine Zeta-Jones.

Doreen glowered at her husband.

"Start saying your prayers," he said.

That's when Doreen saw the gun in D'Amato's hand. Small. Black. Shiny. It was aimed at her stomach.

"On your knees—I won't say it again."

"OhmyGod." Doreen slipped to her knees. Sweat poured off of D'Amato's craggy face, dripped from his Pancho Villa mustache. For all his crazy stunts, he had never pointed a gun at his wife before.

D'Amato shielded his eyes against the blatant sun.

"Now turn around, pig wife. Away from the digging. Face the pile of shit you call a house and repeat after me: 'I, Doreen, wife of Vincent D'Amato, do make love to him with the enthusiasm of a drugged warthog.' "

She looked up at him. "You're scaring me."

D'Amato didn't understand these spoiled, militant feminists of today. Whenever his father, a retired police sergeant, pointed *his* gun at D'Amato's mother, she did exactly what she was told to do, no back talk.

He cocked the hammer. "Say it."

"Awright. Awright." Doreen repeated what D'Amato had instructed. "Now put the gun down, Vinnie."

"No, repeat after me." D'Amato's gun hand was unwavering. "They have murdered our lake. We, the D'Amatos, live in the Land of the Dead!"

"Please," Doreen said. "Stop."

"Prepare to die."

Doreen gasped and her mouth went dry.

"Whoa," D'Amato said and ducked to avoid a pair of aerobatic, backyard dragon flies. "Did you know that a dragonfly has a life span of twenty-four hours?"

"Yes," Doreen said. "No."

"That a goldfish has a memory span of three seconds?"

"What are you talking about?"

"It's impossible to sneeze with your eyes open. Did you know that?"

"You're not making sense," Doreen said.

"Dumb cow. Gimme one good reason why I shouldn't end your useless fucking life, right now."

"Our babies."

"Good one." D'Amato uncocked the .38, had second thoughts and re-cocked it. "Gimme another reason."

"Because I love you."

"Ha. Only thing you love is chocolate cheesecake."

"They'll take your guns away."

"What?"

"Your guns."

*That did it.*

Suddenly the demon voice was gone. What did she say? Take his guns? No. He would never allow them to take his guns.

*Never.*

D'Amato lowered his weapon, uncocked it, slipped it into his jeans pocket, turned his back on Doreen, cast his face to the heavens, and closed his eyes as if to absorb some sun.

Doreen struggled to her feet, picked up the shovel and, swinging it like a baseball bat, hit D'Amato "whap" across the top of the head. He fell face down on the lawn, bleeding.

# CHAPTER 31

Zeke Taylor couldn't help it. He hated cops. From the nose-picking tub-of-lard sheriff in Zeke's hometown of Tupelo, Mississippi, to the Hollywood slick New York City cops, to the rude court officers now leading him into the criminal courtroom, Zeke hated them all. And cops, it seemed, weren't too fond of Zeke either.

Zeke had spent most of last night feeling more hateful than a bobcat with his balls on fire. But because of the book he'd read in prison, *Think Positive*, he knew that hating cops—especially the ones who had murdered his sweet, innocent little brothers—was a negative emotion. So when he woke he was determined to turn that negative energy into positive action. And he was convinced that this morning's apparent run of good luck—he had just been informed that he was being released from jail—was due to that effort. Positive thinking was just plain infectious.

The court officers ushered Zeke past his arresting officer, Detective Doyle, and the assistant district attorney, to the defense table. There he was introduced to his Legal Aid lawyer—a chubby, yarmulke-wearing Jew that Zeke loathed on sight. The Jew said something to the judge. The judge said something to the ADA. Detective Doyle said something to the judge, who then told the ADA that he was wasting the court's time. Before Zeke knew it, his handcuffs were being removed by Detective Doyle.

"What's going on?" Zeke said to Doyle. "You really let-. tin' me go?"

"That I am," Doyle said and put away the cuffs.

"Cause I'm innocent?"

"No, Gomer," Doyle said. "Because I'm trying to make amends."

"Oh." Zeke thought about that. "Amends for what?"

"For the deaths of your two brothers."

Zeke's index finger homed into his nose clear up to the second knuckle. He hooked something, worked it out, and wiped it on his pants leg. "Say what?"

Doyle shivered with revulsion. "I withdrew the charges, Zeke," he said. "Told the judge that your gun did not have a firing pin. No law against carrying a replica." Doyle put his cuffs away. "I told him I was dropping the assault charges—it's my prerogative."

Zeke squinted at the cop, trying to figure what in the hell he was really up to.

"Move." Doyle escorted a reluctant Zeke out of the courtroom, down two floors, and out of the building to the top of the courthouse's cascading front steps. Zeke looked warily around the streets, wondering what would happen next.

"Do you have cab fare?" Doyle said.

Zeke said he was broke. That he gave his last few dollars to some fag in prison for, er, cigarettes.

"Here's cab fare," Doyle said, handing him $20. "No hard feelings, Zeke."

Zeke nodded in bewildered acknowledgment. Looked at the cash in his hand. He was truly being set free. And that fact filled him with righteous indignation.

"Twenty dollars," Zeke said. "That's it?"

"Correct."

"Who's gonna pay for my pain and suffering?"

"Surely," Doyle said, "you jest."

"Like hell, I do." Zeke folded his arms across his bony chest and decided to give this cop what-for. "Now look-e-here, de-tective." Zeke spoke the word with contempt. "I've been arrested enough times, seen enough episodes of *COPS* to know that *you* severely violated *my* civil rights. Police officers are suppose to frisk you, put the handcuffs on, read you your rights and cart you off to jail—thank-you very much. But you beat living hell out of me. Now, de-tective, what're you gonna do about that?"

Doyle twisted Zeke around and kicked him on the ass so hard he went airborne and cracked and scraped down the courthouse concrete steps.

A bunch of passing shackled prisoners and cops applauded. Pedestrians gasped in horror, thinking no one could survive such a violent, wrenching plunge.

A steady flow of commuters stepped around Zeke. A businesswoman cussed him for lying on the sidewalk and blocking her path. No one made a move to help.

Zeke lay dead still for a moment then stirred, one molecule at a time. He moved a finger, hand, arm, toe, foot, leg. After a few minutes he even managed to roll onto his back and struggle, unassisted, to his feet. Goes to show what positive thinking can do.

Zeke limped away from the courthouse and headed to the subway. He caught the uptown IRT subway and got out at Simpson Street in the South Bronx. He walked to Westchester Avenue and elbowed his way through a gaggle of two-dollar hookers congregating on the sidewalk in front of a flop called the Hot House Hotel. The Hot House was a Bronx brothel, drug den, the end of the world for some, and a place where those who didn't want to be found could always be found.

Zeke pushed through a set of splintery swinging doors

and the familiar stench of sour bodies came on strong. Home sweet home.

Zeke walked past the spic Chico—one of fat Tookie Jones's Stoners—and a middle-aged nigger couple screaming and beating one another.

"Yo, dawg." Tookie Jones waddled out of the lobby's cruddy lavatory, eating what looked like a Three Musketeers bar. "Sorry 'bout Bo and Bubba—mutha-fuckin' cops."

"Thanks," Zeke said. "Hell happened to you?" Zeke was eyeballing Tookie's painful-looking bandaged nose and two black eyes.

"Fuckin' cops, dawg." Tookie flopped onto a filthy couch—dust mites filled the air—and picked up a copy of a dog-eared magazine: *Rotund Ladies Exposed.* "I'm gonna kill me some cops one of these days," he said as he absently flipped the pages. "Just see if I don't."

"Uh-huh." Zeke strode away from Tookie, past the registration desk and the ancient, toothless hotel manager who sat behind filthy bullet-proof Plexiglas, his view obscured by a scrawled ROOMS BY THE HOUR sign.

Zeke moved to the rear of the hotel and up a set of rickety stairs. Arriving on the third floor, he pulled out a key, kicked away a scruffy affectionate tomcat, and unlocked the door to room 311.

The room reeked of his brothers—that is, stale booze, crusty underwear and sweat-sodden socks. Zeke glanced around the dark, sparse pigsty and a tear welled in his eyes.

Since their parents were both killed in a crack-cocaine-and-Jack-Daniel's-fueled trailer park fire, Zeke had practically raised Bo and Bubba between stints in prison. And he could picture those little rascals, wrassling each other, gouging each other's eyes like they always did, on the never-been-made bed, just like when they were kids.

Zeke turned on a light. Roaches scattered. He threw a window open and switched on an insignificant, squeaky window fan. He pulled a cold beer from the corroded mini fridge, opened it, was drinking it down in one long pull when the phone rang.

Zeke let out a stomach-draining belch, then picked up the phone. "Good morning," he said cheerfully, remembering that positive, congenial phone manners were important in today's world.

"How'd you like the name of the cop responsible for killing your brothers?" a man's voice said on the phone.

Zeke's blood hardened. He swallowed the last drop of beer and crushed the can. "Who is this?"

"Saddam Hussein," Pete from Queens said.

"What's the catch, Mr. Hussein?"

*Unbelievable.* "The information's gonna cost you."

"How much?"

"Five thousand dollars."

"Now, where in the hell you expect me to get that kind of money?"

"You knock over the Chung King Check Cashing store at Hoe Avenue and Aldus Street in the Bronx, at about five P.M. today."

"Do tell."

"It's welfare check day. They'll be about ten thousand cash in the vault, maybe more."

"Then you'll give me the cop's name?"

"Count on it."

"Keep talking."

"Go to your room door. Open it up."

"My room door?" Zeke said. "What fer?"

"Just do it."

Zeke did as instructed, chinned the phone, opened the door to 311, found a plastic bag hanging outside on the door knob.

"In the bag is a fake detective shield," Pete said.

Zeke opened the bag, saw the shield.

"Use that to gain entrance to the check cashing store's back room."

"Use it, how?"

"Tell them you're a cop, stupid. That you're investigating a robbery, something like that."

"Uh, uh." Zeke closed and locked the door. "How do I get you your share?"

"I'll find you," Pete said and hung up.

Zeke placed the phone back on the hook, then let out a rebel yell—what a day he was having. He'd been released from jail, told where to steal a whole load of money, and soon he'd be face to face with the cop who killed his brothers. Thank you, *Think Positive*.

Zeke reached under the bed and dragged out a rolled-up blanket. He shook it out and a shotgun and two handguns thudded to the floor. He picked up an open bottle of Jack Daniel's, drank to his dearly departed brothers and thought about the Chung King Check Cashing store. He was familiar with the establishment. It was run by a nasty band of slanty-eyed, sneaky yellow devils—Chinks, Japs or some such godless race—too dangerous a place to try robbing on his own.

Zeke took another swig of booze and recalled that Tookie Jones was hanging out in the lobby. Maybe he and his gang would be available as backup.

Zeke picked up the shotgun and checked that it was loaded. Then he chose the handguns, loaded them with Teflon ammunition, which was sometimes referred to as "cop killer ammo" because of its ability to penetrate a cop's bulletproof vest.

# CHAPTER 32

A rust-bucket Ford pulled onto Aldus Street, made a right onto Hoe Avenue and stopped in front of the Chung King Check Cashing store.

"Let's just sit and wait a few minutes," Zeke, behind the wheel said. "See what we can see." He switched off the engine.

"It's hot, dawg," Tookie Jones, seated in the passenger seat whined. The fat gang leader was sweating profusely. "Fuck're you killing the air conditioner for?"

Chico, in the back seat said, "A cop sees a car idling in front of a check cashing store, we be asking for trouble."

Having read in *Think Positive* that complimenting others was a sure-fire way to make friends and build loyalties, Zeke was quick to dole out praise. "You're pretty smart, Chico," Zeke said, "for a Spic." He used the car battery to power down the windows and warm, sticky air flooded the car.

After a moment Tookie said, "We gonna do this, dawg, or what?"

Zeke scanned the street, sidewalks and faces of the multi-national emigrants that populated Hoe Avenue. He did not see any plainclothes cops, cop cars or cops on foot patrol.

Zeke racked a round into his shotgun, and rolled it in a newspaper.

"Me and Tookie're goin' in," Zeke said. "You get'yer Spic ass up here in front, Chico. You gonna drive."

"Awright," Chico said.

"Let's do it." Tookie said.

Zeke and Tookie eased out of the Ford and moseyed over to the check-cashing store. Chico climbed over the seats and settled behind the steering wheel.

Zeke peered into the store through a plate-glass window. It was a narrow room, about twenty-feet in length, lit by fluorescent lights. There were three people waiting on a line. A wino and two fat, fifty-something women each sipping a sixteen-ounce beer in brown paper bags. At the far end, behind what looked like a reinforced steel wall and bullet-proof Plexiglas, were two employees, hard-looking, slanty-eyed yellow men. One was busy at a computer. The other man was at the counter, apparently cashing an old woman's check.

A security buzzer sounded as Zeke and Tookie entered, but the yellow men did not bother to check who'd come in. Tookie took a spot at the end of the line. Zeke stepped to the front and knocked on the Plexiglas window.

When the clerk looked up, Zeke pressed the fake detective shield against the glass and gestured for the yellow men to open the steel security door.

"Po-lice. Gotta use the bathroom," Zeke said, all smiles.

But the yellow men shook their heads.

"C'mon," Zeke pleaded, hopping from foot to foot, turning on the charm and his dark powers of positive thinking. "I really gotta pee."

The yellow men were adamant. "Go away," the taller of the two said. "No pee here. Go."

"Police," Zeke screamed, brandishing the shield, losing patience. "Open the god-damned door. And I mean, now."

"No. You go." The taller man picked up a telephone and said. "You go now, or I call 911."

At that precise moment the front door buzzer sounded. A third yellow man entered the store, walked over to the security door, stood by Zeke with a set of keys in his hand.

# CHAPTER 33

Something was wrong with D'Amato.

He barely spoke to anyone during roll call. He made no cat calls, fart noises, or wisecracks. And as we settled into our RMP, tossed our memo books on the dash and positioned our nightstick, I noticed that he kept his hat on— he never kept his hat on especially in summer. He was sullen, withdrawn.

*"Central to all units. Holding 118 jobs in the 41 precinct. I repeat, holding 118 jobs in the 41 precinct. Any 4 to 12 units available?"*

I picked up the radio. "41 Ida available."

*"Ida, 10-34, assault in progress, 231 Whitlock Avenue."*

"How old is that job?" I said.

*"Three hours old,"* Central said.

I almost laughed; there was no chance that the assault was still in progress, or that the assailants would wait three hours for the police to arrive to arrest them. "10-4," I said and replaced the radio.

D'Amato started the engine and pulled from the curb.

I was planning to tell him about my earlier visit to Gold Tower and my conversation with Solana Ortiz—the fact that she made provocative statements regarding Pete and

Doyle. But because of his foul mood I thought better of it. He'd probably fly off the handle, accuse me of leaving him out of the loop, jeopardizing his police career, operating like the Lone fucking Ranger.

"Let's locate Tookie Jones after this job," I said.

D'Amato shook his head, his sour expression said we were wasting our time. Maybe he was right. Tookie had to know we'd be looking for him. There's no way he'd be dumb enough to hang around—then again, Tookie was no brainiac.

My cell phone rang. "Yes?"

"Hey, ferret face," my pal from the NYPD's OCCB unit said. "I got the lowdown on Pete—'Pete from Queens'—Costello."

"I'm listening."

"Haven't got much," the cop said. "Pete was involved with a Queens loan shark after he was honorably discharged from the service. He was a suspect in a hit for hire; guy named Mario Vitelli. No body was ever found. A Detective Doyle handled the investigation."

*Doyle.* So there was a direct connection.

The OCCB cop continued. "The case went cold. Nothing on Pete since. He's been off the radar crime-wise. Far as I can tell, he's gone straight—if you believe those guys ever go straight, I've got a bridge in Brooklyn I wanna sell you."

I thanked my pal, told him I owed him dinner and hung up.

D'Amato did not ask who I'd spoken to, made no comment. And maybe that was just as well. The way things were going, it would probably be better if I left my soon to be ex-partner out of the arson investigation.

D'Amato made a right, slowed in heavy traffic, and let out a deep, heartfelt sigh.

"You all right?" I said.

D'Amato changed lanes, hit the gas, made another right.

"Doreen left me." He took off his hat: a bloody bandage was taped to the top of his head. Judging from the size of the bandage, I'd guess he'd gotten at least ten stitches.

"Left you?" I wasn't sure I understood. "You mean—?"

D'Amato nodded. "Took the girls."

"Christ. I'm sorry, Vinnie."

"Yeah. Thanks."

"Hell happened?"

"We had a fight. You know, one of those silly little marital spats." D'Amato touched his bandaged head, cringed from the pain. "She flipped out. Hit me with a shovel when I wasn't looking. When I came to, she was gone."

"Hit you? With a *shovel*?" I'd known Doreen longer than D'Amato had known her and I liked her. Although, as she was the daughter of a tough as nails retired cop, the only way I could rationalize her tolerating D'Amato's crazy antics was to assume that she'd learned how to handle macho cops from her mother. And she must be a masochist and/or a bit crazy herself.

"I didn't go home the other night when we were at J.G. Melon," D'Amato volunteered. "Doreen had a problem with that."

"No sense of humor," I said. "Well, where'd you sleep?"

"Mona Love's."

I did a double-take. "You nuts?"

D'Amato snapped around and glared at me. "Now the TV star's an expert on women?"

"She's a convicted felon, for Christ sake."

"Do me a favor, big shot, mind your own fucking business."

I looked to see if D'Amato was even half-kidding. He wasn't. "You know, Vinnie, I've had it with your lousy fucking attitude."

"Yeah? We'll I've had it with you."

"*41 Ida*," Central said. "*41 Ida*."

I grabbed the radio. "41 Ida."

*"Ida, disregard 231 Whitlock Avenue. 10-85 Captain Ward, Aldus and Hoe, that's Aldus and Hoe, 10-85 Captain Ward."*

D'Amato looked at me.

*What was this about?* Being called to meet a precinct captain outside the stationhouse was fairly unusual—unless he had discovered a serious condition, like gambling or drug dealing in the open in our sector.

*"41 Ida, you copy? 41 Ida?"*

"10-4, we copy, Central," I said. "On the way."

"That bitch." D'Amato slammed a fist on the steering wheel. "That crazy fucking bitch."

"Who?" I said.

"Doreen. I'll bet anything she called the captain. She's pressing charges against me."

"Why? What'd you do?"

"Nothing," D'Amato said. "I did nothing."

*Boom.*

The first, distant thundering shotgun blast startled me.

Two more shots caused everyone on the street to stop, fall silent, and look toward the source of the gunfire, Hoe Avenue.

"Oh boy," D'Amato said, suddenly alert, happy, a kid at Christmas. "A gunfight."

I grabbed the radio. "41 Ida. We have shots fired on Hoe Avenue. That's shots fired." My transmission collided with several other transmitting units; the airwaves were clogged.

I reached to hit the siren and D'Amato slapped my hand away. "No siren," he effused. "We'll surprise the fuckers."

I didn't argue. "Central," I tried again. "We have shots fired. That's shots fired somewhere around Aldus and Hoe."

*"10-4, 41 Ida,"* Central said. *"Any units available to backup 41 Ida?"*

D'Amato honked the horn at a double-parked van. The

van eased to the right allowing us barely enough space to inch by.

"Central," I said, "41 Ida requesting backup."

"*No units available*," Central said.

I pulled my Glock, clicked off the safety as D'Amato cleared the van and slammed down the accelerator.

An Asian man staggered out of the Chung King Check Cashing store into the middle of the street and collapsed. D'Amato had to stand on the brakes to avoid running over him. I let my door fly and was out of the car practically before it stopped, eyes everywhere, gun ready. I knelt beside the Asian man, turned him over. There was a bloody mess where his stomach used to be.

D'Amato was at my back, gun extended in both hands, crouched in a combat position. Bystanders watched us from windows, doorways and alleys. Any one of them could be the shooter.

D'Amato trained his weapon at the Chung King Check Cashing store, then on a man standing in a bodega entrance. The guy raised his hands, shook his head. Sensing movement D'Amato pivoted and pointed at a woman behind a car. His finger was on the trigger, always on the trigger.

The Asian man said, "My brothers." He gestured to the check-cashing store. "Both dead."

"Who did it?" I said.

"Two men in a brown Ford."

"A brown Ford?"

The man nodded.

"A brown Ford, Vinnie," I said.

D'Amato's eyes swept north, then south.

"Crazy men," the Asian man wheezed. "No reason to shoot. We gave money," he said and died.

"I see it!" D'Amato yelled. "Moving south on Hoe Avenue."

He holstered his .38, jumped in the RMP and gunned the engine. "C'mon, Beckett."

I used my thumb and forefinger to close the dead man's eyes. Then dragged his body to the curb—knowing I'd catch hell for disturbing the crime scene later—and stepped into the RMP.

D'Amato hit the gas.

I checked my weapon, took a deep breath, psyched myself, prepared for what we were about to do, confront armed robbers who had already demonstrated their willingness to kill for no reason.

I looked at D'Amato. There was no logical reason, but at times like this I'd rather be with him than any cop on earth.

"There." D'Amato was pointing straight ahead. The brown Ford was about half a block away. "They're gonna get stuck behind that garbage truck."

"Let's take 'em, while we can," I said.

D'Amato eased the RMP to a stop.

I picked up the radio. "41 Ida to Central. 10-13. Hoe Avenue just south of Aldus Street. 10-13."

We didn't wait for a response. We slid out of the RMP and approached the armed robber's car from the rear, a textbook approach that all cops are taught at the Police Academy. I advanced from the right, passenger side. D'Amato on the left. Our guns were extended. Combat ready.

## CHAPTER 34

"A fuckin' garbage truck?" Zeke in the back seat said.

"God hates me," Tookie in the passenger seat said.

Chico, behind the wheel muttered, "He ain't the only one."

"Say what?" Tookie said.

Chico shook his head.

The brown Ford slowed to a stop behind every motorist's nightmare: a monster Department of Sanitation garbage truck making pickups. Hoe Avenue, a narrow one-way street, was blocked.

Chico put the car in reverse, tried to back up; a line of cars was stopping him. He put the Ford in park. Leaned on the horn. Cursed the garbage truck driver.

The truck driver ignored him. Two other garbage men went about their business at a snail's pace, picking up garbage, tossing it into the back of the large white truck.

Zeke noted that every tenement had piles of garbage stacked curbside. At this rate they'd be sitting behind that truck another twenty minutes, maybe longer. Zeke was feeling like a yoked steer in a slaughterhouse. And he didn't like it one bit.

"Now what?" Chico said.

"Use that police shield, Zeke," Tookie said. "Order 'em to move the fucking truck."

"No," Chico said. "They could ID us later."

"Dammit, Chico," Zeke said. "You *are* one smart spic."

Zeke took a moment to muster up his dark powers of positive thinking, and came up with, what he considered, yet another brilliant plan. "We gonna leave the car," Zeke said. "Go it on foot."

"What about fingerprints?" Tookie said.

"In the glove compartment," Zeke said. "Napkins."

Tookie popped the glove compartment, found a pile of Dairy Queen napkins, handed some to Chico and Zeke and they began wiping down the Ford's interior.

Behind the Ford cars honked their horns. Zeke glanced out the rear window. Thought he saw a blue uniform, then another.

"What was that you was sayin', Tookie, 'bout wanting to kill you some cops?"

"What 'bout it?" Tookie said.

"Here comes your chance."

# CHAPTER 35

The next thing I knew, someone in the Ford's passenger seat fired at me. I heard two shots. Saw the barrel flash. Thought I was hit. I felt a horrible pressure in my right ear. Time stood still—instinct took over. I veered left. The Glock in my hand bucked out five shots as fast as I could pull the trigger.

The first two rounds shattered the passenger's face. His body went rigid. He was already dead by the time the ensuing shots tore into his skull. He slumped against the dashboard.

The driver fired at me. The shots hit the car door frame.

I blasted away. Two rounds tore into him. Blood spewed forth from his neck and chest. D'Amato, meanwhile, was busy emptying his own gun into the driver and passenger.

I sensed someone in the back seat. When I looked, I found myself staring down the barrel of a twelve-gauge shotgun. I fired a bullet into the guy's chest. D'Amato pumped another into his arm. The guy convulsed. His head snapped violently back. He dropped the shotgun. But the guy fought death. He pulled a backup gun. I ducked. The guy lost sight of me.

D'Amato ducked.

I jumped up. Unloaded more rounds into the back seat.

D'Amato shot the guy at least three more times. The gunman slumped forward against the front seats and stopped moving.

Silence. It pounded in our ears but we knew better than to trust the silence. We spun, guns ready, searching for a possible accomplice who would shoot us in the back. We pivoted in a series of crouching 360-degree turns, aiming at doorways, rooftops, behind cars. But there was no one.

As the acrid stench of spent gunpowder filled the thick summer air, we flung the car doors open, yanked the two men from the front seats and threw them on the ground like bags of garbage.

"Well, we found Tookie Jones," I said.

"I got his pal, Chico, over here."

A crowd began to gather.

We opened the back door and looked at what was left of the gunman with the shotgun. Blood flowed from his eyes and mouth.

"I know this guy," I said.

D'Amato grabbed him by the T-shirt, studied his face, and then threw him onto the street. "Ain't this the guy Doyle locked up? He was in the precinct holding cage. Zeke something?"

It was difficult to tell with half his face blown away.

"Yeah," I said. "I think that's him."

That's when I spotted a canvas bag on the back seat floor board. I picked it up and looked inside. "Money, partner." I pulled out a fistful of cash.

"Hey, look at this." D'Amato held up a gold detective's shield. "Good copy."

Sirens filled the air, drawing ever closer. All at once police cars and cops on foot overwhelmed Hoe Avenue.

After confirming that we were not injured, a patrol sergeant took control of the crowds. He ordered a sector car to drive to the Chung King Check Cashing store and secure it for the detectives and lab boys. He used a radio to notify the 4–12 tour's Eighth Division duty captain who would notify the Bronx Borough Commander, who would notify the Chief of Patrol, who would notify the Police Commissioner, who would notify the Mayor.

An ambulance showed up and the robbers were officially pronounced DOA. A squad of robbery/homicide detectives materialized and began interviewing people in an effort to locate eyewitnesses.

We were relieved and driven to the 41st stationhouse. While en route I realized that I felt light-headed and was having trouble understanding anyone who spoke to me. Knew from experience that I was suffering from some form of shock.

We walked into the station and were greeted by a standing ovation. D'Amato took bows and held up Zeke's shotgun like a trophy. He was smiling ear to ear, his shirt unbuttoned to reveal his almost hairy chest, his sleeves rolled up around his almost muscular arms, his gun low, gunslinger style.

As I handed the bag of money to the desk officer, I noticed that, for the second time in three days, my hands were caked with blood.

CHAPTER 36

The remainder of the 4–12 tour passed in a detached haze.

After being gawked at, applauded, and queried by dozens of curious, sympathetic and/or ghoulish cops and department civilian employees, we were intercepted by the 41 Precinct union representative and sequestered in the sitting room. Our union rep, a concerned Irishman, gave us the same sage advice he gave all cops after shooting incidents: recommended that we report without delay for stress-related sick report and to refuse to answer any questions without the presence of legal representation.

"After the Black Cat Social Club incident," the union rep said, "the politicians might wanna hang you two. They'll be looking for something, anything. A lapse in police procedure, for instance."

"There was none," D'Amato said.

"That's a matter of interpretation," the union rep said. "The brass will see what they're told to see."

"But we've got nothing to hide," D'Amato said. "The perps fired on us first."

"Do what you want, D'Amato," the union rep said. "You

always do. But at least heed this: Do not, and I repeat, do *not* speak to anyone from the media."

D'Amato, who saw the gun battle as a surefire path to fame and fortune and who had every intention of granting interviews to any and all reporters, said, "Why not?"

The union rep switched on the sitting room TV.

A scrubbed female reporter standing at the shooting scene said: "Citizens of the South Bronx got a taste this evening of what it must have been like to witness the infamous shootout at the O.K. Corral—"

D'Amato applauded.

The union rep switched channels.

"It was murder," the Reverend Al Dullard exulted to camera. "The po-lice done shot those three helpless children for nothing."

"Bullshit," D'Amato exploded.

Again the union rep changed channels.

"They never had a chance," a well-spoken Hispanic woman who had the polarizing tone of a pseudo-community activist said to a reporter. "The police did not identify themselves. They marched up to that car and executed those poor boys. They never had a chance."

I was stunned.

"Since when does a uniformed cop have to identify himself?" D'Amato said to no one in particular. "Fuck is the uniform for?"

"Look, the truth always comes out in the end." The union rep clicked off the TV. "But until then, do not under any circumstances, speak to reporters." He looked at us. "Questions?"

We told him no.

The union rep said he'd stay around in case he was needed, then left us to our mountain of paperwork. With the clerical man Neary's help, we confirmed the identification of the three robbers and wrote the arrest reports—it was then that we discovered that the guy with the shotgun was Zeke Taylor, the brother of the dead arsonists, Bo and Bubba Taylor.

"That solves the Coster Street fire mystery," D'Amato said.

"You think so?"

"Ain't it obvious?" D'Amato said. "Tookie was partners with the Taylor brothers. He must've hired Bo and Bubba to start the fire. No one's gonna convince me otherwise. Case closed."

We attached supplemental UF #49 reports which detailed every aspect of the shooting. Vouchered the robbers' guns and the stolen money, bill by bill. Recorded every serial number, all $3,300 in singles, five, tens and twenties.

Having decided not to go on sick report and to submit to department interrogation without the benefit of counsel—we felt we indeed had nothing to hide—we were separated and interviewed by the Bronx Borough duty captain—a crusty veteran—and a disconcertingly youthful assistant district attorney.

I recounted the incident. A stenographer recorded every word. The duty captain and ADA listened intently, asked only questions that pertained to the actual gun battle. At the time they did not seem concerned by the fact that the radio airwaves were jammed—it did happen occasionally—that a replica NYPD detective's shield was found on one of the perpetrators, or the fact that Captain Ward could not have given us a 10-85. Captain Ward, it turned out, was not working that evening. Which meant D'Amato and I were lured to Aldus and Hoe.

We finished our interviews, which seemed to go smoothly, and were told to report for tomorrow's day tour for reassignment to desk duty, and to schedule sessions with the NYPD psychiatrist: SOP for officers involved in shootings.

"How do you feel?" D'Amato said after we'd changed into civilian clothes and were exiting the station house.

"Numb."

"No kidding?" D'Amato considered that. "Every time I think about it, picture those skells lying in that car with their brains blown out, I wanna kill them all over again." D'Amato's eyes were wild. "You know what I mean?"

I looked at my partner; he was spewing macho bullshit, as usual. "You sure you're feeling all right?"

"Fan-fuckin'-tastic," D'Amato said.

"You wanna crash at my place, or what?"

"Hell no," D'Amato said, unlocking and sliding in behind the wheel of his car. "I've got a hot date with Mona Love. She's got a friend. Wanna join us?"

"I'll pass."

"Your loss." D'Amato started the engine, revved it once, but did not drive away. "We were good tonight. Weren't we?"

"We're alive," I said.

D'Amato sat there, bobbed his head like he was about to say something, maybe open up, show some emotion, but he didn't.

"See you tomorrow," he said and put the car in drive. I flagged down a passing RMP and convinced the cops— the promise of a six-pack of beer goes a long way—into giving me a ride home.

I walked into my East 77th Street apartment, carrying a handful of junk mail and bills, around two A.M. I switched on the lights and air conditioner, checked my caller ID. There were calls from my parents and sister Shannon, a few friends, and other cops, but I didn't feel like listening to the messages, and it was too late to call people back.

I shit-canned the junk mail, scanned the bills, kicked off my shoes, reached into a kitchen cabinet, took out a Waterford Crystal shot glass and a bottle of twenty-five-year-old, single malt Irish whiskey—I was too wound up to sleep.

I switched on the TV, poured myself a shot, drank it down. I realized that I felt lightheaded, again. I looked at myself in a living room mirror: I was pale, drawn. I sat on the couch, dropped my face into my hands, and saw dream-like visions of the men we'd killed—the entire nightmare played back in slow motion. I saw things that had not registered before.

Tookie took my first round in the face, head thrown back in a shriek, his hand pressed to the wound like he'd been stung by a hornet—there was something childlike, even endearing in his pained expression. The second round caused him to convulse. He went rigid as I turned my weapon on the others. . . .

My phone rang. I checked my caller ID. It was a cell phone number I didn't recognize.

"Hello?"

"Hi, Michael," Solana said. "I know it's late. I don't mean to bother you."

"No, that all right."

"I saw it on the news, the shooting I mean." Solana paused, seemed not to know what else to say. "I just wanted to see if you were all right."

"I'm fine."

"The car looked all shot up on TV. There was blood—"

"It all went down so fast, I'm not even sure I remember everything that happened."

"If there's anything I can do, Michael. I mean if you just want to talk."

"I appreciate that."

"You promised to be there for me."

"I meant it." I wasn't sure why, but I didn't feel like talking, not even to Solana. "I have to go, Solana. I'll call you tomorrow."

"Bye, Michael."

I hung up, stripped off my clothes and got under the covers. I lay there in the safety of the cool darkness, stared out the window, and listened to the hum of the air conditioner.

# CHAPTER 37

I couldn't sleep. I kicked aside sweaty, tortured sheets and rolled out of bed around six A.M. I made a pot of coffee and then hit the play button on my answering machine. After listening to concerned messages from my family and a half-dozen cops, followed by a death threat for "gunning down three innocent children," I took a shower and got ready for work.

As a I walked into the 41 Precinct, a cop rushed to shake my hand. Other cops stopped to ask me about the shooting. With all the distractions, I barely got into uniform and down to roll call on time.

I never noticed the brown paper bag at the bottom rear of my locker. Nor did I pay much attention to the squat bald man in a suit who entered the locker room as I walked out.

Roll call was chaos with D'Amato taking center stage, working to shake hands with all fifty men assigned to the day tour. He flitted about the sitting room recounting the shootout, laughing about blowing one of the perp's faces off. Taking bow after bow. Acting like he was running for public office, the killings were his *Law & Order* platform, something to brag about, be proud of.

I didn't feel proud.

The sergeant moved to the podium and called the roll.

D'Amato sat next to me and spoke in a whisper. "Can you believe all this attention?" He was beaming. "You know, I'm thinking of writing a book about the shooting. Maybe a movie script."

"Why don't you shut the fuck up," I said.

D'Amato reared back. "Hell's your problem?"

I gave him a look, started to speak, then thought better of it; D'Amato simply didn't get it. I got up and moved to another seat across the room.

"Beckett. D'Amato," the sergeant said. "I know I speak for everyone here when I say I'm glad it's those three skells lying on slabs in the morgue and not the other way around. Thank God you're safe."

The room erupted into applause.

"Okay, men, quiet down. One last thing." The sergeant referred to a clipboard. "Last night a homeless man sleeping on an abandoned pier out in Hunts Point was attacked and nearly torn apart by a pack of wild dogs, apparently led by a black Rottweiler."

I listened up—a Rottweiler. The one-eyed dog with the scab on his head, Lobo, was a Rottweiler.

"For the benefit of any new men and rookies," the sergeant said. "Over fifty percent of the shootings that take place here in the 41 involve dogs."

The cops in the rows behind me began growling, yelping and barking. One got down on his hands and knees and nipped a shirking policewoman on the ankle.

"Where they come from?" a rookie shouted over the mayhem. The sergeant waited a moment before motioning for everyone in the room to quiet down.

"Some were bought by local residents as protection against street crime and burglars," the sergeant said. "God knows, up here they need it." There were nods and murmurs of agreement.

"But most were acquired to guard illegal drug labs. Many of those dogs have had their voice boxes removed so they don't bark. They attack without warning. Right D'Amato?"

"Right." D'Amato jumped to his feet, rolled up a pant leg and proudly displayed a ragged scar on his left calf: a dog bite.

"We never saw the dog coming," D'Amato said. "A German Shepherd mix—didn't hear him. Right, Beckett?"

I gave the thumbs up.

"Those dogs are specifically trained to attack anyone in a police uniform," the sergeant said. "Remember that."

"But how do they wind up on the streets?" the rookie said.

"A family gets burned out," the sergeant said. "Or an animal gets too dangerous for the drug dealers to handle, they turn it loose. The ASPCA does a sweep of the deserted piers out in Hunts Point where the dogs congregate, but with all the budget cuts. . . ."

Mumbling around the room.

The sergeant spoke louder to be heard over the chatter. "The dogs are territorial, so use caution during confrontations." He glanced at his clipboard and, deciding there was nothing else, put it aside. "Any questions?"

There were none.

"Beckett and D'Amato," the sergeant said. "Report to the captain's office. The rest of you men, take your posts."

I KNOCKED AND entered Captain Ward's office with D'Amato in tow. The captain, his river-otter toupee askew, was sitting behind a rusty tin desk that he dwarfed. A set of bolt cutters and a brown paper bag were laid out in front of him. A bald, squat, pleasant-looking man about forty, in a dark suit, was seated by the window. The same guy I'd seen a few minutes ago up in the locker room. Ward gestured for us to take seats.

"You men alright?" Ward said.

We said that we were.

"Need anything?"

"Not a thing," I said. "Thanks."

Ward's eyes went to the brown paper bag on his desk. "Lieutenant Slotkin wants to ask you a few questions."

"I'm with Internal Affairs," Slotkin said amiably.

D'Amato and I exchanged wary glances.

Since cops from the Internal Affairs Bureau were frequently rogue cops who'd been arrested, turned state's evidence against other cops, and then been assigned to IAB—the department's logic being, "it takes a crooked cop to catch a crooked cop"—we knew to be careful; something was up.

"Who recovered the money from the robbery last night?" Slotkin said.

"I confess, Lieutenant." D'Amato pointed at me, a wiseass grin on his face. "He did it."

"My name's on the voucher," I said.

"How much was recovered?" Slotkin said.

"$3,300," I said.

Slotkin arched an eyebrow. "You're certain?"

"Yeah," I said. "I'm certain."

"Well, then," Slotkin stood, walked across the room and sat on the edge of the captain's desk. "We have a problem."

I said nothing, waiting for him to get to it.

"The main office of the Chung King Check Cashing store stated their Hoe Avenue location computer records indicate that there was more than $10,000 in the store at the time of the robbery. You recovered $3,300. That means $6,700 is missing. Can either of you men help me out here?"

I shook my head.

"Their computers are wrong," D'Amato said.

Slotkin dropped the brown paper bag onto my lap. "Mind explaining how that got in your locker?"

I looked at the bag bewildered and opened it. "Money." I pulled out a stack of cash.

"$6,700," Slotkin said. "Where'd you get it?"

"You found this in my locker?" I was flabbergasted.

"I did."

I looked at the cash in my hand. "I can't explain it."

"All right." Slotkin took a few strategic beats before speaking. "Tell me what I'm suppose to think, Officer. There's $6,700 missing from the robbery. I find $6,700 in your locker that you can't explain."

"Why look in my locker in the first place?"

"They got a tip this morning at IAB," Captain Ward said, rolling his eyes. "Anonymous."

"It's a setup," I said.

"Fine—who'd set you up?"

Slotkin, Ward, and even D'Amato looked at me.

For the moment I was at a loss.

"Juan Langlois?" D'Amato said.

"Who?" Slotkin said.

"Juan Langlois," Ward said. "A level-3 sexual predator and drug dealer Beckett collared. He told a reporter Beckett set him up. Swore revenge. It was in the newspapers."

Slotkin made a note. "Anyone else?"

There were killers, armed robbers, burglars, and other drug dealers I'd arrested during the last ten years who'd threatened retaliation—it went with being a cop. But most of them were posturing, trying to make points with fellow criminals. None of them had the brains or clout to pull off a setup this good.

"I want a lawyer," I said.

Slotkin took the money and the paper bag back from me.

"Officers Beckett and D'Amato," he said, "you are hereby notified that you are the subjects of an official Internal Affairs investigation. General Order #15 is in effect. As you both know, General Order #15 waives prosecution in exchange for cooperation. With that in mind, is there anything either of you wants to say?"

D'Amato and I sat in silence, dumbfounded.

"Fine," Slotkin said. "You are both suspended. Turn in your guns and shields to the captain."

"Me?" D'Amato came out of his chair. "Suspended for what?"

"You will both report to IAB headquarters tomorrow for an inquest," Slotkin said. "Beckett, you be there at nine. D'Amato be there at ten. I advise you to be accompanied by legal representation."

"This is bullshit," D'Amato roared.

"Don't say another word," the captain said.

I rose awkwardly with anger, placed my service gun and shield on Captain Ward's desk, turned and left the office.

"Now what am I gonna do?" D'Amato said as we exited. "Wait tables? Tend bar? Being a cop's my life."

"We're suspended," I said, lowering my voice. "Not fired. Besides, they didn't find the money in *your* locker."

"Those scumbags at IAB take you down, I'm part of the package. You know it. I know it."

"I won't let that happen, Vinnie."

"Yeah? How you gonna prevent it?"

I had no answer.

"The money," D'Amato said. "You think it was Juan?"

I shook my head. "Hell, no."

"So how'd it get there?"

I took a deep breath. "You'd better sit down."

CHAPTER 38

We found two seats in the corner of the sitting room
and I told D'Amato everything I'd found out from
Solana; Pete being at the scene of an East Bay Avenue arson, his criminal history and his connection to Doyle. I
saved the best for last.

"I went to visit R. J. Gold yesterday. Tried to bluff him,
implicated Pete in the South Bronx arsons."

"Great," D'Amato shot to his feet. "That's just fucking
great."

"When I left a couple of Gold security men followed
me—I guess I hit a nerve."

"You couldn't leave well enough alone, could you."
D'Amato kicked the chair he'd been sitting on, it skidded
across the room. "I thought we had an agreement, let the
system work."

"I didn't agree to anything."

"No, you self-serving asshole, you didn't."

"Fuck you." I walked away from D'Amato. Took the
stairs three at a time, entered the empty locker room and
made my way to my locker. The combination lock that
Lieutenant Slotkin had cut still hung on the door.
Yellow-crime scene tape crisscrossed my locker. I tore it

away, opened the locker, and carefully inspected the interior.

I pulled out the leather satchel, pushed against the lower rear tin panel—it was loose. I inspected the locker room floor for signs that the locker had been moved—it hadn't. I walked around to the next row of lockers, stopped at the one directly behind mine and saw fresh scrapes on the old linoleum.

"Well?" D'Amato was standing behind me.

"Someone moved this locker so they could access mine."

"Yeah, who? Only another cop could've—"

"Doyle," I said.

I walked back to my locker, put my stuff back, closed it. Although there was nothing we could prove yet, when I tallied the preponderance of circumstantial evidence incriminating Doyle, it was overwhelming.

Doyle met Pete while investigating him for homicide. Doyle was on the front lines at the Black Cat Social Club when the Coster Street arsonists got killed. Doyle showed up at Solana's place, of all places, the very night she got forced out of her apartment and the building burned down. Doyle's collar, Zeke Taylor, brother of the two Coster Street arsonists, was back out on the street pulling an armed robbery—a robbery that D'Amato and I were lured to. And last but not least; Doyle was attempting to close out all the arson investigations.

"If you're right," D'Amato said, "and Doyle's on Pete's payroll, the son of a bitch tried to get us killed."

I shook my head. "I can buy Doyle setting us up, getting us suspended to stop the Coster Street arson investigation. But there was no way he'd conspire to kill cops." I pulled the remainder of the yellow crime-scene tape off my locker, crushed it into a tight ball and pitched it across the room.

"It was a pretty good plan when you think about it," I said. "Zeke, Tookie, and Chico were supposed to take off the check cashing store. Make a clean getaway. We get a 10–85 from Captain Ward, show up after the fact. Stumble on the aftermath of an armed robbery, take the past robbery report. Later the cash discrepancy is discovered, the tip is phoned into IAB, the money's found in my locker. We're suspended—except the robbers got trigger happy, killed the store owners—"

"Then got trapped behind a garbage truck—"

"And we caught up with them—"

"Killed their fucking asses—"

We were both quiet for a moment.

"Let's go talk to Doyle."

"Talk?" D'Amato said. "I'm gonna beat his brains in."

That was easier said than done.

The detective division informed us that Doyle had taken some time off, flew his wheelchair-bound wife up to Boston for some medical tests.

"Now what?" D'Amato said as we exited the squad room.

"We call our lawyers. Get ready for tomorrow."

We located our PBA delegate at a desk in the clerical office. He supplied us with the number of the union's legal division. Then the delegate and the clerical man, Neary, wished us good luck.

"I got a feeling," D'Amato said as we exited the clerical office, "you back off investigating the Coster Street arson, this whole nightmare might go away."

"I think you might be right."

"All right." D'Amato held the door open for me as we hit the street. "Gimme your word you'll back off."

"I can't do that, Vinnie."

"Why not?" D'Amato stopped short. "Are you insane?"

"No. Pissed off." I didn't know how else to explain it. Bringing the Coster Street arsonist to justice had become the focus of my life. I was obsessed. I'd never stop so long as I was breathing, not until an arrest was made—and I was getting close. Close enough for the perpetrators to frame us for grand larceny, get us suspended. Their thinking: that we'd be too busy defending ourselves to continue the investigation.

Well, they were wrong. Dead wrong.

"I'll try to keep you out of it," I said.

Exasperated, D'Amato threw his hands in the air. "You'd better." He stuck a finger in my face. "I ain't letting an ego-maniac like you take me down."

As D'Amato turned his back on me and stormed down Simpson Street, I dealt with the fact that as of that moment he and I were no longer partners. No longer friends. I was on my own.

When I arrived at my apartment, I called the PBA and arranged for an attorney to meet me at IAB the following morning. Then I phoned Solana at the *Law & Order* studio.

First thing she said was, "Are you all right?"

Even with all the pressures I was under, the genuine concern in Solana's voice brought a smile to my face.

"Pretty good." I didn't see any reason to tell her about my suspension. She had enough problems of her own. "I did some checking. You were right about Pete Costello—" I was about to mention the connection between him and Doyle when it struck me: Gold security had followed me to the *Law & Order* studios; did they know Solana worked there, that I'd visited her? Was Pete aware that she could place him at the scene of the East Bay Avenue arson? That she could testify that he and Doyle tried to forcibly evict her from her apartment? Solana could very well be in danger.

"Where you staying the next few nights?"

"If no one objects, the studio."

The studio had security guards, security cameras everywhere. Solana would be safe for the time being.

"Would it be all right if I called you later in the week?" I said. "I could help you—look for an apartment?"

"I'd like that." Solana paused. "If you're serious."

"I am."

"No one I dated ever went out of their way for me," Solana said. "Oh, they'd say they would, but when it came down to it—"

"You dated the wrong kind of men."

"Maybe I did."

"Talk to you soon." As I hung up, my mind shifted into overdrive and became awash with thoughts of Pete from Queens, Doyle and Gold conspiracy theories.

D'AMATO DROVE OUT to Massapequa Shores. The house was quiet, more or less as he'd last seen it, except, this time, his wife and daughters' clothing was missing. They weren't coming back. He felt a hole open in his heart.

D'Amato drove to the Bronx apartment of his new main squeeze Mona Love. Phoned the PBA, arranged for his lawyer, then spent the remainder of the day and night agonizing over his suspension and gulping copious amounts of tequila.

"I can't picture myself as anything but a cop," he blubbered to Mona. "Since I was a kid it was all I ever wanted to be. What else would I do?"

Mona suggested he get himself a real job. The remark earned her a backhand that broke her lip and sent her bounding over a chrome coffee table.

"Prepare yourself for the beast, woman." D'Amato unzipped his pants.

"Keep away from me," Mona shrieked as she lay splayed on a dirty shag rug. D'Amato charged, stumbled over a size thirteen high heel, fell heavily to the floor and was suddenly fast asleep.

MONA GOT TO her feet and shook her head. It was the same the last two nights. D'Amato would get crocked out of his mind, pull his clothes off and howl about what he was about to do to her with "the beast." And every night he fell fast asleep. Life had been going all to hell for Mona since Pete from Queens darkened her door; she'd lost the Black Cat Social Club and then got involved with Vinnie D'Amato.

Normally, Mona wouldn't have put up with the likes of D'Amato. He had already struck her twice and took perverse pleasure in forcing her to perform oral sex on him at gunpoint. Not that being involved with a violent alcoholic was anything new, it was just that D'Amato made all the other psychos she'd been with seem normal by comparison.

He'd roam the apartment at all hours of the night, nude, play with his gun and talk to "the beast," his penis. D'Amato and "the beast" would discuss politics, weather, sports, the comics. Even to the likes of Mona Love, D'Amato was one weird white boy. And, to make matters worse, he was a cop.

Watching D'Amato snore on her bare wood floor, a bandage taped to the back of his head, Mona reminded herself that, for the time being, he was a necessary evil. She needed him to protect her from Pete.

Since she'd introduced Pete to the Taylor brothers and Tookie Jones and they'd all wound up dead, she could be next.

# CHAPTER 39

W hen I arrived at the New York City Police Department's Internal Affairs Bureau at 8:45 A.M., dressed in a designer summer weight suit and tie, the temperature had already hit ninety-three degrees.

I used a rickety elevator to reach the third floor and announced myself to a middle-aged, yawning receptionist. She instructed me to sign a visitor's log, then pointed to a bench at the far end of a quiet, dimly lit corridor.

My PBA attorney, a young slacker-type suffering from a serious case of bed-head, arrived about ten minutes late.

"Nice to meet a Medal of Honor winner, dude," he said as we shook hands. He sat alongside me and we discussed the facts of the case; that is, what I was willing to tell him. I knew I'd sound like a paranoid crazy if my trial-room defense was that I'd stumbled upon a vast Gold Organization conspiracy, claimed the cash was planted in my locker by a veteran First Grade detective—all without proof.

"Officer Michael Beckett?" An unkempt man in a rumpled tan polyester suit was standing before us. A man whose face every cop knew. "Sergeant Bork," I said flatly.

"You know me?" Bork said.

"I know your reputation."

Bork scowled.

Years ago Sergeant Bork had been assigned to the Midtown North Narcotics Division and was arrested for shaking down Colombian drug dealers. When confronted with a twenty-year prison sentence, Bork accepted IAB's offer of immunity in exchange for cooperation, and merrily testified against other crooked cops. Although Bork was one of the leaders of the million-dollar-a-year shakedown ring, his associates drew stiff jail terms while the charges against Bork were dropped. He was subsequently assigned to IAB and now, as a born-again something-or-other, lectured other cops on ethical awareness.

"Nice suit, officer," Bork said; an accusation, not a compliment. "Come this way."

The interrogation room was small, bare, institutional. The old wooden table which took up most of the windowless room seated eight. I nodded hello to Lieutenant Slotkin who directed me and my attorney to uncomfortable wooden chairs. Sergeant Bork sat across from us and turned on a tape recorder.

The fact that the interrogation was a non-event unnerved me. There was no hostility, no trick questions. I took my time, recited my account of the shooting incident and the events that followed. I stated several times that I could not explain the $6,700 found in my locker. That it had to have been planted, but I could not say by whom. Although Slotkin and Bork did cover the phony detective's shield and the bogus 10–85 call from someone pretending to be Captain Ward, their questions were few. They didn't play good cop, bad cop, or badger me in any way.

Afterward, my attorney said he was most concerned with Lieutenant Slotkin's lack of aggressiveness. To him, given his experiences with IAB, it meant the interrogation was merely a formality and that the powers that be in the NYPD had already made up their minds.

"My opinion," the lawyer said, "if you weren't a

Medal of Honor winner, dude, you'd already be in hand-cuffs."

That statement sent me reeling. The fact I was totally vulnerable hit home. For the first time the possibility of being sent to prison was a reality.

I left IAB with my head in a fog. I hailed a cab, headed to my apartment where, I hoped, D'Amato, having had time to calm down, would show up, or call after his interrogation.

D'AMATO ACTUALLY ENJOYED his IAB experience. He got to tell the entire story of the shootout, in gory detail, all over again. And he could tell that Lieutenant Slotkin and his youthful PBA attorney and even the infamous Sergeant Bork were most impressed with his heroism.

D'Amato actually felt deflated when the interrogation was over and the tape recorder was switched off. His PBA lawyer said he had to rush to another case and that he'd speak to him soon.

Lieutenant Slotkin left the room.

Bork and D'Amato were alone.

"You're a brave man, Vincent," Bork said.

"Aw, just doing my job." D'Amato pushed back his chair, stood, hiked up his faded Levi's and headed for the door.

"Say, you got a minute?"

D'Amato stopped. "For what?"

"I've got a proposition I'd like to share with you."

"I don't think so."

"You afraid of something?" Bork said.

"I ain't afraid of anything." D'Amato walked back to his chair and sat back down. "Two-thirds of the world's egg-plant is grown in New Jersey," D'Amato said. "You know that?"

"Doesn't everybody," Bork said. "Look, this is strictly off the record, Vincent."

"Yeah, sure it is." D'Amato leaned back, crossed his

legs, and scanned the interrogation room for a hidden microphone.

Bork picked up a file, D'Amato's file, and opened it.

"You know, Vincent," Bork said, "you have an impressive arrest record. What, over four hundred felony arrests in ten years?"

"That's 'cause I'm good."

"'S what I'm saying. You're damned good." Bork turned a page and came to the list of department complaints for insubordination. "You've had a few 'minor' disciplinary problems." Bork closed the file and put it aside. "But that's to be expected when you're an active cop working in a hellhole like the 41."

"There a point to all this?"

Bork nodded. "I'm here to do you a favor, Vincent."

D'Amato tweaked his mustache. "Lucky me."

"First let's examine the situation. I personally interviewed the regional manager of the Chung King Check Cashing Corporation. He asserts he has records that prove the claim that an additional $6,700 was stolen from his Hoe Avenue location. Put that together with the fact that $6,700 was recovered from your partner's locker and, well, it doesn't take a brain surgeon to figure it out."

"That money was planted."

"So your partner keeps saying."

"He's telling the truth."

"C'mon, Vincent. In the interview you stated that you did not actually *see* Beckett find the bag of money."

"That's right. I was checking a body when Beckett said something like, 'Money, partner.' I looked and he was holding a bag and a fistful of cash."

"You see him put the cash *back* in the bag?"

"Well, no."

"So he could've slipped some into his pocket?"

D'Amato uncrossed his legs, leaned forward. "Beckett wouldn't take money. Not ever. Not Beckett."

"Vincent, if due to the preponderance of evidence, IAB finds that Officer Beckett stole that money, we'll hand you *both* over to the Bronx DA. Next stop, grand jury. And you know what that means."

D'Amato did. Knew if the DA presented their case to the grand jury, he and Beckett would be indicted for grand larceny. Guaranteed.

"I don't wanna see a guy like you kicked off the force, Vincent. Indicted. Go to jail. You getting all this?"

D'Amato's response was a solemn nod.

"Good. Now, I don't believe for a moment that an officer of your caliber, with your history of unselfish dedication to the community, would ever even consider such criminal conduct. But I'm not so sure about your partner Beckett."

"What're you saying?"

"We think Beckett's dirty."

"Your ass."

"C'mon, Vincent. He practically advertises it."

"Yeah? How?"

"Look at the way he dresses. I mean, I'm no slave to fashion—"

"That's a fuckin' understatement."

"All right, explain to me how a street cop affords that suit he's wearing, and that wristwatch."

"Stick ups." D'Amato leaned forward, lowered his voice as if divulging a secret, breaking a confidence. He made a show of checking that no one else was in the room. "Beckett's doing stickups; jewelry stores, banks—"

Bork switched on the tape recorder. "What banks?"

"You know, if your brains were any smaller, they'd roll outta your fucking ears." D'Amato reached across the table and switched off the tape recorder. "Beckett's single. He lives in a rent controlled apartment. He don't own a car. Whatever he makes he spends on himself."

Bork blinked several times. "It's more then that. It's his attitude. Beckett's got ambition."

D'Amato made a face. "A lot of people do. So?"

"He acted on *Law & Order*. Maybe he thinks that now he's too good to be a cop. Maybe he thinks he was entitled to that money."

D'Amato shifted uneasily in his seat.

"He say anything to you about a show business career?"

"Not really." D'Amato shrugged. "I mean, he said he might be working on *Law & Order* again. Nothing definite."

"He's moving on, Vincent. Leaving you behind. You know it. I know it."

"You don't know shit."

"Really. Then why are you dumping Beckett as a partner?"

D'Amato straightened.

Bork had blindsided him.

"Well?" Bork said.

D'Amato took a moment, fiddled with his Timex. "Fitzpatrick, the guy I'll be working with, lives ten minutes away from me. We're gonna car pool."

Bork grinned knowingly. He whipped out a filthy handkerchief and blew his nose. "Now, I don't wanna put words in your mouth, but if you wanna tell me how Beckett slipped that money into his pocket, how you tried to stop him but he wouldn't listen? I'm here for you, Vincent. I'm your white knight."

"Beckett didn't take any money."

Bork stuffed the handkerchief back in his pocket. "You know what, Vincent? I like you."

"Yeah?" D'Amato's eyes narrowed. "I'm getting kinda fond of you too."

Bork removed a piece of paper from his jacket pocket,

unfolded it and pushed it across the table. "Beckett tell you he visited R. J. Gold yesterday?"

"He mentioned it." D'Amato looked at the piece of paper: the Gold Tower security sign-in sheet. There was Beckett's printed name. Next to it was Beckett's signature.

"My sources tell me a major studio is producing a TV show about Las Vegas casinos; Gold Organization owned casinos. Beckett asked Mr. Gold for a job; an acting job. Apparently he's quitting the NYPD. Becoming a full-time actor."

Another blindside.

"Tell you what I'm gonna do. I can guarantee, if you testify against Beckett, not only will all the charges against you be dropped, you'll keep your job and pension and there'll even be a medal in it for you."

D'Amato rose an eyebrow. "What medal?"

Bork's smile revealed yellow, pointy teeth.

"The Medal of Honor."

# CHAPTER 40

About a dozen reporters were on me before I'd gotten out of the taxi. I'd totally forgotten that D'Amato's and my suspensions would be carried in the nightly police department special orders, and that those orders are public record. Still, the fact that reporters, in a town as hectic and happening as New York, would be interested in the suspension of two Bronx beat cops made little sense to me.

"This must be a slow news day," I said, ignoring the reporters' rush of questions.

"A Medal of Honor winner gets suspended," a cute, female reporter from the *Post* said, "it's newsworthy. How do you explain the money found in your locker, Officer Beckett?"

I looked at her—the details of our suspensions were not part of the NYPD's special orders. Someone had fed the newspeople inside information. I didn't have to guess who.

"Excuse me," I said and pushed through the gaggle of newspeople and entered my building.

Once in my apartment, I pulled off my suit, slipped on jeans. I checked my answering machine for new messages, and then I phoned the ME to check if they'd been able to

identify the girl in the red dress. This time I was transferred
to a supervisor.

"The girl in the red dress was named Rosa Lopez," the
supervisor told me. "A fifteen-year-old runaway from Al-
abama. Been missing about two months."

"Parents?"

I heard the flipping of pages. "Her mother's been arrested for prostitution a dozen times, shoplifting six times,
twice for DUI—she's a loser. The stepfather's a registered
sex offender. He was arrested for molesting Rosa. He got
her pregnant—they're trailer trash, the worst kind."

I had assumed it would be something like that; a broken
home, physical abuse. "What's being done about the stepfather?"

"He was stabbed to death while incarcerated."

"Good riddance," I said.

"Amen," the supervisor said.

"Anyone claim the bodies?"

"The girl's grandmother is flying them back home."

I thanked the supervisor and hung up. Thought about
the fact that at least Rosa and her infant had family, that
they'd receive a decent burial. I hated to think of them being interred in Potter's Field; New York City's version of
Boot Hill.

I checked the time and estimated that, if D'Amato's interrogation went anything like mine, and he'd calmed
down and felt like talking, he should call or arrive at my
apartment in about half an hour—I needed to kill some
time.

I took a quick shower to cool off. Then sat down at my
computer, booted a word processing program, and opened
a file on the Coster Street arson. I started at the beginning,
recorded my theory of who, what, where, why, when and
how, everything I knew up until that point. Then I wrote
about what my next move should be. The answer seemed
obvious: Doyle—vulnerable because of his sick wife, the

hard-wrought pension and medical benefits he stood to lose—was the key. If I could get to Doyle, flip him, then flip Pete, there was no telling how far up the food chain the Coster Street arson conspiracy went. Maybe up as far as Tomo Nagasue, or even R. J. Gold himself. I edited and organized the data, reworked it until it all made sense, just in case I ever needed to show it to someone. I ran a spelling and grammar check, saved and closed the document.

I checked the time. D'Amato should've at least called by now. I looked out my window onto the street. The reporters were still down there. If D'Amato showed up, I wondered how he'd react to the press now that we were suspended—he'd probably pose for photos, glad hand the reporters, make a play for the cute *Post* reporter.

Where the hell was D'Amato?

I dialed D'Amato's cell. Got no answer. I called IAB and asked a clerk if an officer D'Amato was still there.

"Officer D'Amato," the clerk said, "left an hour ago."

# CHAPTER 41

"Mona," D'Amato called out. "Honey, I'm home."
No answer.

D'Amato removed his key from the front door, closed and locked it, and then made a beeline to Mona's liquor cabinet. He picked out a bottle of tequila, poured himself a shot, and decided he was glad he hadn't called Beckett—he needed time to think.

D'Amato threw back his drink, shivered from its throat-burning tang, and wondered where Doreen had taken their daughters; probably her parents. He wiped sweat from his brow—God the apartment was stuffy. He switched on an air conditioner, then used Mona's phone to call his soon to be ex-in-laws, but an answering machine picked up. He did not leave a message.

D'Amato took off his T-shirt, poured himself another shot, dropped onto a garish pink leather vibrating E-Z chair. When things go wrong, he sulked, they really go wrong.

In the past twenty-four-hours he'd lost his wife, daughters, was suspended from the NYPD and faced a possible jail term. On top of that, thanks to the rat bastard, Sergeant Bork, he now wondered if Beckett, his partner and former best friend, had betrayed him.

Beckett had made it crystal clear to him and Fire Marshal Collyer that he intended to avenge the death of the girl in the red dress and her infant. And he vowed to arrest everyone involved in the Coster Street fire—he was adamant about that.

Yet, according to Sergeant Bork, Beckett had visited R. J. Gold and asked for an acting job, tried to feather his own nest—what the fuck was he up to? Why make an issue of the Coster Street fire at all? Unless Beckett saw it as a way to put pressure on Gold. Sure, tell Gold he knew about Pete's involvement in the arsons, and the two sets of building plans, then offer to bury the evidence, for a price.

Simple blackmail.

Maybe Gold didn't like being blackmailed.

Which could be the *real* reason they'd been set up.

If there even was a setup.

D'Amato sipped his drink and considered Beckett's story about Doyle planting the money in his locker—it could be bullshit. Beckett *could* have stolen it. Anything *was* possible. Which meant the tale about Doyle was a ruse, meant to confuse, distract, lay the blame on others. That seemed uncharacteristic of Beckett, although D'Amato had to admit that he didn't know his partner anymore. Maybe he'd never really known him.

PETE FROM QUEENS left his Lincoln on Casanova Street, walked south and barreled through a group of slow-moving senior citizens.

"What's your hurry?" one of the old ladies grouched just loud enough to show a youthful spark of defiance.

"He look like King Kong," another woman commented and they all sniggered. "Big and hairy." They guffawed.

Pete ignored the blue-hairs and continued down the street, a man on a mission. He saw demolition crews knocking down the shells of abandoned tenements on Gold-owned land. Earth-movers were being unloaded from trucks—the construction of Gold Bronx City had begun and on time.

He passed vacant lots and the boarded-up Black Cat Social Club, still roped off with yellow police department crime-scene tape and guarded by a female cop who, with her long unruly hair and ill-fitting uniform, resembled a troll.

Two blocks later Pete crossed the street and stopped in front of a corner tenement. He glanced up to a second-floor apartment, Mona Love's apartment.

Pete cut back across Casanova Street, dodging traffic, and entered a partially occupied residential building directly across the street. He climbed the dimly lit stairs, careful not to touch the disgusting, grime-crusted handrails, on his way to the top floor. He stepped out onto the building roof—melting tar stuck to his shoes—and stepped over a pile of bricks the locals used, no doubt, to drop on cops and firemen.

Pete pulled out a pair of tiny Nikon field glasses, took a position at the roof's edge, wiped the sweat from his brow, and raised the binoculars to his eyes, trained them on Mona Love's apartment.

D'AMATO WAS ROUSED by a knock on Mona Love's door. When he opened up there was Sergeant Bork; his stained tie awry, his cheap suit showing sweat through the armpits.

"How'd you find me?"

"Mind if I come in?" Bork brushed D'Amato aside, walked in and glanced around the pre-war one-bedroom apartment. "Nice." he said. "Looks like a bag lady exploded in here."

"Whaddaya want?"

"A cold beer," Bork said, "for starters."

D'Amato went to get Bork a brew.

Bork looked around, studied some plastic-framed

photographs of Mona that were set on a bookcase. Mona as a singer, dancer, musician playing the drums in what looked like a grunge band.

D'Amato handed Bork his beer.

"How many polyesters did it take to make that suit, Sergeant?" D'Amato said. "Tell the truth."

"Funny." Bork took a swallow of beer, then sat on an imitation leopardskin sofa.

D'Amato sat on the EZ chair. "Well?"

"Was wondering, what's with that bandage on your head?"

"That what you came here to ask me?"

Bork shrugged. "You look bad, Vincent. Been boozing?"

"What's it to you?"

Bork grinned. "We're alone, I take it?"

"Yeah," D'Amato said. "We're alone."

Bork said, "I ain't giving up on you, Vincent. A man like you is too valuable to the police department."

D'Amato's expression turned sour. He looked deep into his shot glass. "'Bout time someone noticed."

"I noticed, and I'm not the only one." Again Bork glanced around, made a face. "You should go back to your wife and kids, Vincent."

"You snooping in my personal life?"

"It's my job," Bork said.

"Blow me."

"Seriously," Bork said. "This thing with you and Mario, well—at the risk of sounding politically incorrect—it ain't natural."

D'Amato was puzzled. "Who's Mario?"

"Mario Vitelli. Your, er, pal."

"I don't know who you're talking about."

"You mean you really don't know?"

"Know what?"

Bork laughed. "I hate to be the one to tell you this—"

"Yeah, I can see it's tearing you up inside."

"Mario Vitelli is a transsexual."

"Wonderful. So what's that got to do with me?"

"He goes by the alias 'Mona Love.'"

D'Amato jumped to his feet. "What?"

"Mona Love's a man." Bork made a face. "Or, was a man. Now he's an it."

D'Amato, stunned, collapsed into the chair. He gulped down his tequila, splashed more into his glass and gulped that down too. "You're lying."

"No, I'm not." Bork was enjoying this. "Look, forget Mario or Mona or whatever 'it' calls itself—I'm here to make one last effort to save your job, keep you out of jail."

It took a moment for D'Amato to refocus on Bork.

"Life ain't easy outside the PD," Bork said. "Not for guys like us. Guys like Beckett are different. He's already making plans. Hell, Beckett plays it right, he'll be a TV star, banging beautiful actresses two at a time. You think he's gonna think of you, his old partner? Beckett won't even take your calls. And what do you have to look forward to?"

D'Amato, eyes on the filthy shag rug, had no response.

Bork was getting to him, hitting a nerve.

"How're you gonna make a living, Vincent? You gonna drive a cab twelve hours a day? Paint houses? Clean carpets? You're gonna have to pay alimony and child support. Think of your family, Vincent."

D'Amato gazed into his glass.

AS IT TURNED out, Pete had every right to have been concerned when Solana showed up at P. J. Clarke's to meet Beckett. Especially since he became aware that, according to his teamster contact on the *Law & Order* set, they were seen playing kissy face. Solana could place him at the scene of the East Bay Avenue arson, a circumstantial fact he felt could explain away.

But when Doyle informed him that he'd spotted

D'Amato entering Mona's apartment building, that, rumor had it, Mona and D'Amato were an item, he'd become thoroughly alarmed. Mona could put him in prison for life—she'd introduced him to Bo and Bubba Taylor.

Pete focused the binoculars on Mona's apartment windows.

Spotted two men sitting in what looked like a living room.

That had to be the former crooked cop, an IAB sergeant named Bork that Detective Doyle told him about.

And there was D'Amato.

Pete couldn't help but laugh a little. D'Amato was playing "hide the salami" with Mona Love; a degenerate freak, a fruitcake, which meant *he* was a fruitcake. Pete would never have believed it of that crazy son of a bitch, D'Amato. But, hey, who really knew anyone?

Pete pocketed the binoculars and retreated to the shade of the building hallway. He planned to wait until the IAB cop left and Mona came home—he couldn't afford any more gaffes. He had to assume Mona had told D'Amato everything. And that D'Amato had told his partner Beckett.

BORK TOOK A miniature tape recorder from his pocket. He leaned forward and placed it on the coffee table.

"What're you doing?" D'Amato said.

"Relax. All you gotta do is tell me you saw Beckett take the money from the bag and put it in his pocket."

D'Amato stared at the recorder. "I can't do that."

"Think of your family, Vincent." Bork switched on the tape recorder. "Officer D'Amato, did you see your partner, Officer Beckett, handle the cash from the Chung King robbery?"

"I already told you at IAB. We were checking the bodies when I heard him say, 'Money, partner,' and he pulled a handful from the bag."

"And then you lost sight of him."

"Not really. I mean, yeah. He was on the other side of the car. We were kinda busy."

"That's when Beckett could have pocketed the cash, when you were busy." A statement.

D'Amato did not answer.

Bork repeated, "Beckett could have taken the money, when you weren't looking. Couldn't he, Officer D'Amato? Isn't that possible?"

D'Amato poured another shot of tequila, drank it down.

"Let me ask this way, Officer D'Amato. Isn't it possible that Officer Beckett pocketed $6,700 without your knowledge?"

An aching stillness settled over the room. D'Amato remained motionless, transfixed by the IAB tape recorder.

# CHAPTER 42

D'Amato appeared to be in a trance as he lay, nude, on Mona Love's bed. He was staring at the ceiling which was covered with drawings of couples in various stages of sadomasochistic sex—weird.

*Rat.*

The voice startled him.

*Rat.*

The word was so loud and clear that D'Amato sat up and thought about searching the apartment, although he knew that no one else was there.

*Rat.*

D'Amato covered his head with a pillow.

*Rat.*

"Stop it," D'Amato screamed and the voice stopped—just like that. D'Amato heard the front door open and close. Someone was in the apartment. He reached under the pillow and wrapped his hand around the handle of his off duty gun.

"Vinnie?" Mona Love said sweetly.

D'Amato relaxed. "Mario's home," he murmured.

D'Amato had not yet come to grips with the fact that Mona is a he, or *was* a he. Didn't know if a sex change altered a person's sexuality. Was he sleeping with a man or a woman? Did it matter? Yes, to D'Amato it did. But thinking about it confused him and he had other, more important things on his mind.

"Hot out there," Mona commented as she strode to the bathroom.

D'Amato watched as Mario/Mona pulled off his/her clothes. Homo or no homo, Mona had an awesome body: curves in places where most women didn't even have places.

Mona closed the bathroom door, turned on the shower.

D'Amato sprang from bed, danced across the room, stood in front of a full-length mirror and sang, "I'm just wild about Mario, and Mario's wild about me."

Drying off, Mona heard music and laughter. She cracked open the bathroom door. The stereo was blaring. She peeked and saw D'Amato posing in front of the wall mirror, pasty white naked save for his police hat and gun belt. He practiced his quick draw several times. Twirled a gun back into the holster. Held the "beast" in his right hand and sang along to "Do Ya Think I'm Sexy." Mona groaned. D'Amato was at it again.

Mona came out of the bathroom wrapped in a towel.

D'Amato grabbed her, pulled her towel off and was about to kiss her. Stopped. What the hell was he doing? Mona was a he-she. He shoved Mona aside.

Another oldie, the Police's "I'll Be Watching You" started playing. D'Amato turned up the music and danced and laughed as his gunbelt moved around his bare body like a hula hoop.

The song ended and D'Amato, exhausted and wet with perspiration, fell back onto the bed. He thought about the fact that he missed his daughters already, that tomorrow he'd have to face the other cops. And, sometime very soon, he'd have to face Michael Beckett.

D'Amato swallowed a shot of booze, and then another,

and another. But the melancholy would not go away. Mona joined him. D'Amato laid his head on her stomach and she rubbed his temples.

He thought about the fact that he had betrayed his family. Betrayed his profession. Betrayed his partner and best friend—he'd cooperated with IAB. Told Sergeant Bork that Beckett *could* have taken the money. But hadn't Beckett betrayed him first? Going behind his back, blackmailing R. J. Gold?

*The gun.*

The demon voice was back.

*The gun*, it said to him. *The gun.*

A shiver seized D'Amato. He pushed away from Mona, dashed into the bathroom and locked the door.

*The gun.*

D'Amato felt trapped. He spun around, again and again. The bathroom was small. Window tiny. There was no escape. He turned the shower on, then turned it off. Decided against taking a shower, ever again. He sat on the toilet and put his head in his hands, knuckled his eye. His world was coming apart.

"What's happening to me?" D'Amato punched his fist into his palm.

*Kill her,* the voice said.

"No," D'Amato whispered.

*Kill her now.*

But D'Amato didn't want to kill Mona. He didn't want to kill anyone. The gun weighed heavily on his hip.

D'Amato dropped down and did pushups—an attempt at depleting all energy—until he collapsed on the filthy tile floor.

*The gun.*

He struggled to his feet and shook his head violently. "Stop," he screamed in agony.

"Vinnie?" Mona was at the door.

"Get out, Mona."

"Hell're you talking about? This is *my* place. I'm not going anywhere."

*The gun. The gun.*

The gun was there on his hip. He tried not to look at it. He wished he didn't have that gun.

"Open the door, Vinnie," Mona said.

"Leave," D'Amato screamed.

*The gun. The gun.*

"What's wrong?" Mona was pounding on the door.

D'Amato pulled the gun. One shot would do it. Kill Mario. Blast the faggot's head clean off.

"Vinnie, are you all right," Mona said.

D'Amato pointed the gun at the door. Cocked the hammer. Began the trigger squeeze. But he stopped and lowered the weapon. He couldn't kill Mona. Couldn't kill anyone in cold blood.

D'Amato raised the gun and put the barrel to his temple. But he did not like the way the cold steel felt. He tried sticking the barrel under his chin, then opened his mouth and shoved it deep inside until it touched the back of his throat. The gun metal tasted of oil and was cold on his tongue. The experience was somehow exhilarating. Yes. That was better. D'Amato wondered if his wife and children would ever forgive him.

MONA HEARD THE shot. Screamed. Tried to break down the bathroom door but couldn't. She dashed to the phone and dialed 911—the telephone line was dead. She ran into her bedroom, slipped on shorts and a T-shirt, then ran through the living room, ran to the front door and opened it.

Ran smack into Pete from Queens.

# CHAPTER 43

The blistering summer sun had barely settled on Simpson Street when I stepped from a cab in front of the 41st Precinct.

I took the four rows of stationhouse stairs with one step, strode up to the desk officer and asked if he'd seen D'Amato.

"Ain't seen him." The desk officer scowled. "Doesn't mean the crazy bastard's not here."

I began my search for D'Amato in the fourth-floor locker room, checked the toilets, and every office on every floor until I wound up in the first floor clerical office.

"Seen D'Amato?" I asked Neary.

"No." Neary said. "What's up?"

Again I phoned D'Amato's cell, then his residence and left messages. Using directory assistance, I called D'Amato's wife's parents' house. D'Amato's mother-in-law answered. I asked if she'd seen Vinnie or if Doreen was available.

"Hold on," she said. Doreen came on the line.

"He's having a breakdown," Doreen said.

"What do you mean?"

"He pointed his gun at me, threatened to kill me," Doreen said, telling me more than I wanted to hear. "My father wants me to report him, have him arrested."

"I'll check back with you," I said, not knowing what else to say. "Soon as I find him."

I dialed 411 again and this time asked for Mona Love's phone number. No phone was listed under that name. I checked the police department, Black Cat Social Club incident reports and found Mona's address. She lived out in Hunts Point, a few blocks from the Black Cat. I asked an RMP team to drop me off.

I walked into Mona's tenement and climbed the muggy, lightless stairwell. On the second-floor landing I inadvertently kicked aside a bunch of empty beer cans and sent them skidding noisily across the chipped tile floor; so much for stealth. A guard dog growled menacingly behind an apartment door on my right. Another barked somewhere above.

I moved down the graffiti-lathered hall, approached Mona's apartment. I put my ear to the door, heard rock music, and smelled something; the scent was vaguely familiar; sweet but unidentifiable because it was mixed with other tenement odors.

I pulled my Browning. Knocked. No barking, which meant no guard dog, unless Mona kept one of the dreaded silent attack dogs. I was about to try the apartment door when I realized this situation was alarmingly like my *Law & Order* episode where my alter ego, Detective Eric Stone, was killed. I stepped to the right out of the line of fire, grabbed the doorknob and twisted; the door was unlocked. I pushed it open. No one fired. No silent fanged monster charged.

I eased inside.

All the lights were on. The music was emanating from a stereo which was set on a bookshelf on the other side of the room. I closed the door behind me, crept across a dirty shag carpet, turned the music off, and swept cautiously through the apartment.

I came upon Mona's body first. She was lying just inside her bedroom. I approached her, felt for a pulse; there was none. Her neck appeared to be broken.

I heard something which sounded like running water. I flattened myself against a wall. The sound was coming from the bathroom. As I approached I noted that the bathroom door was splintered—someone had kicked it open. I stepped inside and saw D'Amato.

I turned off the running water and forced myself to look at my partner. D'Amato's head flopped to one side, eyes staring, and the back of his skull was blown off. Dried tear tracks ran down his face. He was naked, save his gun belt. His uniform hat lay between his splayed legs. A .38 was still in his hand.

I considered exactly where and how D'Amato lay, the blood and brain splatter on the wall—D'Amato had eaten his gun. He must have locked himself in the bathroom and committed suicide.

I knelt down beside my partner and was struck by a wrenching clash of emotions: shock, disbelief, and most of all guilt. Had I helped to cause D'Amato's suicide? I'd gotten him suspended. He'd told me that being a cop was his whole life, asked me to back off the Coster Street investigation. I told him no. I couldn't.

I looked at Mona, then back at D'Amato. Was this a murder suicide? No, D'Amato couldn't kill anyone or anything in cold blood. So who killed Mona, and why? And who kicked the bathroom door in?

I said a silent prayer for my friend. Then I used my cell phone to call 911. I identified myself, gave them Mona's address, told them to send the homicide dicks and the ME.

I slipped my cell back into my pocket and walked around the apartment looking for clues. I stepped over Mona's body and entered her bedroom—it had been ransacked—and caught a whiff; the same smell from the hallway. This time I thought I recognized it. A cologne. Pete Costello's cologne.

# CHAPTER 44

"It isn't easy being a financial guru," R. J. Gold was explaining to his paramour of the moment, Miss Georgia Peach. She sat across the table doing her best to appear fascinated by her dinner companion.

"There are all types of pressures." Gold leaned back in his chair. "For instance, see that bald guy over there at the corner table, sitting with his, uh, niece?" Gold was gesturing with a shrimp fork across the ornate dining room at Le Cirque. "That's John Ross," he said. "Owns a cosmetic firm. A film company."

Miss Georgia Peach gazed across the room: Ross, a bright-eyed, diminutive man with an unlit, log-like cigar sticking out of his mouth like an obscene appendage, was dining with a stunning young Asian woman.

"Guy's worth around six billion." Gold waved a gratuitous greeting to Ross who responded with a level stare and a cool nod. "A real killer when it comes to doing a deal. But he drives me crazy. Calls constantly asking for investment advice." Gold stuffed an entire oversized shrimp in his mouth and again forked across the room. "Or that guy over there. That's Rick Stein."

Miss Georgia Peach saw a distinguished man in his

early sixties dining with a brassy, cheap-as-wood-chips redhead.

"He owns a baseball team," Gold said. "If it wasn't for me bailing his fat ass out every week, telling him what deals to invest in, he'd be in the poorhouse."

"Tee-hee-hee. Tee-hee-hee," Miss Georgia Peach tittered. A waiter brought their main course. His a burnt, cave-man-portion sirloin steak with French fries. Hers, a roast Cornish game hen with herb-bread stuffing. Gold covered his meat and fries with half a bottle of ketchup.

Aghast, the waiter fled.

Miss Georgia Peach over-salted her food, chose the wrong fork, and wondered if all rich northerners were as repulsive as this loathsome creature R. J. Gold. She smiled graciously at him, twisted to show a tad more cleavage, forked a sliver of game hen, and decided she'd rather make love to a scabby plow horse than spend another second with him. But a Southern belle had to do what a Southern belle had to do. "Never turn down free food," her mother used to say. And Gold was supplying more than free food.

He was paying her rent on a suite in a swank Central Park South hotel. Buying her clothes. Jewelry. She had even visited his Gold Tower apartment while his wife was away. They'd made love in the marital bed—if Gold's slobbering, grunting and grappling qualified as making love.

Gold was saying, "But, hey, what can I say? That's just the kind of guy I am. When my friends need me, I do the right thing." He cut off a huge hunk of the burnt meat, shoved it into his jowly face, then washed down the barely masticated flesh with gulps of designer water. "You understand?"

"Tee-hee-hee. Tee-hee-hee," Miss Georgia Peach flashed her best pageant smile. She guzzled her sixth glass of champagne and signaled the waiter for another bottle. "Right away," she said.

Gold's cell phone rang. He unglued his eyes from his

dinner companion's breasts and prayed it was not his wife calling.

"IT'S ME, BOSS."

Pete from Queens and Detective Doyle were parked in Pete's Lincoln down the street from Mona Love's apartment building. An ambulance and several police cars were on the scene.

"Yes, Pete?"

"Sorry to bother you, but you told me to let you know if something came up."

"Not a problem, Pete."

"Beckett's partner, Vinnie D'Amato?"

"Vinnie, sure." Gold stuffed more steak into his mouth.

"He committed suicide."

"Really." Gold stopped eating, put his fork down. "Sorry to hear that—think his suspension had anything to do with it?"

"Who knows." Pete used a white handkerchief to absorb blood from fingernail scratch marks on his neck. "He was a psycho, Boss. And I mean certifiable according to Doyle. Anything's possible."

Gold sat back; another death. He didn't wish to believe Vinnie D'Amato killed himself over being suspended; a suspension that was meant to be a warning. And just long enough to keep him and Michael Beckett busy defending themselves while Pete tied up any loose ends, covered his tracks, and the construction of Gold Bronx City went into full swing. He wanted to believe Pete's version of events: that D'Amato was a mental case, a man not in control.

"Anything else?" Gold said.

For a moment Pete considered telling Gold about the Mona Love, D'Amato, Beckett connection. The fact that, although Mona swore she had told D'Amato nothing before she died, he had to assume she was lying. Which meant that Beckett had to be dealt with, posthaste.

"Pete?"

"That's it, Boss," Pete said. "Everything's under control."

Pete pocketed his cell phone. He continued to dab at his neck, checked his handkerchief for blood, then folded it and put it away.

"Where'd you get the scratch marks, Pete?" Doyle said.

"I'll call if you're needed."

"You kill Mona Love?"

"Get out of the car."

Doyle glared at Pete. "Do me a favor," he said as he opened the door and stepped out. "Lose my phone number."

Pete smiled. "Gladly."

# CHAPTER 45

M ona's apartment was a beehive of activity.
Besides Captain Ward, there were four CSI technicians, two homicide dicks, two guys from the ME's office, and half a dozen cops in uniform controlling access.

"Sorry about D'Amato," Ward said.

I was standing in a corner of the living room, watching the lab boys do their thing; examining the bodies, dusting for prints, the usual.

"Captain?" A CSI technician walked over to Captain Ward. "It was a suicide," he said, referring to D'Amato. "No doubt about it."

Ward shook his head in acknowledgment, then looked at me, a grave expression on his face.

"Got what looks like skin under the fingernails," another CSI investigator called out from Mona's bedroom. I stiffened, walked to the bedroom and watched the tech pull plastic bags over Mona's hands. Skin meant DNA. DNA was proof.

"Recent stitches on the back of D'Amato's head," a CSI called from the bathroom. "But no scratch marks."

"If the perp's DNA is in the database," Captain Ward said, coming up behind me, "we'll get a match."

"Make sure," I said, "to check the Defense Department database."

"Why?" a homicide dick stopped what he was doing. "You know something?"

"Whaddya got, Beckett?" Ward said. "Speak up."

I looked at Ward, thought about finally spilling my guts, telling him my theory, everything I *thought* I knew. But all I still had was circumstantial evidence. If Pete killed Mona, his DNA was under her nails; which would be the first solid evidence of a Gold Organization conspiracy. And then no one would be able to silence me.

"Just check the database," I said.

I left Mona's apartment with the intention of traveling out to Long Island to where D'Amato's wife and children were staying, telling them the gut-wrenching news: your husband and father is dead. Like all cops I hated being the bearer of such news. But as D'Amato's partner and godfather to his eldest daughter, I had no choice, it was my responsibility.

"Not necessary," Captain Ward told me. "The NYPD chaplain has already been dispatched."

I have to admit I felt relieved. I decided to make the most of the chaplain's timely intervention and take the coward's way out: I'd contact Doreen tomorrow.

I couldn't catch a cab or ride back to the city. So I climbed the el, caught the next train, and found a seat, an orange plastic bench against a bulkhead beside a nodding commuter. As the train rumbled by block after block of crumbling tenements, I was consumed by sadness.

It was difficult to believe that D'Amato was dead. Gone.

The more I thought about it, the more I was sure I'd contributed to his despondency, had had a hand in his suicide. I didn't know how I could deal with that. D'Amato was out of my life, but it would take a long time before he was out of my head.

I stepped off the train at 77th Street and realized I'd

pass Saint Monica's Catholic Church on my way home. I headed to the church, climbed some steps, knocked on the rectory door, asked a receptionist to see my friend Father Gorman, said I wanted him to hear my confession.

I met Father Gorman in the church not five minutes later. He shook my hand, said he was glad to see me. Then he entered one side of the confessional box, I entered the other.

I knelt on a padded kneeler and waited for the priest to get settled. I glanced around the tiny darkened space, remembered my very first confession—I was so young I had nothing to confess, so I made things up and the priest actually laughed at me.

"I'm ready, Michael," Father Gorman said.

"Bless me father for I have sinned," I said to a thin, silk veil that separated me and the priest. "It's been three months since my last confession."

"I thought I'd be seeing you," Father Gorman said. "I read about the Hoe Avenue shootout."

"I'm not here about that, Father."

"Oh?" Father Gorman waited.

"I think I triggered my partner's suicide."

"He the one I met at your Medal of Honor ceremony?"

"Yes. Vinnie D'Amato."

"How?"

I told the priest about the Coster Street fire, the death of Rosa Lopez and her infant, the fact the infant had died in my arms, an event that sickened and outraged me. My obsession with tracking down the arsonist, at any cost.

"D'Amato asked me to back off. He was afraid of losing his job—the job was his life. I ignored him. I got him suspended."

"I understand your feelings of guilt," Father Gorman said after I'd finished. "Truth is, when someone is determined to commit suicide, there is very little if anything someone else can do to prevent it. None of us have any control over the choices and actions of another human being. To believe that you could have prevented this simply by backing off an investigation, isn't realistic. For reasons known only to him, your partner acted on an impulse. His suicide became a permanent solution to a temporary problem. But if you need to assign blame, blame whoever is responsible for the Coster Street fire."

I remained in the confessional for another few minutes, listened to the priest's words. Granted, he made some sense. But I couldn't relate to what he was telling me, not yet anyway.

"What about the Hoe Avenue shooting?" Father Gorman said. "How has that horrific experience affected you?"

"It was us or them, Father."

"I know that, but you were forced to take the lives of three human beings. Have you experienced any feelings of remorse?"

"Honestly?" I looked at the priest's silhouette. "When I think about killing those three skells, I feel nothing, Father. Nothing at all."

# CHAPTER 46

I entered my East 77th Street apartment, still thinking about D'Amato, lying naked, the back of his head blown off. It would be a long time before I'd get that gut-wrenching image out of my mind.

I tossed my keys on the kitchen counter, pictured Mona Love lying on her bedroom floor. And recalled that when Vinnie and I had first seen her, an alleged hostage sitting at the bar at the Black Cat Social Club, she'd been filing her nails, looking bored. She did not act like a hostage, did not appear nervous or frightened. It was as if she knew Bo and Bubba Taylor.

*That was it!*

It had to be.

Mona must've known the Taylor brothers.

Knew who hired them to set the Coster Street fire.

Which is why she was killed.

My telephone rang. "Hello."

"It's me, Neary," the 41 Precinct clerical man said. "Sorry about D'Amato."

I shouldered my cordless phone and sat on my living room sofa. "Thanks."

"How're you holding up?"

"I don't think it's hit me yet, if you know what I mean."

"I hear you—did you suspect? See any signs, I mean besides the fact he was a raving nutcase. Was he depressed?"

Who knew? Disposition-wise D'Amato was pretty consistent: larger than life and, no matter what his mental state, over the top. I recalled that night years ago when he drunkenly put a gun to his head and dared me to dare him to shoot. I had considered alerting the police department's Psychological Services Unit, but I knew they'd seize his weapons, take him off the street, end his police career. In the end I didn't report him. Now I wished I had. True they would have kicked him off the force, but at least he'd be alive.

"His wife left him a few days ago," I said. "Took his daughters. Being suspended didn't help."

"Well, if there's anything I can do. If you need to talk, whatever—long as you're buying the beers."

"Bite me."

"In your dreams—look, there's a grand jury subpoena here for you. None for D'Amato."

That took me by surprise. "Are you sure?" I leaned back. "That can't be."

"Maybe they decided to target you, leave D'Amato out of it—or maybe—" Neary hesitated. "Maybe D'Amato made some sort of deal."

"Deal?" I sat upright. "What kind of deal? What're you saying?"

"Look, I'm the last guy to badmouth the dead, but—"

"But what? C'mon, Neary."

Neary was silent for a long moment. "I got a phone call from a guy works in the Borough office. He told me D'Amato made a deal with IAB."

For a moment I was speechless, my mind raced. "But D'Amato knows—*knew* I didn't steal that money. There's no deal to be made."

"Have it your way. I'm just telling you what I heard. One

way or the other, you'll find out tomorrow at the grand jury—good luck. And remember, if you need anything—"

I hung up, walked over to my window and stared down onto 77th Street. The usual dog walkers were out. A meter maid was ticketing cars.

I told myself that Neary's source at the Borough office had to be misinformed. Besides, even if I'd gone bad and stolen that money, D'Amato would never turn informer. Not D'Amato.

Not the D'Amato I knew.

Yet he was dumping me as a partner. I'd gotten him suspended. Doreen had said he was experiencing some sort of mental breakdown. I turned away from the window, paced aimlessly, slowly, and came to the disheartening conclusion that, under the right circumstances, and with enough booze in him, D'Amato might've said anything, done anything to save his job—maybe even made a deal with the rat squad, concoct one of his infamous yarns, and turn on me.

My phone rang again and I picked it up without thinking. I took a deep breath and prayed it was not Doreen.

"Hello."

"Michael, it's Solana."

"Solana." I relaxed a bit. "Nice to hear a friendly voice."

"Help me, Michael," Solana sobbed.

I stiffened. "Help you—what's wrong?"

"Hey, pencil neck," Pete from Queens said.

My stomach sank. "What's going on, Pete?"

"Meet me in Hunts Point, Pier 1, in forty minutes," Pete said. "And come alone."

"Go to hell."

Pete chuckled. "If you're late, if I even think I see another cop, I'll snap Solana's neck."

My stomach knotted. My mind swirled; was he for real? I pictured Mona Love lying on her bedroom floor with her neck broken and fear for Solana's safety gripped me.

"Don't do anything stupid, Pete."

Dial tone.

*Shit.*

I placed the phone on the charger. Although I still had no real proof, if I had had any doubts whatsoever that Pete killed Mona Love, that he was involved in the Coster Street fire and had orchestrated our suspensions, that phone call erased them.

But what was he up to?

Why snatch Solana?

Had to be to get to me.

Pete must think that Mona told D'Amato about him hiring the Taylor bothers, and Pete figured that D'Amato had told me.

I walked over to a closet, pushed aside a false wall revealing a weapon's safe. I dialed the combination, swung open the door, chose a handgun, then pulled out a sawed off, five-shot pump shotgun, and remembered what I'd told the actor who played the drunk on *Law & Order*: *"Real cops don't take on lunatics alone."* Yet here I was about to do just that.

Unless Pete killed Solana and me first.

I grabbed my Rolodex and found the direct line to Captain Ward. I picked up the phone, began to dial, then stopped. Forty minutes gave me more than enough time to alert the captain and get backup into position. But then I thought about the fact that, the way Pier 1 was situated, Pete could see the reinforcements coming; hell, he'd see *me* coming a mile away.

I hung up the phone. Sat at my computer, opened the Coster Street arson file, printed a copy, addressed it to Captain Ward and locked it in my weapon safe. If something happened to me, my father would see to it that the document got to the captain.

I checked that the shotgun was loaded, placed it in a duffle bag, shouldered it and headed out the door.

# CHAPTER 47

Pier 1 in the Bronx, a wooden wharf on the East River, was constructed in 1949 for use by the Department of Sanitation. For twenty years it was utilized to transfer the city's refuse from garbage trucks onto huge ocean-going barges which were towed twelve miles out to sea, where the trash was discarded in the ocean. The pier was abandoned years ago and has since served as a shelter for packs of wild dogs and the occasional rambling derelict.

My taxi stopped at the entrance to Pier 1.

I got out and scanned the area.

Eerie. The sky was overcast. A soft, warm saltwater breeze blew in across the East River. The streets were dark, deserted. Not even a parked car or truck was in sight. The only sounds were those of dogs barking somewhere to the east and that of the departing taxi.

I scoped out the mammoth tin and steel building at the end of the pier. I removed the shotgun from the duffel bag and discarded it. And as I drew closer to the structure, I could see a dim light was burning somewhere inside.

I peered through a filthy wire mesh window, saw nothing. I felt my way along the building wall, stumbling in the darkness until I found an open door. I heard a noise. Turned and saw that I was surrounded.

The dogs must have been lurking in the shadows: German shepherds, Doberman pinschers, pit bulls, mastiffs, all with eyes as red as demons.

As still more dogs skulked toward me, I remembered the roll call sergeant speaking about the homeless man who was attacked and nearly torn apart by a pack of wild dogs.

I raised the shotgun.

Out of the center of the pack lumbered a one-eyed Rottweiler. Lobo padded menacingly toward me, his head erect.

"Hey, pupa," I said. "Hey, Lobo."

The Rottweiler stopped and looked at me quizzically, tilting his head this way and that, sniffing the air, catching my scent.

"C'mere, pupa." I took a chance and stuck out my hand. The big canine dropped his head, pranced over and rubbed against my leg. "Atta boy," I said, scratching the dog's back. The other dogs began to lose interest in me. I gave Lobo one last pat on the head, backed ever so cautiously away from the pack, eased the tin door open, stepped inside and closed it behind me.

Whew.

It took a moment for my heart to stop pounding and for me to get my bearings. I squinted, eyes piercing the darkness.

The pier's interior was strewn with parts of abandoned garbage trucks. The stench of stagnant water and rotting refuse permeated the air. And there was something else. I breathed in and was struck by the strong, acrid odor of gasoline.

In the distance I saw a vague light.

I picked my way carefully through the mountains of debris, moving quietly, bounding over assorted refuse and oil-slick puddles, sidestepping remnants of trucks and dumpster bins.

I stole a glimpse of Solana Ortiz through vistas of rubble about fifty feet away. A single overhead beam of light tented her. She was perched on a rickety chair in the center of the cavernous structure, and a hangman's noose was suspended from a high rafter and tied around her neck.

I moved closer and realized just how precarious her predicament was: her hands bound tightly behind her back, blindfolded, gagged, the noose scraping a collar of angry abrasions. The chair she was perched on had only three legs. Solana would eventually have to shift her weight. The chair would topple. I had to get to her, fast.

But she was out in the open.

Pete would have a clear shot at me. And it would take two hands to free her. That meant laying down my weapon.

"Hello, pencil neck."

I spun. Pete grabbed me, lifted me effortlessly overhead and threw me. I crash-landed on a pile of rotted truck tires, rolled away as fast as I could, got to my feet, pointed the shotgun: Pete was no longer there.

"This ain't personal, Beckett," Pete said, his voice echoed like a phantom's throughout the cavernous structure.

I spun in circles, my eyes everywhere, gun ready.

A punch from the rear caught me in the kidneys and flipped me onto my back. I rolled as I hit the ground avoiding Pete's jackhammer feet. I scrambled between two rusting truck hulks where I didn't think Pete could get at me. I paused, a quivering, helpless pile of sweat, and prayed the kidney pain would subside. I lay there for what seemed like an eternity and sucked in sour air. I heard a noise: Pete was coming for me. I forced myself to creep forward, out from between the trucks, and crawled toward Solana.

I crawled until I was forced to get to my feet. Pete lurched from out of the darkness and grabbed for my weapon. I leapt back and slammed him on the side of the head with the shotgun.

Pete staggered, but recovered and charged. He bounced me against a Dumpster and locked me in a bear hug. I felt my ribs crack and dropped the shotgun. A head butt caused Pete to slacken his vise grip just enough for me to yank my arms free. I jammed my thumbs into his eyes. Pete screamed a curse, broke his hold, fell back, momentarily blinded. I dove for the shotgun, rolled and fired. Pete was blown backward over a pile of junk and disappeared into the darkness.

I started to pursue Pete, knew I had to finish him, but I heard a soft thud. Looked. Solana had shifted her weight, her chair had fallen. She was hanging.

I charged, leapt over a gigantic old truck engine, was only a few feet from Solana when a hail of bullets lashed the area around me, forcing me to the ground.

I scurried back behind the truck engine and was safe, for the moment. I poked my head up, saw Solana struggling, dangling on the end of the rope, her life slipping away before my eyes. I pulled a handgun, took careful aim at the rope just above her head and fired. Missed. I fired again. Missed. Solana stopped struggling. Her body went limp. I took aim once again, drew in a deep breath, held it, lined up my sights, squeezed the trigger and fired.

The rope broke and Solana dropped heavily to the ground. I crawled through oily, stagnant water, exposing myself, bracing for the punch of a bullet I knew would come.

I rolled Solana over and removed the rope from around her neck. I felt for a carotid pulse. Shook her. She began breathing. I untied her hands and loosened the gag.

"Michael," she croaked groggily, coming out of it. That's when I heard the tin door I'd used to enter the building slam shut.

# CHAPTER 48

Pete leaned heavily against the tin door, catching his breath. He felt pain, checked under his jacket; blood oozed from the gunshot wound—fucking Beckett. He took in several deep breaths, mustering his strength. He bent down, picked up a heavy chain and used it to secure the door and lock Beckett and Solana inside.

Now he was glad he'd taken the time to saturate the building perimeter with gasoline beforehand. He'd used over twenty gallons, poured it on thick, watched as the gas seeped under and into the structure—there could be no screwups this time.

Pete picked up yet another can of gasoline and spread the contents liberally around and under the chained door. Then he lit a match and dropped it. There was a gentle whooshing sound. The fire caught and spread with alarming speed.

Pete heard noise behind him; a growl then a bark, turned to see that he was surrounded by about two dozen dogs.

*What the fuck?*

Lobo lumbered out of the pack, padded close to Pete, raised his snout, sniffed the air, caught Pete's scent. The silent attack dog made a noise that sounded like a muffled growl.

"You?" Pete recognized Lobo. He pulled his weapon.

# CHAPTER 49

I heard a whooshing sound, faint at first, then louder. I looked and saw two streams of fire spurt into the building and race around us along the interior circumference of the structure. Within seconds Solana and I were completely encircled by ten-foot-high blue flames.

I pulled Solana to her feet. Searched for an escape route, but I could see that the fire now blocked access to all doors and windows. There was no way out.

Frantic, we crouched down, crawled around the grease-stained floor, below the dense smoke, searching for a break in the flames.

"Michael," Solana said, using her hands to brush dirt off of something on the ground. "Look."

It was a manhole cover.

Together we tried to lift the iron hatch but couldn't. We looked around for a tool of some sort. And heard sudden and repeated gunfire coming from outside—what was that? Had an NYPD patrol car happened on the scene and confronted Pete?

An overhead scraping noise snagged my attention. I looked up just as part of the flaming roof came sailing down—we dropped to the ground, covered up.

Solana screamed. She was on fire. I grabbed her and rolled her on the ground, smothering the flames. Solana sobbed and I pulled her close to me. Smoke was burning our eyes, slowly contaminating our lungs.

"Wait here." I held my breath and ventured into the smoke. I needed to find something I could use to pry open the manhole cover. I kicked aside flaming debris and picked up a long, rusty pipe. I dashed back to Solana, wedged the pipe under the manhole cover, pressed down but the cover did not budge.

"Help me," I said. Together we pressed down, used our combined body weight to exert pressure.

No movement.

A sharp, grinding noise startled us. We looked and saw that the steel beams directly above us were buckling.

"Again," I said and we bore down on the pipe, harder this time, our bodies shaking from the all-out effort. "And again." The cover finally budged. Another great effort dislodged it. I dropped down to the concrete, lay on my back, leg-pressed the cover aside, just as the entire building collapsed upon us.

I shoved Solana into the manhole. She struck her head against a piling, and sank below the surface.

I dove in next.

I hit the deep, polluted water hard, had the breath momentarily knocked out of me. I gulped in air, looked around. Solana was nowhere in sight.

"Solana!" I dove several times in random directions. My eyes burned from pollutants, but I stayed submerged each time until my lungs felt like they'd burst—I couldn't find her. I resurfaced for what could have been the third or fourth time, caught my breath and spotted bubbles to my right—if that was Solana the tide was pulling her away from the pier out to sea. I dove toward the bubbles, searched blindly, felt hair. I grabbed hold and pulled the body to the surface: a dead German Shepherd.

Revolted, I let go the decaying, molted carcass, and fought the urge to be sick. Then I spotted Solana floating motionless about six feet to my left, face down. I reached her in one stroke, placed her in a rear lifeguard hold and managed to sidestroke her away from the burning pier.

I dragged Solana onto the rocky coastline, laid her on her back, and began to administer CPR—she coughed water out of her lungs almost immediately. She rolled to her side, was seized by retching coughs, but then began to breathe normally. I collapsed beside her, my arms and legs leaden. Solana took my hand and we watched as the building and the wood pier burned with startling speed and a sea-breeze-fueled vengeance.

Through the smoke I caught a glimpse of Pete: it was like a scene from the old black-and-white horror movie, *The Thing*. Pete was engulfed in the firestorm, fighting dogs who clung to him like fanged parasites.

"My God," Solana said. She was sitting up, wide-eyed, leaning on her elbows, aghast.

I couldn't think of anything to say.

We lost sight of Pete and I knew he and the dogs would soon be reduced to ashes. There would be little, if anything left of their remains, little left of the arson investigation. The way I saw it, with the Taylor brothers, Mona and Pete dead, I'd never be able to prove Doyle's involvement, if any. And I'd never know if R. J. Gold was complicit in the Coster Street fire.

I checked my wounds and considered calling for an ambulance. But neither Solana nor I had any broken bones or life-threatening injuries. Besides, an ambulance would bring the NYPD. Since I was already up a creek, a suspended cop about to be indicted for grand larceny, and I'd just shot Pete with an unregistered, illegal weapon, alerting the PD was certainly not in my best interest.

"Can you walk?" I said.

Solana said she could.

As we moved stealthily from the area, the fire department arrived. Before they could pull even a single hose, the pier, aglow with white-hot embers and licking flames, bowed and dropped into the East River.

## CHAPTER 50

There are no acceptable excuses for missing a grand jury appearance that I know of, especially when you are the subject of the proceedings.

I arrived at the Bronx Criminal Courthouse at 9:30 the following morning, my ribs bandaged, my shoulders, elbows, knees and just about every other part of me bone-bruised. I hobbled up a challenging set of sweeping steps, to the second floor and entered the grand jury sign-in room, a familiar place which I'd frequented countless times.

I signed my name on a sheet, two spaces below IAB's Lieutenant Slotkin and Sergeant Bork. Normally, as an active duty cop, after signing in, I would have been escorted into an office by an assistant DA who would go over the details of the case, review the questions I'd be asked that session, as well as my responses—not this time. There was no ADA, legal counsel or anyone else to prep or counsel me. Today I was on the other side of the law.

I walked into the police officers' waiting room, found an unoccupied seat on a short wooden bench, and tried in vain to find a position where my aching body would not convulse into crippling spasms. I glanced at the three other cops who were in the room. Although I had never met them, it was apparent to me that they knew I was a soon-to-be-indicted rogue cop; they were making great efforts to avoid my eyes.

My cell phone rang.

"Hello."

"Are you sitting down?" Solana said.

"If I didn't, I'd fall down."

"You know a Carmen Rodriguez?"

"No," I said. "Should I?"

"She works as a waitress at that greasy spoon, you know, the diner on Southern Boulevard?"

"Carmen! Sure I know her."

"She organized an e-mail campaign. It's unbelievable."

"What for?"

"The sponsors of *Law & Order* received over one million e-mails asking that they bring back Detective Eric Stone."

I almost fell off the bench I was sitting on.

I lowered my voice. "I'm back on *Law & Order*?"

"Nothing's set, but I'd say your chances are excellent. Unless. . . ."

She didn't finish that sentence, didn't have to. We both knew, once I was indicted by the grand jury, I'd never work in television or law enforcement again.

"Officer Beckett," Sergeant Bork said.

"I'll call you back," I told Solana and ended the phone call. Both Slotkin and Bork were hovering over me.

"What?"

"Your grand jury appearance has been cancelled," Bork said a disgusted look on his face. "You are directed to return to your command."

"I don't understand."

"You're full of shit."

"Enough, Sergeant." Slotkin looked mildly at me. "Seems you have some friends, Officer Beckett, in high places."

# CHAPTER 51

I walked into the 41st Precinct, stuck my head into Captain Ward's office, asked if he had a moment—it was time for me to resign from the NYPD.

Ward waved me in, pointed me to a chair.

The first thing I noticed was that the captain had changed toupees; this one was more youthful: a Little Lord Fauntleroy helmet.

"Hell happened to you?" the captain said, eyeballing the small bandages and black-and-blues that, more or less, covered the exposed areas of my body.

"What do you mean?" I said with as straight a face as I could manage. I winced with pain as I eased myself onto a chair.

"Again, I'm sorry about D'Amato," Ward said.

"Thanks."

Ward sat back. "You aware you're off suspension?"

"Since when?"

"Since Doyle completed his investigation of the Chung King check cashing store robbery."

*Doyle?*

"Seems they're part of a national chain," Ward said. "A subsidiary of some bank and mortgage company, big business. There was a computer glitch somewhere down in Texas." Ward picked up an NYPD Property Clerk envelope and opened it. "Turns out there was no missing money." He pulled a wrapped stack of bills from the envelope and tossed it to me.

"What's this?"

"The $6,700 IAB found in your locker." He slid a voucher and pen across to me. "Sign for it and it's yours."

I fanned though the cash, then tossed it back to the captain. It wasn't that I couldn't use the money, but that cash was planted to help cover up the Coster Street deaths. And I wanted no part of blood money. "It's not mine."

"Mind telling me where it came from?" The captain shoved the cash back into the Property Clerk envelope and placed it in a desk drawer. "Who planted it and then tipped off IAB? Why one day you're on suspension, next day you're off? What the hell went on with you and Doyle?"

"Sure." I reached into my jacket, took out the Coster Street arson file document I'd printed and addressed to him the day before. Ward accepted it without comment, put on glasses and read.

After a moment, Ward said. "Pete Costello. The Taylor brothers. Mona Love. Tookie Jones. D'Amato. All dead."

"They are."

"Can you prove any of this?"

"No."

Ward made a face. "Well, at least I know why that uppity bastard Doyle resigned. Got out while the getting was good."

"What?" I hadn't seen that coming. "Doyle resigned?"

"Put in his papers." Ward slipped off his reading glasses. "Left this morning. Took his wife on a four-month cruise around the world." Ward shook his head in disgust. "The son of a bitch's got a job waiting for him when he gets back."

I swallowed hard. "Doing what?"

"You're not gonna like it," the captain sneered. "Director of Security. Gold Organization."

I WALKED OUT of the stationhouse, through thick, muggy air and stepped into the back seat of a beat-up gypsy cab that was idling curbside.

"Everything all right?" Solana said.

"No." I slipped my shield in my jeans pocket, clipped my holstered gun inside my belt—it was hot as hell in that damn cab. I looked at the dashboard. A scrawled "out of order" sign was taped to the air conditioner.

"You didn't resign," Solana said.

"Doyle took Pete's job at the Gold Organization."

"My God—but that's not evidence, is it?"

I shook my head. My eyes slid to movement on a building stoop. Juan Langlois, the level-3 predicate sexual offender and drug dealer was at it again: surrounded by a group of pre-teen boys, handing out ice cream bars, playing the court jester.

"Realistically," Solana said, "do you have a shot at proving Doyle was involved in the arsons?"

"Doubtful." I looked at her. "But I'm gonna make his fucking life miserable trying."

Solana patted my arm. "Maybe this will cheer you up." She handed me a folder that had "*Law & Order* Story Line Proposal" written on the cover. I flipped it open, scanned the cast list. Saw my character's name, Detective Stone. "How long's the contract?" I said.

"If it's approved, ten episodes," Solana said.

I saw McShane and Ryan grappling with a gargantuan prisoner, dragging him toward the stationhouse. The prisoner broke free of his handcuffs—a superhuman feat—and punched McShane in the face. The perp then spun, threw a kick, knocked Ryan down, and ran in our direction.

I waited until he was almost abreast of the gypsy cab, then threw the rear door open. *Crack.* The big man nearly tore the door from its hinges when he hit. He fell back, stunned, and sat on his ass. McShane and Ryan were all over him. I got out of the cab, drove my foot into the guy's kidney, and flipped him over.

The guy lashed out. Kicked me back into the side of the cab; I hit hard. He tossed McShane and Ryan aside like rag dolls.

Police Officer Destiny Jones was suddenly there.

She swung her nightstick, caught the prisoner on the back of his knees; he buckled. Destiny's next two strikes caught the guy on the shins. He screamed in agony and fell to the ground.

"Good form, Destiny," I said.

Destiny's smile lit up Simpson Street. "So I've been told."

I helped Destiny, Ryan and McShane put another set of cuffs on the prisoner.

Solana stuck her head out of the cab window. "You all right?"

"Yeah."

"Who's she?" Solana pointed. Destiny, Ryan and Mc-Shane were jostling the prisoner across the street toward the stationhouse.

"That's Destiny Jones."

"You know her well?" Solana said.

"No," I said.

"Keep it that way."

I looked to see if Solana was serious. She was.

I heard a child shriek with joy, saw Juan Langlois muss a boy's hair, then rub his back in a too-familiar way. Something inside me snapped. "Be right back." I walked over to the building stoop, cut through the group of pre-teens and grabbed Juan by the throat. I swung the pervert around, slammed him against the building, knocking the breath out of him; the kids scattered. I searched his pockets, found no drugs.

"You get the fuck outta my neighborhood." I dragged the

scumbag down the stoop. "Next time I see you, I'll snap your spine." I shoved Juan and watched him skulk away.

"Hey," the cab driver said as I stepped into the backseat. "Who's paying for the dent in my door?"

I told him to turn his air conditioner on or I'd give him a dozen fuckin' tickets. He bobbed his head contritely, lifted the "out of order" sign, switched on the air conditioner, and mumbled something harsh in broken English.

I looked toward a cop helping a bloodied crime victim out of his RMP, into the 41 stationhouse and an inner voice said, *"Who are you kidding?"* Avenging Rosa Lopez and her infant's killing were not the only reasons I hadn't resigned from the NYPD. Although I was thoroughly burned out and needed a long vacation, I must confess that I'd finally come to terms with the fact that being a cop defined me, fulfilled me: the NYPD was in my blood.

"Any chance you can take a month off?" I said.

Solana raised an eyebrow. "What do you have in mind?"

"Flying down to Tortola, renting a sailboat, cruising the Virgin Islands."

"You know how to sail?"

"I was in the Navy."

"You told me you were a cook."

"Cook, schnook; we'll figure it out."

"In that case," Solana smiled and squeezed my hand, "I'll see what I can do."

"I've got some brochures at my place." I wiggled my eyebrows.

"Why am I not surprised?"

"Why," I said, "indeed."

I told the driver my address. The cab moved down Simpson Street, slowing to avoid contact with drunken, disorderly pedestrians and a mob of children playing atop the shell of a stripped-down, burned-out car. As we passed abandoned, disemboweled buildings, I glanced at the usual crowd dancing to drum music.

Solana moved close and squeezed my hand. I put my arm around her, turned her face to mine, kissed her on the lips, and thought about Caribbean cruises by moonlight, long loving summer nights, saxophone music and blazing tropical sunsets.

# EPILOGUE

The only time I remember crying, during my adult life, was when my mother died. I was unable to control those wrenching, primal sobs. I did not weep at Vinnie D'Amato's funeral.

No one did.

The simple graveside service was held at Woodlawn Cemetery in the northeast Bronx. There was no NYPD honor guard. Few cops attended. Most did not care to attend the funeral of an IAB informer, a rat. But D'Amato's family, his wife Doreen, the two kids and Doreen's father were there, as were a few neighbors and childhood friends. Twenty people in all.

It was not much of a funeral.

A bird-faced minister who never even met D'Amato droned a mercifully brief eulogy. That done, the mourners formed in single file, moved past the gold-trimmed mahogany casket and each dropped a single white lily on it, a last good-bye. When everyone but the cemetery workers had left the grave site, I figured it was my turn.

I stood over D'Amato's casket and peered beyond it into the ominous black hole in the ground—it was so deep. I realized that all the death I'd witnessed over the past ten years had failed to prepare me for this moment.

"Step away, please," a gravedigger said to me.

"In a minute." I reached into my pocket, took out my Medal of Honor and placed it on the casket among the flowers. Then I stepped back, stood at attention, saluted D'-Amato and watched as the grave diggers slowly, solemnly lowered my partner, my friend, into the ground.

# ACKNOWLEDGMENTS

To the friends who stuck with me through my "rolling pennies for food" days. Thanks for the free drinks, meals, the occasional loan and all the abuse I could handle. Alphabetically: Edward Breen, Sam and Joanne Cohen, Michael Collyer, Esq. (posthumously), Tom Counihan, Paul Derounian, Esq., Tony and Kathleen Iwanczuk, William "Bill" Lenahan, Dominick Porco.